A Cat's Play is
the Death of Mice

Kon Blacke

DDP
DEEP DESIRES PRESS
Winnipeg, Canada

Developmental editor: Craig Gibb
Proofreader: Francisco Feliciano

Published April 2024 by Deep Desires Press, an imprint of Story Perfect Inc.

Deep Desires Press
PO Box 51053 Tyndall Park
Winnipeg, Manitoba R2X 3B0
Canada

Visit http://www.deepdesirespress.com for more scorching hot erotica and erotic romance.

Subscribe to our email newsletter to get notified of all our hot new releases, sales, and giveaways! Visit deepdesirespress.com/newsletter to sign up today!

A Cat's Play is
the Death of Mice

Chapter One
A Prostitute's Home for Me

1854

I didn't know where I was going through the rain-slicked cobbled alleyways, but I trusted my mother's hand. As a flush of anxiety washed over me, I managed a quivering, nervous smile. We turned into alleyway after alleyway, our pace quickening as we went.

"This way. Hurry," my father said, gasping, his breath a visible cloud because of the cold. He was holding my mother's other hand. "We're being followed."

Footsteps ahead of us clanked against the cobblestones. A shadowed man blocked our way, stopping us dead in our path. My fear rose to grip me tight by the throat at the sight of him. Was this who we were running away from?

"No," my mother said, sounding petrified. "We've been found."

Before I could find the strength to question her, a bright light and a series of screams rang out. My mother's hand slipped from my grasp, chilling me suddenly with its unexpected absence.

The drizzle that wet the cobblestones slicked my face to obscure my vision; the umbrella my father held above us no longer protected me from the weather. Water found my face. I wiped my eyes and looked around desperately. More drizzle, now shifting to rain. I kept wiping my eyes. I couldn't see my parents.

"Mother?" I cried.

Another bright light. Then dull, wet thuds of heavy weights fell at my feet. I jumped in my own skin, startled. Two bodies lay like dark stains against the cobblestones. Were they my parents? *Lord Almighty, no!*

I felt claws of fear walk up my spine as that terrible realisation struck me; not like those of a housecat, but of those that belonged to a great bear after it had felled its prey. The claws held me fast, except my bladder. My only warmth now.

A sinister chuckle, that of the shadowed man, frightened me to my bones. I became confused for a moment. Through that, and my numbing fear and grief, a strange stirring welled up within me, an awakening from deep within my body.

My hands began to luminesce, blue as gaslight.

With a flourish of his coachman's cloak, the shadowed man slunk back down the alleyway. "We shall meet again, Master Merritt. But for your fear, you will know me forever more as the Skilamalink Man."

There was silence once again, save for the unending rain pattering against the cobblestones. Eventually, the light over my hands extinguished, but the power I felt within me remained. It continued to roil for what seemed an eternity, stirring my gentlemanly parts, until even that diminished once my awakening eased. My fear subsided with the power, leaving sadness in its wake.

Rain dripped off my nose. I tried to grasp for any meaning as to what had happened. I found none, too numb to do anything but wipe my face. My hand that once held my mother's was cold. My throat then constricted once more, held tight by the reality threatening to crush me.

After my breath hitched, I cried.

The harsh clacking sounds of the wooden rattles used by the peelers—the men of the law—pierced the rain at that moment. I could do nothing but fall onto my knees beside my mother. I parted her long, wet blonde hair matted about her gaunt face. Her eyes stared up at oblivion, cold as the rain, dead as the atmosphere within the gloom.

Not too far away, but out of reach, was the body of my father.

I was slumped over my mother for what seemed an age, feeling her warmth leave her, trying to cling onto it as best I could. I shuddered with grief, my insides knotting painfully as tears flowed from me in mourning.

The rattling noise stopped.

Several peelers had gathered, as well as a lady pointing at me with a shaking finger. "See 'im there? See 'im? Took my very breath it did to witness it," the lady said, aghast. "May the Lord Almighty rest their poor unfortunate souls. There 'e is, by 'is mother. See 'im?"

"Over here, lads." A peeler's voice struck me with its coarseness, rough and deep. "Bring the cart."

"This one's 'ad a terrible fright, 'e 'as," the lady said, shrugging on one of the peelers' coats. "Best I take 'im to Lady Penelope. Give 'im what 'is mother's love can't no more, I say."

The peeler looked around; I could see him surmising the rain-soaked scene, puzzlement drawn on his brow.

"Then take him, woman. But know we will be there shortly to question him," another peeler's voice answered, but not the voice of the first. This one was more commanding, even if it sounded unsure.

"You don't expect the boy did this to 'is own blood, do you?"

After a pause, the commanding voice replied, "No…I don't."

"I'll take 'im right away, Constable. 'E will be the Captain and Lady Penelope's boy now. There's nothin' for 'im here, the poor blighter."

"I'd wager that you might be right," the peeler in command

said. "Jenkins! Go get Orson from the morgue. There's two more for his draws tonight."

"Yes, sir."

I found a warm hand against my cheek, a gentle touch at my back. I looked up at the lady to study her properly. She had a tender face, soft and sweet. Her beautiful skin, unspoiled and wonderfully dark, intrigued me. Despite her thick, common accent, she was dressed handsomely in an evening dress of flowing lace over velvet, her shoulders covered by a rain shawl and the peeler's coat she'd been given.

I knew a toffer when I saw one.

Being attractive, she'd no doubt be employed in a well-to-do upper-class establishment. But at the moment, and with another shudder, I realised a prostitute who promised me a home was all I had.

Her bonnet dripped rain as she whispered, "Come, lad." She pulled me up to my feet, supporting me, for I was still weak from grief that had consumed every fibre of my being. "It'll be for the best…bad luck to 'ang onto the dead, it is. There's naught you can do for 'em now, anyways."

I nodded assent. She escorted me away from the scene of my parents' murder; peelers were everywhere, including their wagons and the gawking onlookers who had come with them, breaths billowing vapour from their agape mouths like the chimney stacks of industry further down the Thames.

"What's your name, lad?"

"Oliver Merritt, ma'am," I replied, pushing out the words through my numb, cold lips.

"I'm Minerva, but folks all 'round 'ere call me Mimsee."

From that moment on, my life got really strange.

Chapter Two
More Than an Errand Boy

I came into adulthood during the time I stayed in the chamber Mimsee made me comfortable in. I was a weeping mess back then; I still am at times when I think about my parents, or something triggers the memory of that fateful night.

The room–my home, really–was on the third floor of a brothel, large and clean, with a vermin-free bed and a heavy wooden chest of drawers next to a nightstand. It had a copper tub in one corner for bathing and a couple of chairs, carved wood ones with padding made of a silk-like material where it mattered. Luxury it was, really.

Clothes were provided, as were regular meals.

Mimsee would come into the chamber every day and chatter to me about whatever took her fancy. Most of the time she told me stories of the men she'd had the previous night, laugh mockingly at their ineptitudes.

"Oh, you should 'ave seen 'is tackle, Oliver," she'd say, as she opened the window's drapes, tidied my chamber, then fussed over me. "'Onest as I stand 'ere, it looked like a bulldog 'ad chewed on it then spat it back out. Poor man didn't know what to do with it for starters!"

Most days she'd bring me sweetmeat treats. I'd eat them with relish, beginning to smile when she was around. And as the seasons changed from my window's view, my sullen, withdrawn mood began to blow away, like cobwebs giving way to a fresh morning breeze. It still hurt so badly to think of my parents, but as Mimsee had said to me during one of my brighter moments, "You'd better get on with your life. You won't give your parents' memory any 'onour by mopin' around 'ere all day. You've got somethin' special, you have."

"What's that?"

"You got the Talent."

When I asked her what that was, she shrugged. "Not for me to tell—only Lady Penelope or the Captain can do that. Not my place, it ain't."

That very day, Lady Penelope came into my chamber.

She moved as if she walked on air, her carriage as elegant as her composure. Lady Penelope was pretty for a woman older than my mother, dressed in all the finery and silk flowers money could buy, jewels dripping off her ears and neck like the London weather.

A man slid out from behind her, all greasy and spider-like with bloodshot eyes. I later found out, through Mimsee's chatter and jests about the man's physical appearance, that he was some sort of fancy High Street lawyer. All I know, he was wearing a smart black suit, stovepipe hat, and an inverness coat with matching cravat. He also smelt of pipe smoke. I almost choked from it when he came close to look at me, my eyes burning.

"This is the honourable Mister Bannister, Master Merritt," was all Lady Penelope said, her voice as silky as the flowers that adorned her breasts. Apparently, during my time of mourning, the lawyer had been finalising the paperwork for me to remain at the house under the Captain's and Lady Penelope's care.

Mimsee said something strange to me after they'd chatted between themselves, looking at me only for reference to their words before they left my chamber. "You'll 'ave to earn your keep now. Right good-lookin' lad like you should bring in many a pretty shillin' to the 'ouse. You mark my words."

"But I don't know if I'd be any good at what you do," I said, disbelievingly.

"Don't need to be good. Just need to make 'em happy."

"That's easy for you to say." I began to squirm, for I knew my fate now. Not that it worried me, I was just nervous. "You're a woman. Men like the pretty flowers—more than likely yours the most, guessing by how busy you are." I didn't mean that to sound disrespectful in any way, but didn't dwell on it, either. "Who'd be interested in me?"

She snorted out laughter, but like a lady, did so behind her hand. "Some men, 'specially the ones 'round 'ere, don't care as long as there's a pink 'ole to stick it in."

"Are you sure?" I hadn't thought about that. I thought I was the only one who liked my own kind. Many times, I'd sneak a look at some of the more handsome men that frequented the establishment. My father had always suspected I was different, but mother scolded him, telling him to let me be. I fought back tears at the deep pang of pain when I thought about her.

But it was true. I was different. Now that I was mature, most nights that maturity made itself evident over my stomach as I imagined one of Mimsee's clients giving me the attention they paid her for. Mimsee aired out my chamber often, but never complained when she saw my sheets after changing them. It was frowned upon in society for boys to touch themselves, but here, in my new home, nothing was ever questioned about what I did.

The next day, Lady Penelope called for me. I was to wear my Sunday best; Mimsee went and bought it. The suit itched but made me look good.

Mimsee wolf-whistled when I presented myself to her. "My word, you take my very breath, you do. Good enough to eat, I'd say."

"Thanks." I blushed.

She escorted me to Lady Penelope's chamber, rapping three

times on the door. I didn't want to let go of Mimsee's arm; I felt safe by her side. Not even the Skilamalink Man could strike fear into me when I was with her.

"Enter!" Lady Penelope called.

Mimsee urged me beyond the threshold but didn't enter with me. There I was, standing before my guardian, my tongue preventing me from swallowing as it seemed stuck to the roof of my mouth, my hands fidgeting behind my back. Her chamber was massive, but crowded with all sorts of furniture, both lavish and beautiful. Lady Penelope surveyed me for the longest time, lips pursed tight. Nerves struck me. I licked my fingers and then patted my hair in an attempt to plaster it in down further, the cowlick at my fringe stubborn to remove even with plenty of spittle.

After more tense moments than I could count, Lady Penelope said, "I was to ensure, by my Captain's orders, that you were to be well looked after. Have you been, Master Merritt? Have I kept up my end of that agreement?"

I was taken aback. "Of course," I mumbled in reply, forcing myself to unstick my glued tongue.

"Speak up, you've been addressed."

I managed to swallow. "Yes, ma'am, Lady Penelope, ma'am, I've been looked after. Thank you, ma'am."

"That's better." She touched a broach made of ivory and gold on her laced lapel. It must have meant something to her as her fingers lingered over it and her expression softened. "Now it is time for you to reciprocate. I look after you, and you look after me. Do you understand?"

I nodded.

"What was that? You have a voice; use it when you've been addressed or asked a question."

"Yes, ma'am, I understand."

"Good. Now, you will help us all around the house." I found

it funny that she referred to the establishment where she was the abbess as her house but I didn't say anything to provoke the matter. "You will help Cook prepare evening meals for the clients before they see my girls, then you will run errands as I see fit. This will keep you busy for most of the day, as you should be. Idle hands are the Devil's tools, and Mimsee tells me you've been very idle lately." I felt my cheeks heat at those words. "Time for that to change. You've mourned enough, and I've given you enough time. Now it is high time for you to get on with things. What do you say to that, Master Merritt?"

"I will do as you ask of me," I replied honestly. I did, however, want to ask why I was given menial tasks, when Mimsee herself had told me I could bring in far more coin to help earn my keep if given the chance. I asked the question, for better or worse. "Why won't you let me do what Mimsee does? She says they'd pay a lot for me, and I know she wouldn't lie."

"Only gentlemen frequent my house, Master Merritt." She seemed to dismiss me with her clipped answer. Her attention was now out the window, at a raven flying past.

But I added, "I don't mind—and I will perform your errands each day as you ask, but I also want to...*contribute* just like everyone else here. Why should I be treated any differently?"

She turned back slowly to meet my gaze, lips pressed thin to whiten them. "The Captain wants you looked after, and by extension, that means leaving you untouched. So that's what I shall do. Do you think our agreement entails that I have you with your head stuffed in a pillow and your bare buttocks in the air? No amount of money is worth what could be lost to me...*to us*...if I were to let you be deflowered. Do you want to lose everything, Master Merritt?"

I didn't understand what she meant. How could I lose everything if I worked in the house like the others? Mimsee had said some men liked other men, as I did. Surely there would be plenty of shillings for what I could do for them.

"No, ma'am, certainly not," I finally answered. But I steeled my resolve. If Mimsee could do it, live like a queen because of her fleshly talents, so could I. Then one day, I would be able to pay my own way with what I had earned. I could hunt the Skilamalink Man, using my riches to fund the expedition.

Being an errand-boy wouldn't give me enough coin to do that.

I had an idea that might satisfy both of us. "Mimsee says a lot of the wealthier men would just like to look at me, in my nakedness, I mean. They'd pay handsomely to see my gentlemanly assets, she told me. I wouldn't let them touch me, ma'am, if that's what worries you."

Lady Penelope un-pursed her lips. I could see the cogs of her mind working as she considered my words. "You do give me an idea, that's true." A pause. Another touch of her broach. "All right, Master Merritt, let's see you then. Show me your youthful trinkets; let me judge their worth, if that is what you want certain gentlemen to see for their shillings."

With a feeling of victory coursing through me, and without further hesitation, I disrobed proudly in front of her. As I stood there—more confident than when I walked in, empowered even—I could see the pennies, shillings, and sovereigns glint in her eyes as she studied me.

"Do you believe I'm worthy, Lady Penelope, ma'am?" I asked, already knowing the answer; Mimsee always gasped when she helped me dress and saw my nakedness.

Chapter Three
A Sailor's Boy?

Lady Penelope didn't reply to my question immediately. Instead, she seemed transfixed by my form. Staring at me as if a strange apparition had possessed her.

But I would never know what had transfixed her.

She quickly snapped out of her reverie. "I do have a very few select and exclusive clients who would appreciate your proposal, Master Merritt. Ones who will pay purse-fulls of sovereigns to see what I witness before me now. They, however, will require the utmost discretion for such things. As such, you won't be with the others; your work will be done separately. It won't be easy, but I can see you're keen to earn your keep."

Opportunity welled up inside me. "Thank you, ma'am."

An ugly line then worried her brow. "You are most certainly a fine lad, handsome and striking, there is no doubt. Not only have you ripened, your *arbour vitae*—as they say in circles where discretion is required—is a proud size for your age. And you are of age, Master Merritt, being eighteen. But let me warn you: a few of the clients I have in mind won't be satisfied to just look. They'll want you to use your hand upon yourself, give them a show of your youthful exuberance. That is fine by me, and up to you if you wish to perform such service.

"However, one or two will want to touch you, some very intimately. I will insist the price they pay for your company does not include that sort of contact. You will insist it also. You must remain untouched by others and unbedded, and there is no negotiation on that matter. It protects you with the agreement I have with our Captain, and it also protects my establishment. I don't want this to be a house known for rent-boys and molly rooms. My reputation is my honour, and I expect the same for those who work for me—including you. You will stick to this agreement to the utmost of thought and consideration. Do you understand me?"

"I understand, ma'am."

"Good," she said victoriously. "Now get back into your clothing and report to Mimsee as soon as she's available. She will teach you a trick or two—and how to deal with any wayward hands and determined libidos."

"Yes, Lady Penelope, ma'am."

"Oh, and Master Merritt? The Captain will be arriving back home four weeks from tomorrow. It will be his duty to talk to you about your Talent and how you will be able to get it to work for you. He will also ensure our agreement has been honoured. Don't let me down."

I didn't know how to reply to that. Those last few words she spoke were the strangest I'd heard since I was brought here my first night, that fateful night when my parents were murdered. What had she meant? I remembered Mimsee saying I had the Talent, and I remembered what had happened when it came out of me: it frightened off the Skilamalink Man. But what was this talk of controlling it? What did the Captain do? I wasn't to go to sea to become a seaman, was I? I heard sailors were rough, more so with young men like me. I suspected it was something else, though. Something deeper and darker maybe.

Mimsee wasn't available until the next day.

As such, I was compelled to begin my errands. I reported to

Cook that afternoon. She was a big, burly lady with plump breasts one could sleep on if they so desired; like the chimney-sweep boy was known to do from time to time.

Cook required fresh courgettes for an entree she was preparing that night. It was a Friday; the clientele would be plentiful.

I was to go to the market. She gave me the pennies with instructions given in her booming but warm voice to make sure I picked the freshest ones. This was the first time I'd been outside since that fateful night what seemed so long ago now. I took the longest moment staring up at the building I called my home once I was out on the street proper.

Lady Penelope and the Captain were most certainly rich enough to afford a three-story mansion deep in the ultra-fashionable garden areas of London.

My parent's home wasn't too far away...

That thought sparked a dormant memory about the night they were murdered, one that had been hidden previously because of my grief. I remembered that there was a heated discussion between my parents about debtors, some sort of trouble as a result, and my father deciding we'd be better off leaving England. Mother talked of France, but I couldn't be sure. Everything from those days was a haze—only small snippets of information leaked into my consciousness when certain sights, sounds, or smells triggered them.

Sadness struck me, but as Mimsee had said, I had to get on with my life, for it was getting better and better each day. I proceeded down the street toward the market, coming around a corner. A puff of smoke greeted me, looking like it was from a strange fire. A man breathed it out. The chilly air combined with it to give it more volume than was natural. I couldn't see his face.

He was shadowed. A shadowed man in a coachman's cloak.

I froze, those terrifying claws of fear clutching at me once more in bitter memory of what had been. I couldn't think of what to do. My mind was as clouded as the smoke that surrounded me. I only managed a weak, strangled cough.

Time seemed to slow as I was suddenly confronted with my horror, my dread. And just when I thought my life had become comfortable, my path at least surer. Damnation to my complacency. Tarnation to my stupidity. I should have woken up to myself earlier, gone to Lady Penelope sooner so I could work as we'd agreed, saving up all my shillings. Then I could have afforded a flintlock with plenty of ammunition. A weapon I wished was in my trembling hands right now.

I'd shoot the Skilamalink Man. Shoot him until he was as dead and cold as my mother.

That's what I'd do.

I went from fear to hate with a quick pound of my heart. My whole body stirred, and my loins ached. The awakening Talent rose up from deep within, fuelled by my emotions. I could feel the tendrils of light tickle down my wrists toward my hands.

"You want a ride, laddie?"

Just like that, the magic that raced within me dissipated.

I gasped, thinking of what I could have done: the man was a coachman. A horse's nicker and then an impatient neigh from the cobbled, straw-strewn street revealed him as such. The coachman clambered up into his box expertly. He grabbed the reins.

For a moment I couldn't speak, my body waiting for things to return to normal.

"I said, did you want a ride?" the coachman repeated.

"N-no. I'm fine…thank you, sir."

"Then I'll be off," the coachman said. To his horse he commanded, "Get going, Bessie!"

The coach lurched. With the clip-clop of hooves fading away, I was left alone. Sweat trickled down my brow. My hardness, however, lingered. Was the Talent waking up inside me more each day, like it was once a slumbering dragon but now roused to action? I breathed in deeply, taking a moment before I moved on, heading for the market as was my instruction. My heart still pounded, though; that would take an age to still.

That night, the Skilamalink Man haunted my dreams. I tossed and turned until deep sleep finally found me, but only because of exhaustion.

Chapter Four
Keep Your Pecker Up

"Well, I never. Clean sheets this mornin'," Mimsee stated matter-of-factly.

She had already opened the drapes and window; the sweetmeat treats waited for me on the nightstand. I was groggy, and the light that streamed into my chamber blinded me. My very bones were now sore from the residual effects of the Talent that was called forth prematurely yesterday. I could taste a strange tang on my tongue from it, worse than anything I'd ever eaten. I devoured the sweetmeats to rid me of its foulness.

"I had a bad night," was all I mumbled through a mouthful in reply to my best friend.

"You poor blighter, you. Well, cheer up," Mimsee said. "It's been given to me to teach you the tricks of the trade, as Lady Penelope sees shillin's of profit from you. As I knew she would, I did." There was a knowing wink from her.

With something sweet inside my stomach, I felt better. I smiled and clambered wearily out of my bed. Slipping off my nightshirt, I went to the chamber pot and did what my bladder needed me to do.

It didn't worry me Mimsee was there. She knew what I looked like under my clothing and what my body did naturally. Soon, she was calling the house servants to empty what I'd filled. It wasn't her job to remind them of their duty, and as a prized toffer of the house she wasn't required to wait on me either—but she did. That was her kindness; I loved her because of that.

I climbed into more appropriate clothing—drawers, trousers, shirt, and jacket, clean pressed and comfortable, and feeling the better for it. "Where do we start?"

"Not where, silly…'ow."

I didn't know what she meant.

Over the course of the morning, however, I quickly found out. She had me taking off my clothing, as slowly and seductively as I could manage under her tutelage. Many times, I had to get dressed again and again, repeating her instructions.

Each time, I believed I got better, less rushed and more appropriately sensual. Well, she didn't laugh as much by about the fifth or sixth disrobing. When it was time for midday dinner, a bell tinkling above the chamber door to announce it, Mimsee was beaming a smile.

"My word, Oliver. I think we'll make a good dancer of you yet, we will."

Her praise meant the world and I felt warmed by it.

After we had dined on the food prepared by Cook, a repast consisting of poultry, greens, and Yorkshire puddings, Mimsee produced one of the courgettes I'd purchased from the market yesterday.

"Now, Oliver, I've done and taught you enough to get you by for most of the men Lady Penelope 'as in mind for you. But you just keep far away from 'em if you get the notion that they're all 'ands. If you need to, kick 'em between their legs; that always drops 'em like a sack full of spuds."

"I understand." I winced at the thought of being struck between my legs; my bollocks separated in such a way would no doubt be painful. Yet, I looked at the courgette curiously.

She winked. "But now it's time to 'ave a little fun after all that work. I know you're not to be touched when you're workin', and never to be bedded, because that was Captain's orders. But, 'ey, why can't we have a good laugh? Besides, this'll be useful to know, as one day you'll be with that someone special…if you know my meanin'." She waved the courgette, drawing my attention to it. "And this 'ere will really teach you a trick or two about 'ow to please even the fussiest of men in the boudoir."

"What do you mean?"

"See, it's about the right size for the average man's tackle. I've gone and seen plenty in my day to tell you that's the truth." Sure enough, the courgette was about five inches or so long, not too thick, but one that was larger at the rounded end. For more realism, no doubt. "Now 'ere, too, see the skin of it's very soft. It'll tell you to keep your teeth away, as I'll see the marks on it. Men don't like teeth over their delicate bits—unless they ask for it, o' course."

"I think I understand."

"Now." She handed the phallic vegetable to me. "Go on, give it a good suck, Oliver, lovely. Let's see what you can do and 'ow you do it."

Again, just like my seductive dance, it took me a while to master the courgette. At first, I was simply too keen. Mimsee scolded me for trying to get it all in my mouth at once. It wasn't something for me to eat but to pleasure, she instructed. A worthy point of difference, I noted.

"It's tackle and attached," she explained with laughter. "You've gotta lick it, too. Get it all wet and slippery. Now, also, and don't you forget this bit, you'll 'ave to get your tongue around the rim of 'is end bit. That drives 'em crazy, 'cause most upper-class men these days are circumcised, they are. I know that as truth as well. But if they so happen to have the extra skin, then you can lick less—it's a lot more sensitive, you know. If you please 'im so 'e sees no other for 'im, you'll be set. You mark my words, you'll want to get a man who 'as plenty of shillin' to keep you when the time comes. That's my goal, it is."

Just like when she spoke of having to possibly kick a man in his delicate bits if he misbehaved, I felt queasy when she spoke of it being circumcised. My own parts seemed to have shrunk up in sympathy at the thought of someone cutting off a bit of it. But like a Light Cavalry hussar given his mission, I pushed that to the back of my mind and continued to service the courgette.

We had a grand old time.

By the Lord Almighty, we laughed and laughed. So much so, tears filled my eyes and that poor courgette probably wished it'd found Cook's soup instead of the games I played on it with my mouth. I did, however, succeeded eventually; not too many teeth marks marring its surface by the time our fun was done. I learnt quickly to flatten my tongue for better comfort.

My jaw sure got sore, though.

"Good, Oliver. Very good. Lady Penelope will be right chuffed with 'ow you caught on so quickly with your dancin'. Got me near on flushed it did, I 'ave to say. I shall go tell 'er of your progress…but the fun with the courgette, that's between you an' me, 'ear?"

I smiled, wiping dribble off my chin.

That afternoon, when Mimsee returned, she informed me that my first client would be at the house tomorrow night.

I had another day to prepare.

He was some important land-owning lord and in the area for a short time; the chance to gain his sovereigns was only a small window of opportunity. Lady Penelope had told Mimsee that I could have half of what was paid, as a trust for keeping my end of our arrangement.

I would do nothing less.

But I became nervous all of a sudden.

Even though this was what I wanted—to earn good money—I didn't think I was ready. What if I got frightened and my Talent came forth with my arousal because of it? I knew it was linked to my emotions and libido, but how exactly, I didn't know. Were they able to be separated? Could I control it better if they were? I could only hope this so-called Captain could shed light on all that. It surely mystified me.

But a worse thought struck me.

What would happen if the blue light from my hands burst forth uncontrolled to murder the poor, unsuspecting man while he watched me with my gentlemanly parts waggling about for his paid pleasure? Lady Penelope would be in the middle of a scandal. The press of Fleet Street would be crawling all through the house like ants over jam sandwiches at a High Society picnic. It would be my fault, and I'd be out on my ear. Then there would only be the fate of the Skilamalink Man for me, as I would know nothing more than I did now, the Captain not arriving for a month.

My nerves tingled to prick at my stomach like pins, but Mimsee came to reassure me I was going to be fine. She said I was a natural performer and that's all that mattered. I was to practice my routine. Be myself and relax. Don't even think of the man in the room.

She'd told me the high lord was a known voyeur who liked young men. He gave his word as a gentleman that he would behave and wouldn't touch me.

"I do hope you're right," I said, my nerves lingering through my words to make them stutter.

"Just keep your pecker up, Oliver," she said softly and reassuringly—not meaning my main gentlemanly attribute, but my spirit. "The first time's always the 'ardest. Ask me some day 'bout my first time…it'll give you the 'ives you'll laugh so much."

I said I would do that.

For the whole of the next day, I practiced. Mimsee judged, clapping and cheering me on as I got into it. Again, we laughed. But I couldn't help but get a dark, strange feeling about what was going to happen that night. I didn't know the how or why of it, but I knew something wasn't going to go well.

Chapter Five
Do You Smoke?

My fear was unfounded—at least when it came to the gentleman who paid handsomely to see me without a stitch on. I think it had something to do with me never uncrossing my fingers.

Not until the time to perform for him arrived quicker than blinking, anyway.

Because Lady Penelope wanted utmost discretion, I wasn't allowed in the main foyer to chat with potential clients and look enticing, as the girls did with their tight bodices and cleavage up to their chins. Instead, I was told to wait in the smoking room located on the second floor. I'd be hidden from prying eyes and questioning whispers that way.

Lady Penelope was there with me, but we held no conversation. Even though it was impolite to smoke in front of a lady, no one would be able to enter the room to do so.

Tonight, the room was mine for as long as the high lord required me.

After what seemed like an eternity, a slender man, tall, dark-haired and fanciable, carefully pushed back the red velvet curtains that covered the door's entrance. He entered as quietly as a church mouse. The man had a gentle face, almost womanly. He reminded me of Lady Penelope, if I was to give an honest assessment of his looks.

Lady Penelope got up and curtsied to him. As graceful as ever, and without a murmur, she took her leave.

"What is your name, my dear man?" Even though his lips

moved to ask the question, his eyes already had my measure. I could see them brighten.

"My name's Oliver Merritt, sir."

He sat down in the chair Lady Penelope vacated. I was dressed in clothing Mimsee had purchased with the money the house coffers allocated for me to do my job and look presentable. As Mimsee said, peeling off layers of fancy clothing built up the clients' interest even more.

It also loosened their purse.

I found the shirt to be a bit too ostentatious with frills around the cuffs and collar and silver struck buttons down the front. The rest of the suit—complete with bow tie, undershirt, waistcoat, and jacket—was comfortable and stylish. Not as good a quality as my Sunday best, but certainly more than respectable.

After my introduction, there was silence.

The high lord stared at me. Enough time passed to bring an unsettling discomfort into the room's atmosphere. I had to say, he was as quiet and still as a corpse—I'd mistake him for one if I hadn't seen him breathe. If I didn't know any better, I would have believed he was as nervous as I was; seeing his hands tremble confirmed it.

"W-would you like me to show you w-what I've got, sir?" I had nothing else to say to try and get on with proceedings; we were at a sort of stalemate before anything had even got started.

Mimsee never told me about the shy ones.

I'd have to inform her of that.

The high lord gasped at my question, but again his eyes reflected his curiosity and deeper hunger. Through murmuring lips, restricted by the sudden intensity between us, he whispered, "I would like that very much, Oliver."

I performed for him.

As I did do so, a small confidence washed through me. I realised I held the power here. I was in control. Lady Penelope had selected my first client well; he was most certainly content to watch, eyes wide as he did so.

The high lord was so enraptured, by the time I was completely naked he was rosy cheeked and held a satisfaction on his face that was unmistakable. I couldn't help but become aroused myself but controlled it enough so as not to encourage my Talent. That would be the last thing I needed—a dead high lord with a smile plastered on his face for the Fleet Street press to tell the world about.

When I had completed my routine, the high lord had buttoned up his trouser front and returned a retrieved handkerchief into his front jacket pocket. When he got that out or did his thing, I couldn't say. I was too involved in making sure I did the best I could for him, sticking to my routine but also concentrating on not causing any mishaps, Talent-related or otherwise.

But I did it.

"You are very…*handsome*…Oliver," he said with a satisfied sigh. His nerves seemed to have left him, as he now spoke with more confidence. "And my goodness, you are also very fortunate with what the good Lord has blessed you with. It was an absolute pleasure to witness what you showed me, and in the wonderful way in which you did so. Lady Penelope did well when she suggested I see you. I would be pleased by your continued company tonight…if that is what you want, of course."

"Thank you, sir. I'd like to stay." Although, for all his talk, he didn't say whether I was to get dressed or remain as I was. Mimsee informed me that I was to always do as the client wanted within the bounds of the agreement, and if that meant remaining without a stitch on for as long as they wished, then so be it.

In the end, he answered my question, but added another option. "Would you like to get into your clothing or stay as you are, Oliver?"

Mimsee never explained about a client giving me a choice. I didn't know the etiquette of answering the right way once proceedings had been completed. I decided to play his game, asking, "What would you like me to do, sir?"

"Oliver, you have done for me tonight something that I had only envisioned in my wildest dreams before now. For that I am grateful. But I am also a gentleman, as no doubt you are. So please, get dressed. Now is the time to get more accustomed to our surroundings. Do you smoke?"

I was taken aback by his request, but curious. "I haven't tried it, sir." I began to climb into my drawers, beginning the long road of putting all I had taken off back on again.

The high lord watched me do this task with just as much interest. By the time I was buckling up my spats, he had reached into his dinner jacket's inner pocket once more. This time, he retrieved a silver case with a small paper bag inside it. On opening, two cheroots were retrieved as well as the striking matches to light them.

I sat on the leather chair adjacent to him; it squeaked as I did so.

He lit both cheroots, puffing away on them in turn until curls of smoke wafted around him like he was a demon enjoying a vacation away from the fires of purgatory. "Here, Oliver. Like this," he said, showing me how to hold the cheroot between my index and second finger. "Draw back on it with a good lungful so the smoke tickles the back of your tongue and throat. Then breathe out through your nose to expel it."

Smoke billowed out of his nostrils. He slumped deeper into his chair, relaxing and clearly satisfied after my performance. He certainly no longer held any nerves. Neither did I. I liked this man. He was gentle and held a care about him that was almost intoxicating.

I, however, didn't get much more time to contemplate the

man's good points once I tried to smoke. The thing was vile in my mouth, burning and acrid, and I coughed so much the high lord had to pat me on the back several times just to still my convulsions.

Through watery eyes, my voice hoarse from my parched throat, I managed, "I think I need to practice this a bit more." I handed him back the cheroot. I'd had enough. He stubbed it out in the ashtray but continued to smoke his own.

"I do believe you're right," he said, a knowing smile on his lips.

After an hour or so of us both talking the business of small talk, with him asking me of the things I liked, from favourite colours to the types of cuisine I enjoyed, as well as what dreams and aspirations I had, he got up. I rose, too.

"I think it's time to call it a night, Oliver. Again, thank you for your most enlightening company. I was greatly educated by it."

"You're most welcome, sir." I then did something I never thought I would do for my first time with a paying client. I kissed him on his cheek. "It is my hope that I see you again."

His expression changed from the measured control he had held throughout the evening after his nerves abated, to surprise by what I did. His face brightened, eyes glistening brighter than jewels. "As is my hope as well."

Chapter Six
Be Still My Beating Heart

That evening, after Lady Penelope informed me she'd been watching through one of the many spy holes her house had in abundance, and concluded that I did well with the high lord, she gave me my earnings.

I held in my hand five gold sovereigns.

I'd never seen so much money. She also told me I should place it into an account—one she'd open for me at her private bank. It wasn't wise to leave money lying about the house, even behind the locked doors of private rooms.

I thanked her and thought her suggestion a prudent idea. The coins became warm in my hand, and I pocketed them.

As Lady Penelope escorted me toward the foyer, telling me to make sure I was refreshed before I retired for the night, there was an announcement by one of the house servants that she had a visitor.

Perhaps my fears about the night would come to fruition, after all.

As we entered the waiting room, a middle-aged, dashing peeler who cut a fine form dressed in his dark uniform greeted us with a smile over his handlebar whiskers.

"Sorry to disturb you, Lady Penelope. There's something you should see, if you may," the peeler said nervously.

Lady Penelope looked at me. "It seems your night isn't over yet, Master Merritt. I will need you to come with me. A lady should never go out into the night unattended."

"Of course, Lady Penelope, ma'am." I slipped my arm into the crook of hers.

When outside, the peeler led us down a side alleyway behind a row of pretty terraces that weren't far from the house.

That all too familiar fear began to prickle at my skin, sending gooseflesh over the exposed parts of it. We were led deeper into the alleyway, and my stomach turned. I had a terrible feeling the dark shape sprawled out on the cobblestones ahead of us wasn't that of an animal.

"There," the peeler said, gesturing toward the scene. "Me and Charlie found her only a moment ago—body's still warm." The aforementioned Charlie was standing over the dead woman, looking grim. "I thought you might recognise her. That's why I came to you straight away, Lady Penelope."

I didn't need to look too hard to know the body was one of the girls who worked at the house. I couldn't recall her name, but she was one of the newer ones and about my age. Very popular, she was, with her innocent looks.

The poor unfortunate lass.

My throat tightened and my mind wheeled back uncomfortably to the time of my parents' murder, dreadful emotions of loss and sorrow welling inside me once more. Lady Penelope must have sensed my discomfort, for she patted my hand, bringing me back out of myself. Her reassuring touch calmed me momentarily. I remembered to breathe, as my breath had been caught by the discovery and the memory it created.

"She is indeed someone I recognise, Constable," Lady Penelope stated, sadness in her words. "How did she die?"

"As far as we can tell, the poor girl must have died of some strange fright. There's not a scratch on her—neither a slash from a knife nor mark from a struggle. Right deuce of a conundrum it is, ma'am." He paused, looking intently at Lady Penelope. "Begging your pardon, rude of me to not realise you'll probably need some time to give your condolences to her before the others arrive and she's put in the draw."

"I'd like that, thank you, William."

From her candour with the peeler, I came to realise that Lady Penelope had many more contacts than high lords and wealthy men. More than likely she had a network of people from all class of folk who would assist her with her wishes and needs. I admired my guardian more and more each day I got to know her.

"Master Merritt, I'd like you to do something for me," she said once the two peelers had moved far enough away to give us their promised moment.

"Anything, Lady Penelope, ma'am. Just ask it of me."

"I need you to use your Talent to determine what you can about Nicole's unfortunate end. There's something suspicious going on here, and I will need to know its source."

That fear rose up again, this time for a different reason. "I-I don't know if I can, ma'am. I've not ever been able to use my Talent. Not to do anything useful w-with it, anyway."

"It's all about control, Master Merritt."

"It only comes when I get really emotional. And then…and then it arouses me and…and I try and stop it and it…it then goes away." I blushed when I said that; admitting such a thing in front of her was, for lack of a better word, embarrassing. Which was silly. She ran a brothel, one I now worked in. She had seen me without a stitch on, knew what I did at nights in private, had watched me with my first client. Because of that, she'd no doubt caught an eyeful of my manly exuberance rising to say good evening while I danced seductively for the high lord. So why was it *embarrassing* to speak of my body's primal functions to her at this moment?

Without a doubt in my mind, such a thing was because of

the situation, as if the dead body could hear. Which again, was ridiculous. Yet, my fears were usually correct. They defined me.

Lady Penelope patted my hand once more, bringing me back from my reverie. "Try, Master Merritt. Think of what you must do. The Talent is an extremely receptive extension of yourself. I only ask this of you because I believe the Skilamalink Man might be responsible for poor Nicole's demise, but I need you to help me confirm that. The only way to do so is with the Talent."

"The *Skilamalink Man*?" I croaked, aghast by her deduction and scared to my wits end by the realisation he could be close to me again. I stared at the body. Nicole stared up at nothing, as nothing was behind her eyes…just like my mother's had been.

I became angry.

At first it was a spark.

Then a warm, uncomfortable sensation washed over me.

I gasped as a bolt of energy like lightning coursed through me. Every emotion I had ever felt—from elation to ecstasy to hate and to fear—exploded all at once, vying for supremacy within me. I was frightened by its power. Oh, Lord Almighty, was I frightened. I could almost smell the Skilamalink Man's presence, like lingering pipe smoke.

Stalking me.

Taunting me.

My hands glowed with the familiar blue gaslight that revealed my Talent. As expected, along with my swirling emotions, my gentlemanly asset stirred to awakening. It began to ache uncomfortably, pressing against my drawers.

As I tried to accomplish what Lady Penelope requested, control my Talent, calm my thoughts and my raging libido at the same time, the light extended in curling wisps beyond my fingers.

I gasped again, this time not in shock, but in complete surprise.

For a moment, that sight caused me panic. The result was that the light flickered like a candle flame in a breeze. I didn't want to lose control already.

With deeper breathing, I managed to regain its glow.

Through the luminous extension of myself, and as it touched Nicole's body, I discovered something more terrible than I would have ever imagined. I reeled, now unsteady on my feet. I pulled back, severing the glowing Talent bridge between us.

Thankfully, Lady Penelope grabbed me. In her arms I remained until my body returned to normality. I knew the truth. The terrible realisation of what I faced if I was to gain any justice for my parents' murder.

"The Skilamalink Man murdered Nicole...and my mother and father...by using the Talent. He has it, Lady Penelope. He has the Talent as I do. He...he used it to still all his victim's hearts. Not just still them...but cause them to rupture inside them. Nicole and my parents didn't stand a chance."

Chapter Seven
The Marrow Within the Bones

I had to change out of my drawers straight away when I got back into my chamber. My Talent had caused my manly fluids to release. Mimsee sponge bathed me in the copper tub once it had been filled by the house servants. The water was hot and pleasantly scented with soothing rose oil.

I felt relaxed for the first time all evening; it was a revelation.

"You 'ad such a fright you did, Oliver," she said, rubbing my back with the sponge, her attention on untying the tautness in my muscles. "I was beside myself to see you like that. You were as white as a sheet when you came back, you were."

She was with me now on Lady Penelope's request, even though it was late. By rights she should be in her own bed—she, too, had a third-floor room—but they were all worried about me. Mimsee more so, judging by the way she fussed with the sponge.

I hadn't spoken since my discovery.

The Skilamalink Man haunted me even worse now. I knew with certainty he had the Talent. But there was a difference. He knew how to control it far better than I, as he was able to murder with it. I didn't have a clue about how to control my magic.

When she was done towelling me dry, I slipped into my night shirt. I then clambered into bed, weary and tired. Mimsee was at my chamber's door, about to leave.

"Stay with me here tonight, Mimsee," I said, finally feeling the urge to speak.

"Well, I never." Her startled expression didn't stifle her

common humour though. "If I do, Oliver, it'll be the first time I've been in bed with a man who doesn't want 'is tackle deep inside my fairest flower."

I couldn't help it—I laughed.

She had such a way, even if it was only with a turn of a phrase, to knock me out of my moods. Comfort me. I really did see her as someone important to my life. I hoped she felt the same as I did. Then again, no mere associate would do the things she did for me.

"Please."

"Then who will bring in your sweetmeats, may I ask?"

"I can do without them for one day."

She stripped to her petticoat and chemise and snuggled up beside me in a bed that was more than ample for two. I held her hand, feeling safe. She kissed me on the cheek. I soon began to feel my eyelids gain weight. Mimsee's gentle breathing only added to me hastening my visit to the land of slumber.

I got up early, the morning spent running errands for the house. I had brightened thanks to Mimsee and Lady Penelope's care the night before. But the revelation about the Skilamalink Man hung over me like a black cloud threatening rain over an annual church fete.

I hurried my gait.

At the market, I bought fresh-cut flowers to replace the ones in the rooms that had been there for a week, readying them for the busy Sunday night's trade. Mimsee said I was a natural at arranging flowers, but I had just plopped them into the vase, turning it until the best of them faced out.

I also completed the list Cook needed for the house's mid-day dinner roast. A big leg of gammon, costing a pretty penny and heavy to carry with the rest of the things I bought. But I managed it.

Lady Penelope entertained all her employees over a Sunday roast in her large, stately dining room. We sat in chairs of the finest craft, the silver cutlery set out before us on a massive, French-polished table. We were all to make sure we were clean, presentable, and in our best. She always checked behind my ears and under my fingernails before I could sit down.

I looked forward to that hearty meal, and my mouth watered in anticipation of it. Cook really knew how to prepare delicious roasted meats, potatoes, and vegetables all smothered in lashings of gravy made from the juices of the pan. Sunday dinner was one of the best times of the week in the house. It was a time where work was far from everyone's minds and relaxation was the order of the afternoon.

After dinner, I had several hours' free time before I was to meet my client at seven o'clock that evening. He had paid in advance: six gold sovereigns now lined my pocket. I wondered why I had been paid the extra coin.

Lady Penelope asked me to join her in the smoking room earlier than I was expected to be in attendance. I was delighted to do so. Not so much when I quickly discovered her aggressive streak when it came to competition.

She had decided to teach me how to play chess, a game comprising of complicated strategy and concentration. I also realised she liked to win at all costs. Even when I started to pick up the gist of it, she played harder.

She was tenacious.

"This will teach you about lateral thinking, Master Merritt," was her answer when I questioned why she hadn't gone easy on me and let me win, not even once.

After the games, and with us both sipping on tea from thin bone china cups you could see the shadow of your hand through, she gave me due warning about my client and the reason for the extra money. I was ready for him by the time I reported back to the smoking room, now dressed in the many layers of my *working suit*, as I'd came to call it.

A crease of worry marred her brow, if only slightly.

"I'll be all right. I promise, ma'am."

She nodded. "The physician is a very particular and determined man. Make sure you read his intentions—you know our agreement," she warned. "At this juncture it is high time I tell you that our agreement is more than you realise. You must know some truth, Master Merritt. The Talent doesn't reside in those who have become impure. I should have told you of this earlier, but you chose to work in my house in this way, and I must respect that. Now I am left with little choice." She paused, sipping on her tea. "You're also a man, and I take your word as your honour until you prove otherwise. I have the utmost faith in you. But know this, Master Merritt: if you want to rid London of the Skilamalink Man, the only way to do so is with your Talent. We know he has it, and as such you must keep yours."

"I...I don't quite follow your meaning."

"What I mean, is that if you do become deflowered, or engage to deflower another, you will lose the Talent. That is the sacrifice those blessed with magic must face and endure. You will never know love's deepest physical touch—even when you find someone special to share it with." She fingered her broach once more. Now I could see it up close, it was a portrait of a dashing man with a handlebar moustache and a determined look.

I was both horrified and curious by what she told me. Lady Penelope seemed to know an awful lot about the Talent. Did she once possess it? Had she then chosen to lose it because the man represented in the broach stole her heart from her?

I swallowed hard.

Her news made things more complicated.

If what she said was true, I had to be careful. More so when the physician burst through the curtains and her words of warning about him echoed within my mind.

He was flamboyant for his excess weight, no doubt. Dressed in a men's frock coat, dark in colour and appropriate for the evening, complete with a garish floral buttonhole and antique cufflinks, he swished across the floor to where I was seated. He had a mischievous smirk and beady, pig-like eyes. For some reason his hands were already gesturing wildly, just as his look did when he spied me sitting there.

I smiled up at him.

"Oh, the perspicacity of your words about this perfect one, Lady Penelope, is the truth. The truth, I tell you. It truly quickens my otherwise quietened heart to see such an angelic vision before me, now I've gazed upon him with my very own eyes." The physician was licking his lips as if he were a foxing hound at mealtime, savouring for the marrow within the bones. "I cannot delay any longer to see what my sovereigns will reveal of you, my dearest young man. My wanting has taken me over. Taken me over it has indeed!"

Nerves found me again.

More than when I was with the high lord.

Chapter Eight
The New Cure

I faced the physician, the smell of pipe smoke wafting up to sting my nostrils. "It would be my pleasure to dance for you," I said, emulating his form of speech as best I could, even though I was nervous, "and show you my nakedness, sir."

His eyes widened, a kaleidoscope of his carnal desires reflected within them. "What name do you go by, my handsome angel incarnate?"

"Oliver Merritt, sir."

"Capital! Capital, I say. A name of delight for such a delightful young man, indeed."

Lady Penelope curtsied, but instead of remaining silent, she whispered into the physician's ear, "See that you only use those dazzled eyes of yours while he's in your company. Otherwise, you'll find yourself at Her Majesty's pleasure." Her words didn't hold venom, only warning.

The physician didn't flinch. In fact, his wolfish grin widened. "I can gleam a lot through these old eyes, madam. But on a gentleman's agreement, as well as the value of my coin, I will do as you request."

"Then we understand each other."

"I am elated we are friends, madam, for to be your adversary would be a terror." But his voice brightened further when he looked at me once more, as if savouring my presence dispelled all his concerns. "Besides, this is the first time you've offered me a young man in all the scores of years I have frequented your business. I'll be on my best behaviour to ensure there will be plenty more encounters with him. He is simply wonderful. How did you know I liked them tall, dark-haired, and handsome?"

My dark hair I inherited from my father—one of the few things I liked from him.

Lady Penelope curled the corner of her lip. "Call it woman's intuition."

She left the smoking room, but I knew she'd be watching through one of the many private spy holes scattered throughout the house. In a way, that reassured me.

The physician sat. "Now, Oliver—may I call you by your first name? It is a touch unceremonious to do so for the recently introduced. But considering what you're about to do for me, I deem it more appropriate, don't you?"

"You may call me Oliver, sir. That is my name." I came to stand in front of him, making sure I was out of arm's reach at a stretched lean. "And, yes, I do think so, sir."

"You may dispense with all the 'sirs.' I'm Harold."

I was taken aback. Gentlemen didn't usually reveal their first names to paid entertainment. Not according to Mimsee. "Yes…Harold."

The physician named Harold took in a deep, wanting sigh. Mimsee had also taught me how to read the behaviour of people, particularly men. I took that as a sign I needed to get on with things.

As far as the dance went, I had him salivating.

By the time I was without a stitch on, running my hands slowly and sensually across my own skin, he was panting. His jowls and cheeks were flushed red and sweat beaded on his brow.

"Oh, my…you're a vision of Adonis himself, Oliver. A youthful God…not marred by the circumciser's blade as is fashion of late. You, my angel, are from a time that harkens back to antiquity, blessing me with your presence," he stammered, dabbing his brow with his handkerchief.

"Thank you. It has been my pleasure." I knew what the extra coin was for. As Lady Penelope's warning filled my thoughts, I had to ask, "Is there anything else I can do for you, Harold?"

He gasped, fanning his face with the hand that wasn't rubbing against his groin underneath his undone trouser front. But he wasn't finished. I could still see his carnal needs flashing voraciously within his eyes.

"There is, indeed, Oliver, my beautiful one. Would you be so kind as to pleasure yourself for me until you come to your ending?"

There it was.

To hear the words shocked me even though I knew they were coming. Without undue hesitation, I replied, "Yes, of course."

"Bless you," he whispered. Harold's lips trembled, jostling his jowls once more, while his hand on himself, covered over by his clothing so I couldn't see his arousal, moved with more intent. "Bless you."

Lady Penelope had informed me that Harold—and indeed others—would want me to touch myself for their pleasure after I had disrobed and danced for them. The reason was simple; it was considered distasteful to do such a thing, and witnessing it was a risqué excitement.

One many were happy to pay for.

Some even believed it was a sickness to masturbate. That doing so would make one go mad, and that circumcision was the so-called "new" cure for such a disease.

It all added to the excitement for them to watch me pleasure myself.

Most of the house's clients had many constraints and expectations on them. Being proper reflected their status, and status was everything. But it was also their curse. People didn't want to be proper, Lady Penelope had explained.

Not all the time.

As such, with the two clients I had entertained so far, I'd earned more money showing them my bare skin than half the girls of the house had with men sweating over them all night. She informed me the demand for what I offered was increasing exponentially. I had enough work for every night of the week if I wanted it.

I wanted the work, but I had to be careful.

My Talent was my only weapon, I knew that now. I couldn't lose it. The Skilamalink Man still hunted, and with gold sovereigns filling my purse, I would become his hunter.

By the time my climax rained over my quivering stomach, Harold had also reached his conclusion. I hadn't noticed when that happened. All I knew was that he got up quickly, heading over to the drinks cabinet to fix us both a London Dry as if his life depended on it. The beverage, as he explained it, was a clean mix of gin, freshly squeezed grapefruit juice, and thyme.

With his back turned, I saw my worst fear realised.

My hands were glowing.

Terror prickled at my insides. A cold sweat now accompanied my skin more than my manly release of earlier. Had Harold seen my freshly manifested Talent because of my ecstasy?

I tried to calm myself before Harold returned with the drinks. Which made matters worse, because thinking of a thing brings it to the fore more so.

My fear didn't ease.

Thankfully, Harold took his time mixing the gin, humming a ditty I didn't recognise. By the time the sloshing sound of the liquid within the cocktail mixer filled the smoking room, I knew I had to hurry with whatever it was I was going to do so he wouldn't see my Talent.

I found that amusing, in a strange way.

Here, I had just shown him how I was intimate with myself, yet the other secret connected to my libido I was petrified to reveal. Beads of perspiration trickled from my brow as if to emphasise that thought.

"Control. Control. Control," I whispered as if it were a mantra to myself. I had previously placed a handkerchief next to me.

Thankfully, I didn't have to move off the stool to wipe away the result of that extra coin Harold had paid me. For the moment he was busy. If I was careful, I wouldn't draw attention to my glowing hands and have him asking for an explanation.

"What was that, my dear sweet, Oliver? Did you speak something to me?"

"Just to say that I have a thirst. And that I wait with anticipation for what you've prepared for me, Harold." I cursed myself as soon as those words left my lips. Damnation to my ingrained courtesy and indoctrinated etiquette.

"Capital. Then I shan't keep you waiting any further." He turned toward me, but my hands still harboured the blue luminescence.

Chapter Nine
The Talent Revealed

Like a blessing, Lady Penelope entered the smoking room. I placed my hands behind my back, taking full advantage of the distraction.

"How did you find your experience with Oliver, my friend?" She glanced to me. Her fleeting look told me one thing: I was to calm myself further so my Talent could quicken its dispersal.

"I must say Oliver gave quite an exquisite performance, one even the most hardened critiques of such things would find hard-pressed to fault. Most satisfactory. Most satisfactory, indeed."

"I am pleased to hear it." Lady Penelope plucked the glass of gin that was supposed to be mine from the physician's hand.

He looked incredulous for a moment but must have thought otherwise about protesting, offering a shrug instead. I imagined he was hoping to hand it to me personally. Her quick action, however, ensured he wouldn't see what he wasn't supposed to when I would have been compelled to take the glass.

Again, I found that amusing.

"I would appreciate it very much if Oliver was to perform for me frequently," he suggested, as his beady eyes studied my nakedness. "If you're enthusiastic to the suggestion, Oliver. Naturally."

I nodded. "I'd like that."

Lady Penelope interjected, "I am sure we can work something out." She placed my drink onto a small round-topped table beside the stool I still sat upon. I didn't reach for it, not certain whether my Talent was still present. "For the moment, my friend, would you like to use our private bathroom down the hall to clean yourself up? My servants will be instructed to expect you and wash whatever clothing is required. It is all part of the service, of course." Her words weren't hurried, but I could detect the tone of concern within them.

"Most kind of you." He tore his gaze from me to glance down at his drink longingly.

"You may take your drink with you. Also, a light supper will be provided; I'm sure you've worked up quite the appetite."

Harold nodded, as I had a moment ago. He seemed a little dumbfounded and somewhat saddened. No doubt he was expecting to spend more time with me; Lady Penelope's intrusion had been sudden and unforeseen.

He accepted her invitation, as a gentleman would.

When Harold left the smoking room, Lady Penelope sat with deliberate purpose on an ornate, cushioned chair next to me, her fancy dress billowing around her as she did so.

"Show me your hands," she ordered.

I did so without hesitation. My Talent still lingered. I felt ashamed, like a scolded boy caught stealing sweetmeats from the larder.

"I'm sorry," was all I could offer.

"Don't be sorry. It's not your fault." Her shoulders relaxed and the worry lines softened across her brow. "I did warn you, when you first suggested to me how you wanted to earn your keep, that this very thing could happen. Did I not? What would you have done if he'd seen your Talent?"

"I don't know," I replied weakly.

"Oliver." She heaved a sigh. "In intimacy you cannot be touched, you cannot touch others, and as you now know, being with yourself can be just as dangerous."

That was the first time Lady Penelope had called me by my

first name. It shocked me more than the contents of what she'd said.

"I don't understand…"

"I told you, you must remain pure for your Talent to remain."

"I understand that part—"

"I don't believe you do." I was taken aback. I didn't know what she meant but didn't have time to contemplate it. She continued, "We have to be very careful, which is why I am screening your clients to the point of obsession. The men I choose for you are all good natured, even though they have a penchant for young men they need satisfied. Yet, because of constraints they have upon them, imagined or otherwise, they dare not do anything that would prick at their guilt to unravel too much of their conscience. They are all men of reputation, and by paying us to *only* look at you, they are able to justify that in their own minds.

"But you never know. Sometimes the heat of the moment could cause some of these men to act out on their deeper lusts, without thought of the consequences. I can't predict that, and neither can you. That is why I remain close when you are working. If something untoward did happen during one of your performances, do you think the Talent knows the difference?" She took a breath, touching her broach. "You will report to my chambers after your midday dinner every day. It is high time I taught you how to use your Talent properly so you can not only defend yourself but be able to use it effectively against your enemies as well."

I was humbled, but managed, "I thought only the Captain could do that?"

She stared at me for a moment, as if wrestling with something within her. Finally, she patted my hand. "When the

Captain isn't in my house, I am in charge and will do as I see fit for those under my care, Oliver."

I was now stunned.

"I didn't…I—"

"I will explain everything to you later, and in due course. For now, get dressed and prepare yourself for bed. I have many errands for you to perform early tomorrow morning. Mimsee will attend to you, as I know you have become close friends."

That "later" she promised didn't come quickly. Even though Lady Penelope had told me to report to her chamber each day after dinner, her servants politely informed me she was indisposed and couldn't be seen.

That happened for two weeks.

In the meantime, I worked. I ran errands for the house, as was instructed by Cook or Mimsee, and performed each night. During Lady Penelope's absence, Mimsee became my secret chaperone. She must have also known about the spy holes of the house. Which didn't surprise me.

"For 'elping you, Lady Penelope 'as been givin' me a share of the money you prize so easily from those lobcock men, Oliver. It's a real treat it is to 'ave all those extra gold coins janglin' in my purse, let me tell you. I'll soon be able to buy jewels like all those rich girls wear. Fancy that, 'ey? Me, all done up like butter on bacon. I'll be the talk of London, I will."

"Lobcock men?" I repeated, curious.

"You know, lovely. The men who can't get it up no longer for want of tryin'. The ones whose wives can't satisfy 'em no more, and they crave somethin' extra saucy just to get any kind of feelin' back inside their tackle—like what you do for 'em, see."

"Oh, I see."

Within the two weeks, and while I waited for Lady Penelope's audience, all those I danced for were unremarkable. I don't even remember them. They were blank, nameless faces staring at me while I performed my routine.

I was always polite to them, though. "Did you enjoy that, sir?" I'd say. "Did you want me to get dressed now, sir?" was another common phrase. They were nice in return, promising they'd be back. "I look forward to that, sir." The conversation was becoming an art form, as much, if not more than, the dance itself.

By the time it came to the Friday evening before the second weekend without seeing Lady Penelope, surprisingly, my client that night was the high lord. I didn't expect him back so soon. The one man's company I enjoyed was his.

Dressed in an auburn-dyed angora smoking jacket with a pristine white shirt, pressed slacks, and shiny shoes, he looked more dashing than the first time I took his custom. He'd started to grow the beginnings of a moustache and goatee. Lord Almighty, he was handsome; breathtakingly so. I also began to realise he was younger than I first believed, as dressed so dashingly he looked no older than twenty-one, if not a day.

That time he wasn't as nervous but remained gentle and considerate in both his manner and his treatment of me. I changed my routine for him; touching myself more, even giving him a good look at my posterior as I turned and danced seductively. He was grinning from ear to ear, like a kid with a pocket-full of farthings visiting the boiled sweet shoppe.

His handkerchief was at the ready.

Afterward, as I'd finished dressing and I sat in the chair next to him, he offered me the obligatory cheroot, already lit. I attempted to smoke again. I got three puffs into me that time before I felt my lungs wanted to be on the outside of me rather than the inside.

My discomfort amused him, but he was never malicious about it. "You'll get the hang of it soon, Oliver."

"I hope so, sir," I wheezed.

He shifted his weight in his seat, leather creaking. "Does Lady Penelope treat you well, Oliver?" He took a deeper draw of his cheroot, studying me, his eyes glinting through the smoke.

"She's treating me very well, sir." For a moment I tried to gauge if there was any other purpose to his question. After quick consideration, I believed he talked straight to me. "I couldn't ask for a better guardian than her. I'm well fed, clothed, and have a warm bed every night. Far more than most orphans from what I hear. What's more, she lets me keep—" I cut myself of momentarily, catching myself before I revealed, unintentionally, that she only allowed me to continue my performances under the condition that I do so without awakening my Talent. I hastily added, "the money I earn for myself so long as I do my chores. One day I'll be able to become independent, if I wish it. I really can't ask for better care, sir."

"That's good to hear. However, I feel we can dispense with the pleasantries, Oliver." He took another deep draw of the cheroot. "You may call me Arthur, if it doesn't make you too uncomfortable; it's my favoured middle name."

"I'm not uncomfortable calling you Arthur."

Now two of my clients wanted me to refer to them by name. The two I so happened to like the most. In fact, for various reasons—both poles apart—I could easily fall for either of them if my circumstances were different. Arthur for his gentleness and consideration; Harold for his zest and liking me to the point of worship.

"You are fortunate indeed, Oliver, to have come under the care of Lady Penelope. I only ask, because those with a talent such as you possess aren't usually treated so well."

Chapter Ten
When Opportunity Knocks

Unfortunately, when he spoke those words, I was attempting the fourth draw on my cheroot. Suffice it to say, I almost inhaled the whole thing because of the shock.

Through a billow of foul smoke, eyes watering, throat searing, I coughed, gasped, and barked, "How…do you… know…that?" How *did* he know I had the Talent? It hadn't manifested itself…had it? I had to think quickly but couldn't recall. I was too engrossed in the revised routine I'd performed for him.

Perhaps it had…

He seemed taken aback. "It is well known how those who work in places like this are treated, Oliver. I was only referring to the way you danced for me. It was most enchanting. So much so, I must admit, I used my handkerchief far too soon."

My mistake struck me. I continued to try and clear my clogged up with smoke lungs. "I-I thought you meant something else. The cheroot…it made me come over all strange and giddy for a moment, that's all," I lied.

"Ah, I see."

"It was my pleasure, Arthur. I enjoy performing for you." And that wasn't a lie; I really did like stripping down to nothing and dancing uninhibited, especially for him.

"You do have a special talent in the way you hold attention to yourself. The presence you command is both alluring and beautiful. I am most grateful that Lady Penelope has taken you into her care, as I can plainly see on your body that you haven't been abused and you *are* fed and well looked after. That pleases me. A good-looking young man like you deserves the best." He reached into his smoking jacket's front pocket, retrieving six golden half-crowns, the coins jangling in his hand. "These are for you. A little tip for your performance tonight, if you will. Spend them well, Oliver."

My eyes lit up, and I accepted his money with nothing more than grace. "Thank you." I couldn't think of anything else to say. I was overwhelmed.

The high lord got up and I stood as well. "I have another opening in my schedule, so I will see you again this coming Sunday evening. I'll have something else for you then that I think you'll appreciate."

"What is it?" I blurted without thought.

He patted me on my shoulder. "You'll have to wait and see, Oliver." That time, he was the one who kissed me on my cheek. His lips were soft against my freshly-shaven skin. I shivered, delighted. "And I thank you for returning to my life a sense of how beautiful it truly can be considering what's been going on with me lately."

He turned and disappeared through the curtains.

I was alone for a moment, bathing in the glow of satisfaction as the lingering tickle on my cheek from his immature whiskers warmed me. I smiled to myself.

"Well, I never," Mimsee said, bursting into the smoking room. As always, she never stood on ceremony with her words. "'Is 'igh and mighty's got the eye for you, Oliver. Ain't no doubt."

"He's a sweet man, that's all."

"Sweet on gettin' you into 'is bed where you'll be 'is tupping boy, you mark my words."

"You're such a tease, Mimsee. And you know I can't do anything like that, even if I wanted it. Besides, I don't think he's like that. He's too gentle and kind and worried about my welfare. You heard what he said."

"If you ask me, and I'll tell you even if you ain't, there can be worse things to lose than your Talent."

"What are you talking about?"

She snorted, "Opportunity, lovely. Opportunity."

"I've...I've got to *keep* my Talent. My mother...and...and all—" my words became stuck in my throat. My eyes welled. I had to blink rapidly to stop my vision from blurring.

She embraced me, and I held her for a long time.

"There, there, I didn't mean that, I didn't. I know you can't do that. What you 'ave, Oliver, is somethin' that mustn't be given away with the bat of an eyelid. No. All I'm sayin' is there's more than one way to kill a cat than chokin' it with cream. If the offer 'e's goin' to give you is about 'im deflowerin' you, then it's not on, it isn't. But if 'e proposes somethin' else, let me tell you, 'e's right about folks being mistreated."

"Are you suggesting he's offering me a job?"

"Could be." She shrugged. "Besides, you've gotta think about what'll 'appen when you get older. Your tight backside and firm body won't last forever, you mark my words, Oliver. No man worth 'is salt pays to see wrinkles and skin saggin' in all the wrong places. Only the bunters can get trade when they've gone past their prime—and that's a rough life, that is. All of us 'ave got to think of the future, we 'ave. Even little ol' me."

"But Lady Penelope will look after us, won't she?"

"She's a wiltin' flower—she's not gonna last forever, is she? What happens when she's gone, 'ey? We've got to think of ourselves; best that way. Take the opportunities as they arrive at our door."

I pondered her words for a moment. "Something will happen, it always does. You found me when I was at my lowest.

And now Lady Penelope said she'll teach me how to control my Talent. There'll be opportunities, as you say. I know it."

"I 'ope you're right."

"I am."

She hugged me again. "I do love you so, you know that."

"I love you, too—with all my heart."

As for speculating about what Arthur wanted to give me, I had to wait until Sunday evening arrived. No use worrying about it until then. Instead, I reached into my suit-coat's pocket where I'd placed Arthur's generous tip. Mimsee's eyes brightened at the sight of the half-sovereigns in my hand. I sorted three coins from the six.

"These are for you."

"You don't 'ave to give me no coin. It's yours. You earned it."

"We share when you look after me. Besides, it's for our future. Agreed?"

She nodded. "Agreed."

After my client the next night, a pasty-faced weedy man who stunk of pipe smoke, and before I retired for the night, I decided to see if Lady Penelope was available. Her servants weren't in attendance. I knew she only wanted me to see her after my mid-day dinner, but something within me compelled me to try now.

I rapped three times, but not too firmly, on her chamber door. I didn't want to give her the impression of impatience after a fortnight of waiting to see her.

"Come in, Oliver."

My heart skipped a beat. Lady Penelope was home, but her voice was different…deeper. She also knew who was at her door before I'd revealed myself. That was strange.

I entered eagerly but burned with curiosity at the same time.

Standing by the window, drapes undrawn to let moonlight bathe the room, wasn't who I expected.

Chapter Eleven
The Captain Returns

It most certainly wasn't Lady Penelope. I couldn't imagine who it was in her chamber, as no one got into her room without her express permission or knowledge. My curiosity burned even more.

"Hello?" I enquired quizzically.

After moving into the room deeper, avoiding the exquisite furniture that crowded her chamber, I could see the person a little better now they were no longer in silhouette.

He wore an indoor suit of the darkest blue. Lounge slippers and matching shirt, lighter in shade than the jacket, completed the leisurely look appropriate for late evening after one had retired but not yet ready for bed.

"Is that you...*Captain*, sir?"

The man turned to face me, revealing his face proper.

"Yes, Oliver. It is." Again, that strange deepness of tone—as if put on but done so with a practiced voice. After he lit a cluster of candles atop a nearby stand, I couldn't believe my eyes. He *was* Lady Penelope.

I gasped. "You're—"

"Now you know, Oliver, my dear." Then back into her familiar, feminine and regal voice, she added, "Now you know my secret, as I know yours."

For the longest time I was speechless, standing stock still, mouth agape.

Lady Penelope—no, the Captain—then stilled some of the

many questions in my mind that buzzed around like bees in a jar with her next words. "I have spoken to you previously about society and expectations, haven't I, Oliver? Well, let me enlighten you further. Please, do sit." She gestured for me to take a seat.

I did as she instructed, feeling numb.

Unable to help myself, I stared at a person I had only ever seen in frilly, lacy finery and covered in jewels. "I apologise for not attending to your training as I wanted, but I have been away on urgent business these past two weeks, disguised as my late husband. The reason you must know, as you deserve it." There was a pause while I got comfortable and my numbness faded. "As a woman in today's world, I have many crosses to bear. Far more than a man would ever understand. A woman cannot vote, she cannot sue another who wrongs her, and she cannot, most importantly, own property. I have, therefore, taken on the persona of my late husband to ensure what was ours remains with me." It was clear the ivory and gold broach was a portrait of her husband, the *real* Captain. It was pinned on her lapel, never far from her touch; even dressed as a man she wore it.

She continued, "I have done all this with many sympathetic lawyers and friends to aid me—Mister Bannister, the lord you know as Arthur, and many others included. They helped me retain what I have worked for all my life, including this house and my business. But most of all, the fortune I have amassed."

"I think that's…what you've done is amazing."

And it was. She was a strong woman, but from what I could see of her now, she was an even stronger man. I held nothing but admiration for her. Also, her disguise was good, the wig and make-up done so as not to arouse suspicion except under the closest scrutiny. She'd even bound her breasts close to her chest, probably painfully so. No one who never knew her as Lady Penelope would question that they weren't addressing a man. Of course, the voice, even though strange as I heard it and quite a good imitation, wouldn't have mattered. She would have got her lawyers to do most of the talking. Lawyers loved to jabber, anyway.

"Why, thank you." She smiled. "You're a good lad, Oliver. I knew it from the first day you came to me—and not just because of your Talent."

I blushed. Compliments from Lady Penelope were rare, and I lapped it up. "I'll always be grateful for what you've done for me, Lady Penelope, ma'am. You, and now Mimsee, helped me when I've needed help the most."

"You may refer to me as Captain in private company, Oliver. I'm Lady Penelope when others are listening."

"Yes, Captain." I enjoyed saying that; it was kind of salacious, calling a woman something a man was usually referred to.

"Now, if you please," she slipped off her leisure jacket, placing it neatly over the rail of a straight-backed chair, "help me out of this rather uncomfortable attire. The cloth I use to press down my bosoms gets painful, and I've been strung up in it all day."

"Yes, Captain, ma'am."

Over the next hour, I attended the Captain. It was sort of dream-like and surreal to attend a lady in such a way, helping her transform from a man. There was an almost religious procedure to it, careful and considered and well-practiced. Many times, my hands simply got in the way of all the ties and laces and loops I had to fiddle with to help her complete the transformation.

Here I was, attired in my working suit with its many layers, but that was nothing compared to what she required. Under her nightgown and sleeping jacket of tan dyed silk and blue embroidered flowers, she had also put on her hose, drawers, wool stockings, and velvet slippers. When that was done, over all of that, she wrapped herself in her peignoir robe, again embroidered and lavish to the point of decadence. Her hair was brushed umpteen times and her makeup removed. She then applied *crème celeste*, a sticky paste from a large jar that contained a mixture comprised of white wax, spermaceti from a whale, and sweet-smelling almond oil. To tie it all in, perfume was sprayed until it clouded about her thicker than the smoke from one of Arthur's cheroots.

I stifled a cough many times, not wanting to appear impolite. She had entrusted me to attend her, and I would do so without complaint.

"There. We're all done," she finally announced, sitting with a relieved sigh and fluttering a pretty fan. I was exhausted. I went to bed in a nightshirt, practically naked by comparison, and couldn't imagine taking on such a routine. She glanced at the time on one of the coach clocks resting on the ornate, wood-carved mantle. "I believe we can begin our first lesson, if you're not too tired and need to retire, Oliver."

It was as near to midnight as to be good enough, but at the mention of a lesson, any thoughts of my bed drifted far from my mind. I plucked up. "I'd appreciate that, Captain."

"Good." She smiled. "During my absence from the house, I managed to engage the services of a gypsy man knowledgeable in the Talent. He told me how it is common in men, especially those recent to maturing as you are, for their physical bodies to become too excited when they use their gift. He then informed me of exercises I can teach you to help you draw on your Talent without any other undue concerns. The last thing we want is for you to worry about anything other than your intentions, especially when the lives of others, or even that of your own, may depend on you accessing your Talent without hindrance. What I'm saying is, a moment's distraction when you are on the hunt for the Skilamalink Man could have you paying the ultimate price, Oliver."

"I understand."

"I am pleased to hear it." She got up, crossed the room with elegant grace, and retrieved an empty perfume bottle off a silver tray on her dressing table. "Now, disrobe for me. We shall begin the first exercise. Your *arbour vitae's* hardness will be the gauge you'll use to determine the amount of Talent needed for the particular task I have in mind for you."

Chapter Twelve
The First Lesson

I removed my clothing as quickly as I could manage. When done, I placed my discarded attire, my important working suit, carefully across the back of a chair so as not to crease it, my spats underneath.

Standing without a stitch on in front of my Captain, strangely comfortable but with a knot of nerves wound up inside me, I watched as she placed the empty perfume bottle next to the candelabra. "First, breathe in deep and slow until you gain a rhythm, Oliver. It is important to centre yourself. Most important."

A quiver of anxiety, mostly from anticipation, coursed through me. I pushed it down, trying to do as she asked. After an eternal moment, I began to calm. My stomach no longer a heavy lump holding my insides to ransom.

"Good." She clapped her hands to show her approval of what I had done, even though I thought nothing of breathing. I did it every day as a convenience to stay alive. "I want you to think of something that makes you happy, as we don't want the Talent to manifest itself through your negative thoughts or emotions. Not yet. For now, you must remain positive. Do you understand, Oliver?"

"I do."

I thought immediately of the sweetmeat treats Mimsee brought me each morning. I then thought of her. How she had an uncanny way of lightening any mood I happened to be inflicted with. I smiled. I breathed steady and deep.

I felt something.

A warmth.

A spark rose up from deep within me from my very soul, to tickle at my thoughts and feelings.

I felt a burning of energy.

"Keep your thoughts positive as you feel your Talent begin to emerge." Not only did I feel my Talent surge, fuelled by my thoughts, but my loins stirred as well. "You're going too fast and using too much Talent. Slowly, Oliver, please. I haven't directed you yet. Just call it forth, that's all I asked of you. Now breathe."

I tried. Panic overwhelmed me, striking me cold. I began to breathe deeply once more, feeling a rush of light-headedness. When everything started roiling within me all at once—my Talent and my emotions and thoughts—control wasn't as easy as I first thought.

It took many more eternal moments for me to calm. But to do so I had to think of nothing. I got there, eventually.

"That's better. Now hold that for a moment."

My hands were glowing, adding a strange, flickering luminescence to the air around me, like ethereal candlelight. Thankfully, my hardness had eased as much as the ache. The Captain was right: my gentlemanly asset was a valid gauge to the amount of Talent I called forth. I could plainly see that now. I also understood that very little Talent energy was required to accomplish certain tasks, as I discovered next.

"Do you see that perfume bottle over there? Use your Talent to pick it up now that you have controlled it better. Remember, the Talent can be an extension of your senses—touch, sight, smell, hearing, and taste. With it, you can find out all you need to know about something, as well as affect it. For now, I only want you to use your Talent to hold and examine the perfume bottle, Oliver. Only draw from within yourself enough to accomplish this first task."

I did so.

But...

In reality, understanding something and doing it were two different things. Whether I underestimated the power of my Talent or didn't fully realise what my gauge was telling me, I'd never fully know.

As I attempted the task, I heard the Captain shouting instructions. I tried to listen. But once the tendrils of Talent, the ghostly glow of its form, blue and as faint as steam from a hot bath, extended out from my hands to touch the bottle with its wispy fingers, I suddenly felt as though I'd been struck by a heavy weight, right in my stomach.

That was when everything went wrong.

"Ah!" I cried.

The perfume bottle shattered into a million shards of glass with a loud, unnerving bang. Not only that, the candles blew out, the drapes ruffled, and my manly release splattered over the polished wooden floorboards at my feet.

I collapsed.

The Captain dashed to my aid, assisting me into a chair. I was all right, only momentarily stunned. Sure, my head pounded, but nowhere near as much as my gentlemanly asset. It throbbed unbelievably, as did my bollocks. I was doubled over, even though the Talent had returned to the deepest recesses of my body, going back to sleep as a beast would return to its lair after a hunt.

"I think I used too much," I said feebly while still gasping.

"A lesson learned, I believe, Oliver. Remember, only the smallest amount of Talent is needed, no matter the task. It's quantity, not quality."

"I realise that now."

After re-lighting the candles, the Captain studied the floor of her chamber. The broken shards of glass marinating in the fluids of my Talent-induced release would need to be cleaned up, and not by the house servants. "I do believe that concludes tonight's lesson. Tomorrow, we will continue. Best if we do this at night after you've worked, I believe, don't you?"

I understood what the Captain meant. She wanted discretion; not even her servants were to know of my abilities—powerful abilities from her surprised expression and the result of the gentlest touch of it upon the bottle. The only other person to know of my Talent was Mimsee. I was glad of that.

The next morning, my mouth stuffed with the remains of my gifted sweetmeat treats, and after a quick kiss on Mimsee's cheek in thanks, I began my errands. First, I went to Cook.

"Good morning to you, Oliver," she said jovially, pouring flour into a bowl from a sack. Her apron was already stained with the result of hours of work. I believed it was after six o'clock, if not almost seven. Still early for me, especially after last night. My gentlemanly assets took ages to stop throbbing, keeping me awake until light began to show in the gap between the window's drapes.

I came to fully understand what the Captain meant by distractions. I wasn't prepared, and if what happened last night had happened while in pursuit of the Skilamalink Man, I would have been left a near cripple to become an easy target.

"Good morning, Cook."

She grunted. "Don't you think for one moment that you have any chance of getting at the freshly made comfits I just put into the larder. I know you're only down here this early because you could smell them, young man."

She wasn't to know I was down in the kitchen early because

my Talent almost caused my gentlemanly parts to explode off my body and I couldn't sleep as a result. "I wouldn't dream of it."

"And you wouldn't hold a candle to the Devil, either, I'm sure."

"Not me." I grinned wolfishly. "But if you're offering one or two…"

She rolled her eyes, then tilted her head toward the larder. "Go on…only two, mind you. Then I've got some ingredients I need you to fetch for me from the markets. I've almost ran out of potatoes and sugar—it's getting desperate in here today."

"Right you are, then." But my reply was automatic. I was more interested in the larder. That was until I remembered the real reason for coming into the kitchen so early, other than to report for work. "I say, Cook, can you make something for a client of mine? Something sweet, like those lovely chocolate bonbons you're famous for. Have it ready for this evening, please?" Tonight, after the house's gathering for our traditional Sunday roast, I was to hear of Arthur's offer. I had to admit, I couldn't wait to learn what it was, but at the same time was nervous about it as well.

I opened the larder, revelling in its bounty. My eyes were fixed straight away on the tray piled with comfits of every variety. I stuffed two into my mouth. Only two, as instructed.

"Oh sure, it's not like I'm up to my elbows in it down here, is it, Oliver?"

"Thanks," I mumbled through the flavour burst of freshly-made fudge and nut treats. "You say you required potatoes and sugar?"

"Yes, I did," Cook sighed, smashing her fists into the bowl; she began kneading the Yorkshire Pudding mixture she was creating for our midday dinner. "Get the pennies from the jar over by the window. There should be enough for you to get what I ask."

After I emptied the jar of coins, I dashed off out the back door toward the markets. I couldn't wait for tonight; I had both Arthur's offer and another Talent lesson to look forward to then.

Chapter Thirteen
More Than a Friend

Arthur's offer wasn't what I expected at all.

With smoke from his cheroot in one hand billowing around him, and his other hand hovering over the tray of hand-made chocolate bonbons Cook made for the occasion as requested, Arthur said, "Your performance was most exquisite, tonight, Oliver. You seemed to have a passion, one filled with an exuberance that I have not measured from you before."

"You give me that passion, Arthur." And it was true. Even I recalled sweetly of my arousal for him while I danced, his eyes wide at the sight of it. Thankfully, my Talent didn't manifest itself. As such, I held his attention well after my performance, even managing to smoke a whole cheroot without coughing. I decided to prompt him about his promise. "The last time we met you said you wanted to offer me something." I tried to appear casual, reclining in my chair and drawing deeply from the cheroot.

"Ah, I see," he smiled, knowingly. "I now know the reason for your enthusiasm. Which is perfectly understandable, of course, because I did promise you something, didn't I?"

My cheeks warmed. Arthur could read me well; he was a marvel. A guilty smile quivered over my lips. "You caught me out."

He shifted his weight within his chair. From what I could fathom, nervousness came to him once more. He tried to hide it, but I could still see it. I never took my eyes off him, to be honest.

The cheroot he brought up to his lips to take a draw revealed his trembling hands.

"I would like it—no, I would appreciate it…if you would attend evening supper two weeks from tomorrow night with me, Oliver. If that is all right with you, of course."

I was stunned by his invitation–did he think of me as more than an amusement for his pleasure? His lover, perhaps?

Arthur must have picked up on my hesitation, for I hadn't replied straight away. I butted out the remainder of the cheroot in a nearby ashtray.

He lit another for me.

I took it.

Still without word.

"You will be perfectly safe. I assure you," he added. "I would not do anything to disrupt or affect my friendship with Lady Penelope or yourself. You would be more than welcome to bring along your chaperone as well." He glanced at a portrait on the wall above the fireplace—one of the spy holes cleverly disguised within its artwork, no doubt.

I found it amusing he knew of Mimsee keeping an eye on me. But the thing that got to me the most was the fact he only called me his friend. His *friend*! That word stung. I was hurt by it, to be truthful; I certainly thought of him as someone more than that.

"Is that all I am to you?" The words that finally came out of my mouth sounded harsher than I'd intended. "*A friend?*"

I didn't have the luxury of reflection, but if I had, I wouldn't have said what I did. What had I expected? I was paid to take off my clothing and show him my gentlemanly assets, and that's what I did. Why should I have believed we had anything more between us than a transaction for a service rendered? As Mimsee had warned me, emotional attachment to clients in our trade wasn't recommended. Heartbreak was the only result.

I could now see why.

"Oh no, Oliver. You are much more than that to me. I didn't mean it like that. I didn't mean it like that at all," he stammered, sucking violently on the cheroot, the lit end blinking bright red as if it were a signal to his distress. He blushed. "I-I do believe I am falling for you. I just wanted to take you out on a...*date*. I want to treat you like someone more than just a dancer for my own gratification. You deserve—"

I didn't hear the rest of what he said.

My world spun around me to make me giddy at that moment.

He was falling for me?

Oh, Lord Almighty, that complicated matters significantly. A friendship, if only a second prize, I could eventually accept even though I had first been affronted by the notion.

But this...this changed everything.

I had the Talent, that wasn't in doubt. What I couldn't have, because of it, was love. His love. Not in the way Arthur believed he could achieve it, anyway. He believed he could begin the ritual of courtship with me, asking me to dine with him in the proper way two people did who had feelings for one another. As anyone would who had feelings for another. So much so, he had felt compelled enough to make the first move, to act on his feelings without knowing my secret.

I dug deep and found I wanted more than friendship from him. At the same time, I couldn't be his lover. Of course, I'd love to have him hold me in his arms, both of us eventually able to consummate our feelings—him penetrating me deeply with his affection while I climbed higher toward the agony of bliss.

Oh, how I'd love that.

But I knew Arthur wouldn't settle on friendship. Perhaps he would at first, but not for long. He cared too much for me.

Here he was, worried I was concerned about my safety. I

would never be concerned about such a thing with him. Arthur had always been a gentleman. My concern was losing my Talent. I wasn't ready to do that.

Not yet.

The Captain was right. Magic had its sacrifices and its consequences. This was one of them, and the biggest of it. I couldn't be with anyone intimately if I wanted to keep my Talent.

I didn't know of any way to tell Arthur such a thing that would make it end well. I needed time to think. Come up with a solution, if there was one. I was confused, conflicted, and needed to give him an answer.

As such, I blurted, "I would like that very much, Arthur."

He then talked of details, of a coach that would pick me up along with Mimsee while I nodded, dumbfounded. He then kissed me, as was our traditional parting. But this time, he kissed me on my lips.

If my awakening Talent gave me an awareness that made me sore for hours, the affection he imparted with that one tender, gentle kiss, gave it a yearning that lasted far longer. My stomach felt as though it was filled with butterflies, ones I could never capture. I stood in the smoking room for so long after he'd taken his leave, the cheroot I held almost burnt my fingers.

Mimsee thought I had lost my senses.

"You know, I almost flew through the walls to wallop you one about the 'ead," she said, rounding on me. "Beside myself, I was. What in blazes were you thinkin' when you accepted an offer like that?"

"I wasn't thinking straight," I admitted glumly, as what I'd accepted had finally sunk in.

"If 'e'd offered you a job, like what we talked about before, that would 'ave been all fine and dandy, wouldn't it? But no, 'e didn't, did 'e? You know you'll be nothin' but 'is dirty little secret, you know that don't you, Oliver? 'E can't show you 'round town like you're his wife, all finery and politeness and smiles, do as he pleases, can 'e?" Her eye twitched as she spoke. "'E can't take you to lawn picnics or evenings at the theatre, like all 'em other couples in love. No, 'e can't. You're a boy. 'E's a boy. Two boys don't go paradin' around, 'and in 'and, showin' the world they're in love."

Before I could answer her, she'd stormed out of the smoking room.

Mimsee was right. I hadn't thought of all that. I hadn't thought of the consequences at all. I wanted more than friendship, because only being Arthur's friend wasn't enough despite me needing to keep my Talent.

And that was the problem.

Whether through some sort of strange telepathy, as I suspected the Captain possessed, I was scolded by her as well no sooner had I entered her chamber to report for my second Talent lesson.

"Just because his wife was lost to him, contracting Scarlett Fever and passing on a year ago, the poor dear, doesn't give him the right to ask such a thing of you, Master Merritt!"

Oh, Lord Almighty, the Captain had gone back to formality with me. I was being addressed as Master Merritt again. That didn't bode well for the rest of the conversation.

"I'm sorry," I offered. "But I—"

She held up her hand. "Don't speak for a moment, Master Merritt. In fact, don't utter a word until I request it from you. Anyway, why aren't you undressed yet? I'm not going to teach you how to control your *Talent*," she said "Talent" with a strain of her vocal cords, "if you don't get yourself prepared for your lessons properly as you've been instructed."

No, it wasn't going to go well at all.

Chapter Fourteen
The Love of Family

I'd never been so uncomfortable without a stitch on in front of the Captain. If my bollocks could have, they would've retreated up into my stomach to try and stone the butterflies that now flapped about erratically in their death throes inside me.

No matter how hard I tried, much to the disappointment of the Captain, I couldn't muster even a speck of positive thought to awaken my Talent. I felt too chagrined by my stupidity at accepting Arthur's offer without thought of the consequences.

"I think it's time for you to retire, Master Merritt," she said bluntly after half an hour of me accomplishing nothing and feeling useless, the perfume bottle unmoved.

"Yes, Captain."

Hot tears began to well. I thought I was going to cry. Once I was dressed in my trousers and shirt, because I would soon be clambering into my nightshirt and bed and I didn't see the point of putting more on, I began to hiccough. My emotions strangled me. I was miserable. The two people I held most dear thought less of me.

Or so I believed.

I was about to take my leave, when the Captain said, "Oh, and...*Oliver*..." Her tone had lost its acidic edge, now of tempered steel; more flexible, but no less strong. "You have come to mean the world to me, and if anything, I mean anything, ever happened to you, I wouldn't know what to do. When I married my husband and chose love over my Talent, I thought I would be blessed with many children. I lost both when he died at sea. Now fate has given me you to look after." She came to me, embracing me firmly, her exotic perfume wafting to intoxicate with its cheery rose and lavender scent. My dark mood was chased away.

"I'm sorry," I reiterated, tears now streamed down my cheeks.

"Perhaps we can salvage the situation. But you must attend him as he requests now that you've accepted it. Your word is your honour, and your honour is great, Oliver. That is one of your many qualities I admire about you."

"Thank you." I felt relief and wiped away my tears.

"However," she let go of her embrace but kept her hands upon my shoulders, "Mimsee should have instructed you not to take business away from the protection of the house, no matter how well intentioned. You were carried away by the moment, and I don't blame you completely. Arthur is a dashing young man, caring and thoughtful considering he's rich beyond measure since his father passed on. Some even say the man was murdered, but that is another story for another time." She paused, clearing her throat with a polite cough. "What I'm trying to tell you, Oliver, is that under normal circumstances I would not discourage you to pursue Arthur's wooing. But this situation isn't normal. Just tread carefully, that is all I ask of you."

"He is handsome," I agreed. "And I don't think he'd hurt me in any way. Not deliberately."

"You have indeed captured more than Arthur's eye."

I felt my cheeks warm. Which was nice considering the maelstrom of emotions I'd experienced only moments ago. "I'd like you to attend the supper with me and Mimsee—you are both my family and I'd appreciate it if you were there. And I won't do anything to jeopardise my Talent…just so you know."

"That is the most sensible thing you've said all evening. Oh, and, Oliver…you will find a way to love someone special one day,

I know it to be so. I just know it won't be Arthur; the signs given to me aren't right." I didn't know what she meant by that, but in a strange way, I wasn't saddened by her words. She added, "There. I think you've learnt your lesson for tonight. Good evening to you, Oliver."

"Good evening, Captain." I wiped my eyes again and kissed her on her *crème celeste* covered cheek, the taste of wax and oil lingered on my lips. A reminder of her love for me.

I should have expected Mimsee would be in my chamber. She hugged me tightly the moment had I put my foot beyond the threshold, all arms and elbows. I came to realise I didn't like it when she was mad with me and didn't want to experience it again any time soon.

"Do you forgive me?"

"'Ow can anyone stay cross with you, lovely?"

We sat on my bed together. She was already dressed for sleep, but wasted no time helping me get out of the remains of my working suit and into my nightshirt.

"You know, I've been thinking about things," I said when she was done, and I was comfortable for the first time in hours.

"Oh, my—was it dangerous to do so?"

"Why you!" I jumped up, pushing her back onto the bed and climbing atop her so I could pin her down. "You're such a tease, you know that. I'm being serious."

She laughed, as I did. "Are you, now?" We rolled around on the bed, wrestling each other, taking turns to dominate. All the while, my worries slipped further and further away. "You goin' to tell me what all this thinkin' of yours is all about that's got you so lively? Or are you goin' to keep me in suspense like I'm some six-penny bunter waiting for payment, 'ey?"

I wriggled up the bed so my head could rest on my pillow proper; she snuggled up beside me. Her warmth was wondrous, her breath upon me reassuring. "I've been thinking about how there must be some way of detecting the Talent within others. There must be a way. Right, Mimsee?"

Mimsee's brow creased, marring her otherwise perfectly smooth features. The waning moonlight that streamed in through the undrawn curtained window caught on her face, highlighting her beautiful ebony skin.

After a while, she asked, "So...is there anythin' you remember? Anythin' at all, no matter 'ow small, that you can think of that was there when you examined that poor, poor Nicole's body—or from the time your mama...and..." Her voice wavered and she cut herself off. "Sorry," she whispered.

My stomach turned uncomfortably, my thoughts taken back to that fateful night. I held her with my trembling hand. I knew my Talent wasn't affected by handholding or kissing; it was the other things folks did to show their love it took offense to. "It's all right; I asked you to help me think about it. I can't change what happened to my parents, but I can do something about it now that I have you by my side. Now, what did you mean? See something such as what?"

"I don't rightly know; you're the one who asked me."

"Fair enough." I cast my mind back to the alleyway where Peeler William showed me the body I examined. I envisioned the darkness created by the close buildings and the hard, cold cobblestones her lifeless body was sprawled over. I shuddered. "I can't think of anything strange about it, other than when I used my Talent to see how she was murdered."

"What did you feel, then?"

"It wasn't a feeling...it's hard to explain, but it's more like I went inside her with my senses."

"Well then, lovely, what did you sense? Think of 'em all, the senses your Talent enhances when it comes out from you like it does."

I rummaged through the deeper recesses of my mind, trying to do as she suggested. Finally, I said, "I sensed her heart had been stopped and…" I squirmed on the bed, uncomfortable as I recalled the experience, "how it had been ruptured—no, crushed like it had been squeezed by a strong hand. A hand of Talent. I…wait, I also smelt something. What was it? I can't? Wait. Yes!"

I inhaled the air, as if to duplicate the moment from weeks ago as I stood over the body. "That's it. I smelt pipe smoke! I smelt the lingering of pipe smoke around her when I used my Talent as Lady Penelope instructed me to do. But there's only one problem with that. I didn't smell pipe smoke when my parents…were murdered. That much I know."

"No wonder you didn't. It was rainin' somethin' terrible that night. It takes more than the smell of pipe smoke to get through the stench rain causes when it falls on stinkin' streets, it does."

The revelation of her words dawned on me. The smell of the rain-soaked cobblestones, filthy with horse manure, rotting straw, and human waste leaching from open sewers and cesspits would have overpowered any other.

"You're right."

"I know I am."

Before I could add any more to the conversation, Mimsee had begun her journey toward sleep. I then realised how tired I was, too. That night I dreamed of my newfound discovery.

Could I find the Skilamalink Man with that knowledge?

Chapter Fifteen
The Canary's Warning

The next day, I returned to the brightness I expected of myself because I was really the luckiest man alive. I had a good home and folks who cared for me. What more could I ask for?

I couldn't wait to tell the Captain of my discovery.

In the meantime, errands for the day had to be performed. I assisted Cook—as always—but also helped the house servants clean and service my home in general. I changed the tallow soaps, refreshed perfume bottles, and replaced flowers and exotic oils in all the rooms, including the smoking room. I restocked drinks, replaced linen, and ensured all toiletries were in good supply.

I did my work studiously, and always at the back of my mind was how I could use my new information to my best advantage.

That night, I performed for another new man who'd been added to my growing clientele list. He was an elderly gentleman who had the tremors. His look was kindly, and, rather sweetly, he fawned over my appearance and couldn't stop raining praises upon me. During my performance for him, one I enjoyed enough to give him a good look at my gentlemanly assets, he said something that gave me an idea.

"My goodness, Oliver. I know it is beyond the service to touch you, but even if I could I'm afraid my hands are too frail. I would not trust them to such a task because of my shakes."

"That's all right, sir," I said while I ran my hands across myself, down to where his eyes never left me. "I'm more than happy to do it for you."

It was only a germ of an idea, but with the Captain's approval, I think I could pull it off.

When I completed my duties and finished work, Mimsee escorted me upstairs. She was my permanent chaperone; I had noticed she didn't sell herself anymore. I believed the Captain gave her the other half of my earnings, to ensure she looked after me. She was therefore, in turn, looked after as well.

I had a feeling Mimsee was as important to the Captain as I was.

As was now part of the ceremony, I knocked three times on the Captain's chamber door. Mimsee left me, attending to her own duties. I kissed her in thanks on the cheek.

When I entered, the chorus of a canary's melodic song filled my ears. The bird's cage was placed on a stand near the window. The moonlight wasn't as bright tonight, and many candles were lit around the chamber.

I had begun undressing the layers of my working suit well before I entered. I didn't want to get chastised again for not being ready. Besides, the sooner my lesson began, the sooner I could talk to her about my discovery.

"Are you ready, Oliver?"

"Yes, Captain."

The lesson that evening was for me to reach into the gilded cage to the canary that was housed within with my Talent. I was to gain as much information about the bird as I could. The Captain informed me that something alive for me to practise on would give me more caution, force me to use the right amount of energy needed for the task. I hoped the canary wouldn't meet the same fate as the perfume bottle did two nights prior—bloodied feathers covered in manly juices on the floorboards wouldn't be pleasant to clean up.

Once my breathing exercises were completed to calm me, drawing on the positive feeling of hope I felt after Mimsee and I talked last night, the Talent began to swirl out from my hands with its familiar smoky tendrils.

"Keep calm. Breathe deeply, and use only what you need," I was cautioned. No doubt the Captain plainly saw my gauge rising already. "Steady, Oliver. Stay in control."

The storm of power within me began to whip itself up into frenzy more and more as my Talent reached the cage. I pulled back as much of the energy as I could, hoping I'd released the right amount for the task. I managed it. It was difficult, cold sweat trickling down my back. I was also burdened with the all too familiar ache from my gentlemanly area.

My Talent touched the canary.

I gasped, hoping the touch wasn't too strong. The first thing I felt was that the bird's heartbeat went from resting to racing, its chambers pounding like little pistons, near one thousand beats a minute. Then, I felt its living warmth, its breathing. I even began to ascertain the variety of seed within its gullet: millet, rapeseed, safflower, linseed, and others. The canary, a male, liked the millet the best. I could smell it had also eaten cabbage recently and had used the supplied cuttlefish bone to clean its beak.

After a moment, the bird calmed, as did I. The wisps of my Talent around the canary gave it an angelic blue aura, shifting as if some unseen breeze flowed through the cage. I became mesmerised.

"That's much better, Oliver. You may stop now; I've seen enough." The Captain touched my arm. The contact of her skin against mine acted like a stopper to the flow of Talent from me. My Talent's hold broke. I took in a deep breath to clear my head of the bird's presence. My hands no longer glowed; the canary began to sing once more.

"I did it!" I announced triumphantly, but exhausted.

There was no doubt, however, that even though I had controlled my Talent, my body still raged. I was so stimulated by what had transpired, it was as if Arthur himself had kissed me passionately, open mouthed, tongues dancing, and leaving me wanting more.

So much more.

"Yes, but you have a long way to go. Look at you."

My stomach quivered. I was on the edge of ecstasy, the most trifling touch against any of my erogenous places right now would have sent me over the edge. I tried to calm again, but I became consumed.

I was swimming in my own sexual energy, a pool so deep I was unable to touch the bottom. I felt as though I was floundering. I was giddy, too. My breathing became as shallow and as fast as the bird's upon my exploration of it.

The Captain must have plainly seen my dilemma. "I have an idea, Oliver."

"Anything," I moaned.

If this was how the Talent left me using the smallest amount, unable to function for desire of pleasure, then I was lost. At the same time, if I used too much—as I did when I tried to hold the perfume bottle—I became crippled by the resulting orgasm.

There didn't seem to be a happy medium with my magic.

"I would like you to allow yourself the release your body now calls out for. But I want you to use your Talent to achieve it. Under my strictest supervision, of course."

I felt pangs of panic rise through the swarm of my urges. I had touched the canary without killing it...*but*...could I touch myself? What would happen if I lost control or used too much? Fear struck me for a moment. "I'm not so sure about that, Captain."

"I will be here with you. You know how much energy to use to achieve what is tasked to you, but you must learn to control your own desires."

"It's too late to do that now. Look at me."

"I do have eyes, Oliver."

"If I tried to use my Talent around the Skilamalink Man I'd become useless, all because of my own physical failings. I don't think I'll ever be able to separate what is needed to become useful to you. I've failed."

"Your virility is not a failing, Oliver. Now, do as I ask. You will understand my reasoning soon, I promise."

"Yes, Captain."

Chapter Sixteen
Smoke and Mirrors

I found myself upon a chaise lounge, everything a miasma of ecstasy caused by what my Talent left behind as its parting gift to me when it retreated to its depths. Now I had to call upon it again. I was scared.

What would happen if I used it so soon?

How would my body cope?

The Captain sat in an occasional chair next to me, her gaze scrutinizing. A worrying line creased across her brow as she folded her arms. "Begin, Oliver," she commanded with cold, surgical precision.

"Can't I use my hand, like I always do?" I mumbled through the fog of my mind.

"You'll only need the slightest touch to achieve what you desire, less than what you used on the canary."

I closed my eyes and breathed in the way I was taught.

Once more, I called upon the fire of my Talent within to ignite, fanning its embers with my thoughts. It didn't take long for the rush of surging energy to overwhelm me. I gasped, crying out. I squirmed, gripping tight with both my glowing hands onto the chaise lounge, as if for dear life. Sweat soon beaded on my skin, along with gooseflesh. My hardness ached unbelievably, worse than the first night my lessons began.

The Captain was right. It took the merest whisper of a touch, a grace of a feather of my Talent upon myself, to cause the inevitable. In the moment before that, I discovered it was incredible to explore myself in such a unique way.

I could feel the immense pressure of blood within the columns and chambers of the corpus cavernosum and spongiosum of my male anatomy, and how everything else prepared for release. With my heart pounding, unrelenting to fuel my desires further, I began to shudder uncontrollably. Pulse after pulse of my conclusion discharged to fall upon my stomach.

I'd never produced so much.

After what seemed an eternity of waiting for my body to cool, lying there staring at the waning moon, and with the Captain giving me a handkerchief to wipe away the result of my Talent's touch, I was finally able to sit upright.

My cheeks still burned, and the ache in my gentlemanly region was still prevalent. But at least my mind had cleared.

I could think straight once again.

In that moment, I remembered what I had to tell her. "I think there's a way I can find out who the Skilamalink Man is." My voice was hoarse and weak from what had transpired.

"I thought you might find a way." She dropped the soiled handkerchief into the laundry basket. "Now, tell me of it. Tea?"

Clearly, the Captain wanted me to remain. It was well past the midnight hour, but I didn't feel tired. Not like I usually was after my conclusion. Another effect of the Talent's touch, no doubt.

"Yes, I'd like that, thank you." She poured the tea, what was known as an Earl Grey mixture. I smelt the bergamot oil. I continued, "I believe those who use the Talent smell of pipe smoke, as I noticed such a thing when my Talent went inside Nicole's body." The Captain let me talk, only nodding occasionally as I did so. She handed me a cup of tea, steam wafting off the brew's surface to remind me of my Talent beyond my hands. I felt encouraged. "If I could use the Talent on others,

I think…I believe…I could sense if they had any link to the Skilamalink Man. What do you think, Captain?"

"Do you believe the Skilamalink Man, or one of his associates, is close, Oliver?" She sipped on her tea, no other emotions or tells revealed as to her thoughts about my idea.

"I do. My parents were murdered in an alleyway not far from here, as was Nicole. I have also smelt the linger of pipe smoke on a couple of the men I've performed for. Whether they have come in contact with the Skilamalink Man or not, or even if they don't have the Talent themselves and I am only smelling their habits, I won't know until I have determined it through my Talent's finely tuned perceptions. Perhaps I could invent a way to use it upon them without them knowing it."

"You are certain this pipe smoke smell is related to the Talent?"

"I am." And I was.

I knew the pipe smoke smell was more than a scent stuck on skin or cloth around them, but I had to prove it. It was hard to explain, even to myself, but it was like the person had become tainted by it, stained on a deeper level than their flesh. Did I smell like that to others who had the Talent? It was as if the Talent, used near them, or indeed, if they used it themselves, left a footprint upon them. One I could hopefully see with my Talent enhanced senses.

"How would you accomplish what you propose?" Her question indicated to me she was amused by my idea. She had brightened but concern still marred her brow. "Although, getting a client to not notice the Talent coming from you when you are his secret desire dancing naked before him would be a feat."

I steeled my resolve. Perhaps it was the tea that fortified me. I ventured further with my thoughts. "I could come up with a kind of game," I suggested. "Maybe use a blindfold and tell him I will touch him intimately if he does as I asked. I know all my clients would want for that. I know I cannot do so physically, so I'd do it with my Talent. The man I do this for wouldn't be able to see my Talent because of the blindfold or discern the difference between my Talent's touch or my own. It would then reveal to me what I would need to know." I then recalled the information I'd gathered about the canary and my own gentlemanly assets to reinforce my suggestion.

"I believe what you propose could work, but you will need to practice with Mimsee any addition to your routine. Whatever you do, it would have to seem like a natural part to proceedings so as not to arouse undue suspicion."

"I understand." I became even more heartened. Would it work? I hoped so. "Also, I think it will lessen the chance of suspicion if I pleasured myself for them first before asking them to blindfold themselves. That way they will get to see what they desire and be more accommodating."

"I believe you may be onto something, Oliver." She drained her cup of tea, placing it onto the saucer with a gentle clatter. "But what about your hands? They often glow when you do such a thing to yourself. At this stage you've not mastered how to do so without that happening every time."

I thought for a moment. "I'll wear gloves, say it's all part of the game."

She cocked a well plucked and shaped eyebrow. "A most interesting idea. I will get Mimsee to buy you a gentleman's pair in the morning. Now, I suppose we must come to the crux of the matter: who did you smell the pipe smoke upon, Oliver?"

"Only a couple, but I must do this to all of them, just to make sure."

"Even Arthur?"

Chapter Seventeen
The Peeler's Son

Even Arthur.

Those two words reverberated around in my mind as I gathered up my working suit, said my goodnights and thank-yous to my Captain, and proceeded toward my chamber. I needed my bed, realising I was tired to my bones. My body was so drained I could hardly lift my feet, my gait more a shuffle as I trod the floorboards. I hadn't even bothered putting on anything but my drawers to travel the distance between our rooms.

Mimsee wasn't there.

She must have come in earlier and left when I wasn't present; sweetmeat treats were already waiting for me on my nightstand. I climbed into my bed.

Sleep found me immediately.

For the first time since I arrived at the magnificent brothel I called home, I didn't dream of my mother but of my father. The dream was bitter and disturbed me. He used to be a master at the General Post Office, with a reasonable income. But he was also a man who would go into fits of rage after drinking and gambling, striking me often for the most innocuous reasons. Reasons such as not cleaning my room to his satisfaction, even though I had done so. Or talking too loudly, even though I only ever whispered in his presence.

When he noticed I didn't pay attention to the fairer sex after I'd matured, he got worse.

My mother tried to stop him. In the end, it was better if he hit me than her. I let him do it, usually without protest. He only did so until his fists hurt, which wasn't long most times unless he was really infuriated by his gambling losses. Even back then before I knew what to call it, I came to realise I used my Talent to protect myself, to shield me from the blows. He wouldn't have seen the glow; inebriation and blind anger would have ensured that.

Finally, the debtors came.

They gave my father plenty of time to repay them, but he was as stubborn as he was addicted. It got to the point where they would wait no more for what was owed. It quickly came to that fateful night, the night I lost my mother…and him. It was within that dream I realised the Skilamalink Man was involved, perhaps he was the leader of the gang of men who came to collect their money.

I woke sweat drenched and with the sheets clinging to me.

It took ages for the dream to leave me, haunting me until Mimsee came into my chamber. When she drew the drapes and opened the window, the dream finally left me, floating away in the morning breeze.

She made things better by being there.

"You'd best get cleaned up and dressed quick smart, lovely," Mimsee suggested. "The Captain wants us to attend 'er in the morning room. We've got guests arrivin' within the 'our to see us."

"Guests?" I asked, curiosity clinging to me as close as the sheets had been. "Who are they?"

"You'll see."

Once Mimsee called the house servants, they poured hot water into the tub that had become an important part of my chamber's furniture. I never attended the communal bathroom on the first floor; I liked to bathe in my own room. Not because I didn't want people to see me without a stitch on; I was well beyond that sort of inhibition. It was simply because I liked Mimsee to attend to me. She must have liked doing it as well, because she never hesitated or complained. Besides, we talked in the most meaningful ways while she ran the soapy, perfumed sponge over me. I noticed that she never touched me with her own skin, only ever with the sponge.

"I 'ear you've gone and got yourself an idea," Mimsee said, concentrating on washing me, her tongue poking out of the corner of her mouth in concentration as she did so. "The Captain wants me to 'elp you with it. Sounds like a 'oot and a 'alf."

"It will be a spot of fun, won't it?"

"I left the gloves you'll need for it over there." She gestured to my wooden chest of drawers I had moved so it now lived at the end of my bed.

Sure enough, there they were: black leather gloves, able to be buttoned at the wrist.

They were perfect.

After I was dressed in an informal morning suit—with Mimsee's help, of course—I was ready to go with her to meet our mystery guests. My suit, mid-grey in colour, consisted of striped trousers, shirt, silk tie to match, oxford shoes shined to perfect black, and with a waistcoat and jacket in a shorter length than those worn for evening. I looked smart, but not as smart as Mimsee did. Her dresses always shone. How she managed to bathe and dress me without getting any of it wet or out of place was one of those mysteries women held dear.

I took her arm, and together we descended the stairs to the first floor. The Captain was waiting for us outside the door to the airy morning room that was used to receive guests in a causal manner, hence our less formal attire. She smiled at me and Mimsee. "Time to meet someone who can help us catch our killer—you both can't do all the work, you know."

"I didn't know we were," I offered.

"Remember, I'm Lady Penelope in company." She took my other arm, folding it into hers. Together, all three of us proceeded into the morning room.

Aside from William the Peeler—who stood at the front window looking out; hands clasped behind his back in thought—there was one other man waiting for us. He was seated but stood when we entered.

By the Lord Almighty Himself, he was the most handsome, fair-skinned young man I'd ever seen. As long as my days had had breath, anyway. I think I audibly gasped, because Mimsee squeezed my hand, her smile knowing.

The young man looked about the same age as me. He had fiery ginger hair that was so tousled upon his head it was as if it could never be tamed. Freckles danced across the bridge of his slender nose, and his bright blue eyes bore into my soul to melt it. He was tall and slim, and held a smile that would have made my knees buckle had it lingered any longer.

William turned, his handlebar moustache emphasising his smile. He bowed to us. I bowed in return but didn't let my gaze wander too far away from the other man. Mimsee and Lady Penelope curtsied in reply to William's greeting.

Lady Penelope announced, "May I formally introduce to you my adopted son and daughter, Master Oliver Merritt and Miss Minerva O'Donnell, Constable William Arkwright."

I was a little startled by those few words, for many reasons. One, I knew Lady Penelope had gained guardianship of me, but not ever did I realise what that really entailed. I was her *son*! I couldn't have been prouder, to tell the truth. And two, hearing Mimsee's full name almost made me break protocol and burst out into laughter. I imagined she felt the same. She squeezed my hand once more, this time for a different meaning: to let me know that if I teased her later about it, she'd give me such a wallop I'd be sore for weeks. I didn't doubt it, either.

"They are smart looking children you have there, Lady Penelope," William said. He was dressed in his peeler's uniform, a navy-blue trench coat with a parade of large silver buttons down the front. His trousers and shoes matched his coat. The other man was dressed in a morning suit of lighter tones, if somewhat less refined than my own. "And this here is my son Tom, Lady Penelope. He's a right handful, but you've got to love 'em no matter what, I say."

"Indeed, you do, Constable Arkwright."

His name was Tom.

He was the peeler's son.

I sighed, if only to myself.

Lady Penelope and William went to the breakfast trolley already prepared by the house servants. He poured out fruit juice from a pitcher into five tall tumblers, the expensive ice used to chill it clanking against the glasses as he did so. Meanwhile, Lady Penelope shared out triangles of toasted stone-ground bread, sliced cold ham, poached eggs, and white fish. There were squares of butter and little dishes of marmalade, plum conserve, and strawberry jam accompanying each plate. I realised then how hungry I was. The last thing in my stomach was what I put in there yesterday at midday dinner time: it was now nine o'clock in the morning.

Mimsee leaned over to me and whispered, barely audible, "I bet 'e's got a great big peeler's truncheon between 'is legs, that ginger one. Right looker, 'e is."

I almost choked on my tongue.

Before I could answer Mimsee, sarcastically or otherwise, Lady Penelope gestured for us to be seated and to begin our breakfast, the formality of protocol no longer required.

We could relax.

I sat next to Mimsee on a three-seater lounge. William and Lady Penelope went to the high-backed chairs by the window.

The view through it was of the tree-lined street and sunlight breaking through the clouds in diagonal lines across the sky. They chatted with each other, but she always made sure her mouth was free from food before she spoke.

As was Lady Penelope's trademark, she didn't stand on ceremony when it came to her words. Straight away, she began discussing the murder of Nicole. William said that the crime rate lately, from pickpocketing to vandalism of property, had increased. The constabulary suspected a new gang about the area. Lady Penelope suggested that the Skilamalink Man might be in charge of it, as I suspected as well.

William agreed.

I, however, didn't get to hear much more of what was said. Tom sat next to us, carrying his breakfast while Lady Penelope and William moved to the far side of the room.

As Tom settled in his seat, to my absolute dread and disbelief, I could smell pipe smoke wafting off him, strong and vigorous. But that time, the smell was different to what I had taken in before. It held a sweetness, like smoked honey. My stomach knotted. The attraction I had instantly felt for him when I first met his gaze turned to curiosity.

What Tom said next could have blown me over with its words alone. "You've got the Talent, haven't you, Oliver?"

Chapter Eighteen
The Curse of the Talent

I didn't know what to do. Should I admit I had the Talent to Tom or not? He could clearly smell it on me as much as I could smell it on him.

To be truthful, I was stunned I'd met another like me. So much so, the plate of food I held almost slipped from my fingers to find the expensive hand-woven carpet.

But I also had to be careful. I glanced over at Lady Penelope. She was in deep conversation with William–the poor man clearly wasn't grasping the sage advice she was bestowing upon him.

She looked frustrated.

I returned my attention to Tom. "I don't know what you are talking about, Tom," was my weak reply.

"You smell of pipe smoke, you do," Tom explained. "And I can see from the way your thumb on either hand isn't yellowed that you don't use a pipe either. You've got to have the Talent. That much I know."

I couldn't see his thumbs, and up until he mentioned it, I hadn't thought of looking. I could only answer by being defensive. "As do you…and likewise."

He winked. "Funny that, isn't it?"

Mimsee, with an eye roll and a cheeky smile, interjected, "Oh, for Lord's sake, you've both got it, the Talent, ain't you? Two 'andsome boys with magic. Now that's love, I say. Ain't that right?" Mimsee was matchmaking; she already knew of my instant attraction to Tom.

I wondered if Tom felt the same about me.

"Begging your pardon, Miss?" Tom said.

Mimsee shrugged. "I know boys, and I know the eye you two were givin' one another when you both met. So 'ere, why can't you be sweet on each other?"

I didn't get any sign from Tom that he had any feelings for me. His expression remained blank, the galaxy of freckles over his nose unmoved. I'd venture to guess it was only Mimsee greasing things up for her own amusement. To tease me. Or was it always awkward when two people who had the Talent met, regardless of their gender?

Surprisingly, even though Tom glanced away from me as I studied him, he began to move the food around his plate aimlessly with his fork.

Was there something there, after all?

I became more certain of it. Sure, if he harboured any feelings for me, he hid them well. I only managed to catch the slightest blush of his cheeks.

"Sorry," Tom whispered. "I don't know what you're talking about, Miss."

I decided to take the initiative and test out my thoughts. I touched the top of his hand, clasping it in mine.

Tom didn't flinch. "It's all right," I said.

When he returned my gaze, a trace of his emotion had welled in his eyes, reddening the rims. "What does it matter, anyway? I can't be with no one, and they can't be with me. Not in the way where it means anything, anyway. Having the Talent is a curse. You'd know that, Oliver."

Lady Penelope and William were deep in their own conversation. She hung on his words, giving William the comfort of a guest in her house. Yet, she was in control.

Always.

"You can 'old 'ands and kiss, that don't affect it," Mimsee offered.

"Small consolation," Tom said bitterly.

I had another idea. I just hoped he was open to it. "I believe you can help me, Tom. If you agree."

A look of puzzlement crossed his freckled features. "How?"

"Just recently I've been taught to use my Talent better by the Ca—Lady Penelope. Last night I reached out with it to touch myself as part of that lesson." Tom seemed surprised by my candour, his thick ginger eyebrows raising to disappear under his messy hairline. I realised he wouldn't be used to such open talk; not everyone could live in a brothel, after all. I continued, "I think we could touch each other with our Talent, Tom. Besides, I could use you to practice on before I try it out on men I suspect have contact with the Skilamalink Man—or worse, are him. What do you say?"

His mouth opened. Then closed. When Tom finally spoke, he had brightened a little. "Do you realise what you're saying, Oliver?"

"Course 'e does. 'E's a right smart one our Oliver is," Mimsee said, proudly.

"No. I mean, if you're right, you've found a way for someone with the Talent to be...*intimate*...with someone else." He said the word intimate like it was a revelation, an epiphany that had caused his soul to ignite with joy. But he cautiously added, "But I'm not sure...you and me. That's not...right. Is it?"

I was a little hurt. His features flashed with what I could only describe as disgust when he spoke that last part, but I wasn't certain. Perhaps he didn't like men, and mine and Mimsee's impression of him had been miscalculated.

"You don't want to help me?" I asked, pressing on regardless.

Tom glanced over his shoulder to his father. The man was still deep in discussion with Lady Penelope. "I know my Pa would mind at first…but he might get used to the idea of you…being a lad, an' all. But I'm—"

"Scared?" I guessed, hopefully correctly.

"Yes."

That made a lot more sense. It wasn't disgust; it was fear. And my intuition was correct, as it usually was.

Mimsee mustn't have realised the worry I held…or that Tom, no doubt, had it as well. "'Ere, we should get started then, 'and't we? You need the practice, Oliver, you do, 'cause the client you've got tonight is one of 'em pipe smoke smellin' men." I couldn't blame her for not understanding. I'd been told, to the point of having no doubts, that I could never love someone deeply because I had the Talent. Really love someone as it should be between two people, because to do so was both a need and a necessity, to strengthen their bond between them.

Now, with this revelation, all that could change. Love for me could happen, if the one I had interest in had the Talent like me. Yes, that love would be unconventional, but it would still be love.

Tom said slowly, "Are you sure it will work, Oliver? My Pa says my Talent will help me become a great peeler. He's been promoted so there's a place for me—right chuffed the family are, too."

"Your father had the Talent?"

"Yeah, until he married Ma and had me, that is. He gave it up to have his only son. His precious boy, as he calls me. I don't want to do nothing to disappoint him. Nothing."

"I think that there's both sad and lovely, Tom," Mimsee said.

"Might be so, but I've got to keep my Talent, that's a fact."

"As do I," I admitted.

There was a long silence between us while we ate our breakfast. Mimsee was the one who broke it, naturally. "We still goin' up to your chamber, Oliver, to try this Talent-touch thing out with Tom, or not?"

I looked at Tom once more. He had a hunger, a curiosity in his eyes I knew all too well from the men I had performed for. "If it's not going to make me lose my Talent, then I'm game. You're a right handsome one, Oliver—and I wouldn't mind one bit getting to know you better."

All of a sudden, I felt nervous.

Chapter Nineteen
The Price to Pay

After we'd eaten, but before we excused ourselves, William informed us that if there were any more murders around the borough—and when it was deemed safe to do so—we would be informed. Tom and I could then investigate the scene using our Talent.

No doubt Lady Penelope and William had been discussing the abilities of their sons with each other, like proud parents do when speaking of their children.

After Tom and I bowed to Lady Penelope and William once more, in keeping with the etiquette of the occasion—Mimsee curtsying—I said, "I'll be with Mimsee for the rest of the day, to practise what you requested of me before I begin this evening's work, ma'am. Tom will be joining us, if it's all right with you, Senior Constable Arkwright, sir."

William eyed us both. Whether through some instinct, or intentional gesture, I had moved closer to Tom. So close, his hand brushed mine. Without further thought, I came to hold his palm. Again, Tom didn't flinch.

His hand had a lovely warmth to it.

As we held our light touch, my stomach began fluttering with awakened butterflies, a feeling I hadn't experienced since Arthur asked me on that date.

It was Lady Penelope who spoke. "I knew you would find a way, Oliver."

Her words told more than what she said, as always. Tom's

arrival wasn't happenstance. I had a feeling she already knew two people of Talent could show affection to one another in some meaningful way, even if it wasn't how normal folks did it; why else would she have got me to touch myself with my Talent if not to prove that?

"I knew I would, too." I smiled knowingly.

William stood, looking concerned and agitated, pulling down on his coat front to straighten it. "I don't know if I agree with this at all. And you set this all up, didn't you, ma'am? Your son with mine, I mean."

Lady Penelope immediately asked, "You don't agree with what exactly?"

"With my Tom being with your Oliver, that's what."

"Tell me, William," Lady Penelope said coolly, "how is it that two people blessed with the Talent and engaging in magical contact with each other is an offence in any way? Yes, under normal circumstances, two men engaging in intimacy may find themselves committing an arrestable offence. But how would you arrest Oliver and Tom? On what charge? No court would even be able to begin to understand it, as I'm sure you're well aware."

William shrunk, but managed, "I would never arrest my own son."

"I'm pleased to hear it."

"I only meant that I don't want my boy to lose what he's been born with." William's taut features relaxed as Lady Penelope's words must have sunk in. "And for him to be careful. That's all."

I knew his words were a retreat on his part to save face. William might let his son get away with a lot, but him engaging in "private" activities with me, explainable or not, left the man sour. I could tell from the stormy look he still held within his eyes, even if his demeanour had calmed.

"As is my concern as well," Lady Penelope said, also

standing. "But *my* Oliver is always careful. He knows all too well the stakes involved if he loses his Talent. His parent's gravestones are his reminder if he fails."

"I apologise, Lady Penelope. Please accept it graciously."

She accepted it, then let us excuse ourselves.

I escorted Tom up the stairs. As a gentleman should when taking someone to their chamber, I held his hand to guide him. Tom's hand was clammy, and he trembled, as did I.

Mimsee followed, but surprisingly didn't say a word. Not until we got into my bedroom proper, anyway. "The both of you couldn't be sweeter together if you were covered in 'oney, you couldn't."

My cheeks warmed.

Tom glanced between us. "I'm not so sure about this now, Oliver," he said cautiously.

He was studying my chamber, worry lines striking his features. I imagined the reality of what was about to happen, what we were going to do to one another, had finally found him.

"It's your father, isn't it?"

Tom nodded. "I know he's not that happy about me using my Talent with you. He means well, but he worries a lot about me."

Mimsee, rather brilliantly said, "Would it have mattered to 'im if Oliver 'ere were a girl? And it's not about 'im, is it? It's about you and what you want to do, ain't it?"

"I don't rightly know, Miss."

To reinforce her words, I said, "What do you want, Tom?"

"Again, I don't know. It's just…it's what you do for a living, Oliver." He began to stammer. He had let go of my hand, leaving it hanging. I felt strangely cold without him holding me. "I-I mean…when I get the chance to be with someone, I want them to be mine and mine alone…in all ways. And you…you're a man who…well, you know. I don't need to explain it to you, do I?"

"You mean, you're concerned because I perform for other men. Is that it? I don't touch them or do anything else with them. Just dance."

"But you're all in the raw, ain't you?"

Mimsee interrupted, "Well there was that one time—"

I glared daggers at her. Thankfully, that silenced whatever else she was going to say.

Tom continued, "But would you do anything else with them, if you could? If you didn't have the Talent, I mean? Would you do more than dance?"

A flash of concern mixed with anger disturbed the blue pools of his eyes. I couldn't help but become wounded by his change in expression. I didn't know if that feeling was because of what he thought of me, or whether it was because he found himself in the current situation: in my chamber and about to do something more intimate with me than any skin-on-skin contact would ever achieve.

"What are you saying, Tom?"

"I…but if—"

I kissed him. Right on his plump, ruby lips.

Mimsee gasped and I shuddered a breath.

Tom tasted of salt and manliness as we slowly opened our mouths to each other. I quivered inside. Those butterflies shot up inside me to lighten my heart with their wing beats. I knew what I did was a desperate move, but one I hoped would play out how I intended.

After some initial hesitation, he embraced me.

When my head became light and my insides churned worse than when my Talent manifested itself, we finally parted.

All previous concerns had vacated Tom's expression.

Rather delightfully, it was replaced with surprise and that all too familiar yearning men got when their libido overtook their reasoning.

I knew. I had it, too.

Before he could speak, I said, "You're a peeler's son, and I think that's wonderful."

I thought of Arthur as I spoke those words.

The Captain had been right. Arthur wasn't right for me. Sure, he was kind and gentle, but how long would our relationship last when I had to reveal to him that I couldn't give him everything he desired because of my Talent? No gift would make me give up such a thing—no gift except true love. Yes, Arthur was more than a friend. But did I *love* him?

No, I didn't believe I did.

I added, "I know now for a fact that if I am to love someone it will be with someone who has the Talent. Perhaps you and me are destined to be together, I can't say. I do think you're wonderful, Tom. I do. But for the here and now, I need your help. And by helping me, you'll also be helping your father and all the other peelers."

Tom remained silent, mouth agape. He wasn't rich, and I knew he wouldn't offer me gifts to please me. He was only concerned, and through that concern he spoke volumes about how he felt for me.

Our kiss evident of that, too.

Mimsee was crying tears of joy. "Oh, my word, I'm all choked up. Beside myself, I am." She fanned her face with her hand.

Finally, with a voice that was strained and weighted from emotion, Tom said, "I think you're wonderful too, Oliver. But if we're to make a go of it, be together in any way, then it's gotta be built on what we are, not what we want each other to be. You are who you are—and I must come to my own mind about how I feel about it. For now, let's just take it all one step at a time."

My Lord Almighty, he was amazing. Eloquent, intelligent, and above all else, right. "I'd like that very much."

"And I will help you. But I also got to say, you're one good kisser, Oliver. My lips are still tingling."

"Thank you." I smiled. "And you're a great kisser, too."

We embraced, kissing deeply to make my insides flutter with those wonderful butterflies again.

Mimsee coughed. She reminded me of the true purpose as to why we were in my chamber, kissing Tom aside. "Then what are we waitin' for? No use standin' about chattin' like old women, let's get on with the Talent-touch thing. We've got a murderer to catch."

Chapter Twenty
The Duality of Fate

Without further delay, I arranged two chairs so that they faced each other. I set them far enough away so there wouldn't be any accidental intimate contact between Tom and myself, but close enough so we could touch feet. I wanted some sort of physical reminder of our connection while we used our Talent.

"Did you want me to stay or leave you two at it, my lovelies?" Mimsee asked.

Tom couldn't have been sure of the ramifications of Mimsee's question; not until I began disrobing. Soon, I was standing in front of him without a stitch on.

"That's up to Tom." I shrugged, smiling reassuringly. "I don't mind if you're here. You know that, Mimsee."

His eyes widened. "Lawks, Oliver. You're…it's as thick as your arm, an' all, ain't it?" Tom's cheeks suddenly flushed the deepest red I'd ever seen. Redder than his hair. He stared at me for the longest time. My Lord Almighty, I believed he must have had the hardest time tearing his gaze away from my gentlemanly assets.

He let out a sighing moan. Tom was too transfixed by my form to speak further. Bless him.

"Don't you fret, Tom, my dear," Mimsee came to help Tom out of his morning suit, not waiting for his reply. "Nothin' to it. Just start 'ere." She pulled off his coat from his shoulders. "Then we'll go from there, we will."

Soon Tom was shirtless and down to his drawers. The skin

of his body was even whiter than his fair face, like alabaster in the glow of moonlight. I had to admit, even though he was thin, there were clean muscle lines down his abdomen. I appreciated his form very much, and without doubt he was delectable. Atop his shoulders sat a spraying of freckles, the only blemish on his otherwise perfect skin.

He looked down at himself, studying his own body. "What can I say? I got like this 'cause I'm the lackey boy down at the peeler house. Gotta earn my coin somehow, don't I?"

"You look wonderful...very handsome," I praised, without trying to sound too cloying or needy. But it was true, if it weren't for the Talent, I'd kick Mimsee off the bed and let him knock me off between my sheets. I'd be his tupping boy for as long as he liked it, and then some.

Then again, if it wasn't for my Talent, I'd never have met him.

Oh Lord, the duality of fate.

Tom fiddled with the drawstring of his underwear, still looking flushed. "Well, what's there to lose, right?" And with that he pulled them down.

Now it was my turn to gasp; Mimsee echoed me.

Tom had, for want of a better term, and to copy Mimsee's vernacular of earlier, a good sized "peeler's truncheon" between his legs. Being of a lower class, he hadn't had anything cut off it either. More noticeably, however, was the bright red fire of his body and pubic hair, even brighter than the hair on his head. It was stunning.

"Do you...do you like what you see, Oliver?" he offered, gaining confidence with each word. I knew how he felt; being without a stitch on in front of others was quite liberating after the initial hesitation.

"My word, yes!" What else could I say? I went to him,

kissing him on his lips again, letting our tongues touch so I could experience his taste once more.

As we kissed, I was careful to make sure our gentlemanly assets didn't come in contact. As a result, we didn't embrace. I missed that. I knew the Talent allowed certain contact, but I didn't know if that extended to our intimates touching. I didn't want to risk it, either. Which made things interesting as we both hardened.

With reluctance, we parted our kiss. His lips glistened from my attention. Both of us smiled nervously.

Mimsee sat quietly on the bed, smiling brightly and clearly enjoying the spectacle of what unfolded before her.

"I suppose I'm a mandrake for real now," Tom said. "A real man lover, right?"

"No turning back now, Tom." I kissed his cheek.

His smile never left him. "Pa might be upset I'm with a lad. But like you all told me, it's about me and what I want, ain't it?"

"Sure is, lovely," Mimsee interjected.

Moments later, we were both seated and facing each other. Our bodies already showed more than enough evidence of our enthusiasm, my pre-fluids flowing as much as his.

I began my breathing exercise, as did Tom. I didn't have to dig too deeply to find a recent positive experience. He was staring right at me, wide-eyed and handsome; the shock of fire above his aroused gentlemanly asset also a pleasant sight to behold.

"Ready?" I asked.

Tom nodded.

The Talent flowed from us both, at first meeting like two ethereal rivers coming to convergence after a drought. Our energy went further, mine toward him, his toward me. I shuddered with rapturous delight when Tom's energy touched my skin, my delicate parts, and my arousal. He was all over me with his Talent, so close and beautiful. I hissed through my teeth. Every erogenous place, from my nipples to my deepest desires were stimulated simultaneously.

My nerves burned delightfully as did every muscle.

I was soon in the throes of ecstasy.

But I had to hold on. I wanted to give him what he gave me.

With my Talent, I gently touched him. The sensations and perception I received from the magical contact upon Tom were phenomenal. I could feel every nuance of him, inside and out. What he desired. What he liked. What he needed. All of that told me he wanted me and that he'd been waiting—almost desperately—for someone to share his desires with.

Someone like me.

I admitted I felt the same about him.

More and more our Talent deepened. I was at the point of exploding, back arched, and sweating. Tom's Talent-grip upon my body was pleasurable beyond measure, the tendrils of his desire wrapped around me like a thousand arms of his affection as he explored deep inside me. I felt warm and flushed, unbelievably so. My toes curled, I'm sure.

I gripped the chair tightly, leaving fingernail marks on its cloth. "Holy heavens above, Tom!" I couldn't help but cry out such hackneyed words, sounding like I was a sailor on payday bedding his first bunter.

I didn't care.

If I thought touching myself with my own Talent had me seeing stars, with Tom's Talent-touch it was like a whole galaxy had burst before my eyes.

It didn't take long for my arousal to throb and my release to douse me. I could hear, very far away to my mind, Mimsee letting out a shriek of joy. She would have more than likely been amazed by how much came out of me. Even the chair wore it.

We came to completion at the same time.

When my breathing had evened and my body had cooled

enough, I sat up. I was weak. Tom's body glistened with the result of what had come out of him in as much volume as mine had. Sweat had gathered on his temples, his cheeks rosy with satisfaction.

"Lawks!" was all Tom said.

Lawks indeed.

"I need a cheroot," Mimsee said.

"Looks like it worked. We both still have our Talent, Tom."

Chapter Twenty-One
The Skilamalink Man Strikes Again

Tom and I dressed…slowly. The parts of me that didn't ache were numb, as every muscle and sinew seemed to stiffen the more I cooled from the experience. But it was worth it.

Mimsee helped us both.

"That will never leave me. What I just witnessed with my very own eyes, what you two lovelies did for each other…I've never seen the likes of it. It was beautiful." She embraced us each in turn. "If you ask me, and I know you will, I think you're better off. That was special, wouldn't let anyone tell you otherwise. Better by 'alf than to have someone sweatin' and grindin', all foul breath and sticky, stinkin' flesh pressed against you until they pass out, that's for certain."

Perhaps she was right.

Tom was more pragmatic. "We'll never know, 'cause that's how we've got to do it. Being folks with Talent, an' all."

"Did you think it was all right?" I asked.

"Better than all right," he said with a wink.

And then Tom kissed me.

My lips even hurt, as did my tongue. But we got there with it, much to my continued enjoyment.

When we were both back in our morning attire, there was a knock at my chamber door. Mimsee went to answer it. One of the house servants stood at its threshold.

"Begging your pardon, ma'am," the servant announced.

"You are all requested to attend Lady Penelope. She says it is urgent."

We all looked at each other.

"Well, no rest for the wicked, is there?" Mimsee quipped.

"I thought it was 'no rest for the Devil?'" Tom enquired.

"Same thing, ain't it?" Mimsee replied with a titter of laugher. I smiled at her; I knew she was referred to the many times I'd touched myself once I'd retired for the evening. Now that I had Tom, hopefully that would be a thing of the past.

Lady Penelope, William, and two other peelers were waiting in the foyer for us. They all looked concerned, Lady Penelope even more than the others.

"Whatever's the matter?" I asked in general.

William cleared his throat, but his lips were pressed tight as his gaze roved suspiciously between me and his son. Another flash of concern crossed his eyes. I had a feeling William wouldn't be as understanding about me being with Tom as he'd been with other matters in his son's life. But I couldn't linger on that.

The Constable's next words startled me. "There's been another murder. This time in the alleyway behind the house."

Mimsee clutched her chest. "That close!"

Finding out there was another murder so soon and so close fell to the back of my mind when we discovered who it was lying dead on the dirty cobblestones next to the rubbish and open sewers like he was nothing.

The victim was Harold.

A man I not only liked but was also one of the men I'd smelt the pipe smoke on. I could still smell it. The soot and fog-filled air was thick with it. I coughed, covering my nose with my handkerchief.

"Smell that, Oliver?" Tom asked. He was coughing as well, hiding his mouth and nose in the crook of his arm.

I nodded. "Pipe smoke," I said for the benefit of the others who wouldn't have been able to distinguish the scent of the Talent rife in the air.

"I don't smell nothin'," Mimsee said. "Other than the usual stink off the streets, o' course."

I was almost certain the Skilamalink Man had killed Harold to taunt me. Which meant one thing: he must know I'm on to him. How he knew that, I had no idea. I informed Tom, Mimsee, Lady Penelope, and William of my suspicion.

"This 'ere is gettin' curiouser and curiouser," Mimsee offered.

Tom began to investigate Harold's body using his Talent, while his father examined the man in the more traditional way. Soon, more of the truth was revealed. Tom confirmed Harold had indeed been killed by the Skilamalink Man, the man's heart crushed.

William had other news: Harold didn't possess the Talent.

The thumb of Harold's right hand was stained yellow, tarnished by the act of pressing down tobacco into a pipe's main chamber before lighting it to smoke it. Harold was innocent.

A flush of anger coursed through me. Was the Skilamalink Man playing games now? Or maybe Harold was murdered as a warning. Again, I informed my colleagues of my thoughts.

"Well, it's only circumstantial, what you say," William snapped, looking at me with distaste through his eyelashes. I ignored the man, believing it prudent to do so.

That left only one other man who I'd smelt pipe smoke on that I danced for: the weedy man with the pasty face.

"That gentleman is booked in for Thursday," Lady Penelope said when I described him.

That gave me four nights from tonight to prepare.

Tom then said something I'll never forget: "I want to be there with you when you see that man, Oliver. Just in case he's the one."

Lord Almighty, Tom was wonderful. I knew he'd said that to protect me—be the man for me as it were. Because that's what he was. My wonderful man.

Lady Penelope raised her eyebrows in gentle surprise. "Are you sure, Master Arkwright? Do you know what such a thing will entail?"

By that, I knew she didn't disagree with the idea. At the same time, Tom had to be shown how to entertain clients in the way I did. It would be considered strange for someone else to be in the room while I performed if they weren't part of the routine.

"I'm positive, my Lady." Tom smiled confidently.

Mimsee's eyes brightened. Seemed we had more practice to do before Thursday. She'd be in her element, for sure.

William raised his hand, about to say something—in disagreement no doubt—when there was a clatter of wine barrels and crates from the far end of the alleyway. What he said next was something that shouldn't be spoken in front of ladies, no matter the circumstances of the situation. "What the deuce! Hellfire and damnation, there's someone over there!"

Before I could register what was happening, the stench of pipe smoke thickened to the point of sickening me, cloying to my skin to compete with the soot, smoke, and fog. My stomach turned, and not in a good way. A shadowed man bounded over the barrels to disappear beyond them.

"The Skilamalink Man!" I shouted as William and one other peeler immediately gave chase.

No wonder I could smell pipe smoke so strongly. The fiend had been here all along, watching.

Tom tugged on my coat sleeve. "Come on, Oliver! Now's our chance."

We ran after them.

Tom was quick. He ran like a jack rabbit, nimble and light-footed. I could only do my best to keep up with him. I wasn't used to such sudden strenuous exercise; the most arduous activity I did was shake my bare buttocks for my clients. I clambered awkwardly over the crates, catching my knee on one of them. Pain seared up my leg, and I stumbled. I let out a gasp and Tom turned back to make sure I was all right.

"I'm good," I said, wincing. "Just get him!"

"No. Not without you, I ain't."

Tom offered his hand. I took it. His touch was warm, and rather welcome given the circumstances. Thankfully, the pain eased the more I moved.

Soon, the alleyway before us divided into two. I hadn't seen which direction William or the other peeler had gone. I stopped.

"This way!" Tom said, pulling on my hand.

We took the alley that led deeper into the factory district. The fog and dirt in the air soon got as thick as pea-soup, known as the London Particular in these parts. I could only just make out the massive chimney stacks that loomed above us, pouring out their filth in great billowing clouds of blackness against the clouded, grey sky.

I could smell the pipe smoke again, but not from Tom. This was stronger, viler, while that from Tom was lighter, sweeter. Seemed the nuance of the smell told something about the individual, after all.

Tom stopped.

I was about to ask him why, when up ahead I caught sight of a shadowed man, his hands on his hips. The coachman's cloak he wore surrounded him like a macabre halo. His face was hidden.

"Well, well, Master Merritt," the Skilamalink Man said,

cold and sinister and with a voice that shredded my flesh. "I did say we'd meet again."

The Skilamalink Man's hands glowed.

Chapter Twenty-Two
The Dark Side of the Talent

I tried to breathe but couldn't calm myself in the way required for me to be able to draw upon my Talent with any purpose. My chest rose and fell quickly, my intake of air too shallow. I was like frightened prey before a predator.

Which, for all intents and purposes, I was.

The ethereal light of the Skilamalink Man's Talent weaved its way toward me, as if it were a snake homing in on a mouse.

For the sake of my life—and Tom's—I *had* to call upon my Talent. In desperation, I tried to grapple for a positive thought, searching my mind for something I could use under such sudden strain.

The evil man's Talent was only inches from me now.

I wasn't ready for this.

Tom squeezed his hand within mine, and that was it. All of a sudden, like a flash of lightning, I found the positive connection I needed. Tom's touch was the catalyst that made my Talent burst forth.

Like an explosion from a street's gaslight, the Skilamalink Man's Talent collided with mine. A massive spider-web of energy, blue and scintillating, formed before my eyes. I staggered back from the push of air created by the collision. Thankfully, Tom's grip held so I was saved from falling onto the cobblestones.

"A good turn of luck that you have your companion with you, Master Merritt. But even though the Captain has taught you well, I fear you still have a lot to learn."

Tom steadied himself, still weighed down by my burden. I also gained composure. Without delay, I called forth my Talent once more, determined to stop the Skilamalink Man.

Tom must have thought the same.

Together, we pushed our Talent toward our enemy. My gentlemanly asset immediately became engorged to the point of aching, but I had to push such things from my mind if I was to succeed.

Tom moaned. I knew his would be hardening, too.

"Bravo, Master Merritt," the Skilamalink Man said weaving more of his magic. "I see you're working together. That will be the only way you can defeat me." He sent more tendrils of Talent toward us. "But not today, my friends. Not today!"

The Skilamalink Man's Talent was powerful, and Tom was shoved aside by it. He yelped in pain as he found the cobblestones. Thankfully, his own Talent had protected him from the worst. He was alive. Tom had used his for defence, as I used to do when my father got drunk and beat me.

"Tom!" I cried.

I wasn't so fortunate.

The Skilamalink Man's Talent pierced my protective web-like shield I'd created as though it were made of cotton threads. His evil touched me. I was spun around, like a marionette with twisted wires and my puppet master was enjoying my torment. Which he was.

He sent even more of his Talent toward us. His laugher, one of twisted joy, echoed through the narrow alleyway.

I didn't know what to do. I couldn't attack with my Talent because I hadn't been taught how. I gulped, waiting for the inevitable release of my life as I lay flat on my back on the dirty cobblestones.

Tom's hand found mine. I squeezed it. At least I wasn't alone at my ending.

I closed my eyes.

The next thing I knew, there was the familiar clatter of peelers' rattles pounding inside my head. I opened my eyes. Pain shot through me. I touched my temple, only to see blood on my hand. With the realisation I was injured, I went numb.

"Today wasn't the day of your undoing after all, Master Merritt. For you or your companion. But soon it will be, I promise you that," the Skilamalink Man proclaimed before the sound of his retreating footsteps echoed over the cobblestones.

Tom came over me, a rather pleasant sight after what had transpired. "Oliver? Are you all right, Oliver?" He grabbed me by my shoulders, gently shaking to rouse me as my mind began to cloud. "Please say you're all right. Oliver?"

I couldn't answer him. I couldn't move at all. What had happened? Had the Skilamalink Man stopped my heart? Was I experiencing the last moments before my death?

William, numerous peelers, Mimsee, and Lady Penelope crowded around me. I could see their mouths moving, but no sound found my ears. Then, even the sense of my sight was robbed from me.

My world sunk into darkness.

I woke to find Mimsee and Tom sitting in my chamber's chairs, talking quietly to each other. I couldn't hear what they were saying but could make out their voices. Thank the Lord Almighty, I wasn't deafened by the Skilamalink Man's Talent.

Relief came to me. I was alive. At the same time, a terrible fear crawled across my skin like an intrusion of cockroaches upon uncovered sweetmeats. What damage had the Skilamalink Man's Talent done to me?

I knew I had been unconscious for a while; I was dressed in

my nightshirt. Lady Penelope, Tom, and Mimsee were in attire more appropriate for the afternoon. All except for William. He wore his peeler's uniform, as always.

Lady Penelope was at my door, watching carefully as the house servants moved a large wooden trunk into my chamber. William stood next to her; a dark look stained his brow.

"Oliver's awake!" Mimsee said, the joy in her voice at seeing me awaken, and mine for being able to hear her were both in equal measure, I'm sure. I breathed in deeply more relief.

"What happened?" I asked, my voice hoarse.

Lady Penelope approached. I tried to sit up but couldn't. I was sore and stiff all over, more so than when Tom and I Talent-touched earlier. "Stay still, Oliver. You've had quite a turn to say the least. From what I hear, you're lucky to be alive. As is Master Arkwright."

I looked at Tom after she spoke his name. It was then I realised his hand was in mine. He looked as relieved as I felt, but his face also held something else, something deeper, something I knew I had to know. "Whatever's the matter, Tom?"

Tom's eyes flicked over to his father for the briefest moment. "We've been talking about things..."

"What does that mean?"

Lady Penelope interjected, "Tom will be staying here with us in the house. He feels, rather nobly so, the need to make sure you remain safe, Oliver." I heard William snort at that. She continued unabated, like a steam train running late for a connection, "Therefore, Tom will be trained to work with you, upon his own request. He will also attend the Talent lessons I give so that the both of you will know how to attack. To not show you that earlier was a shortcoming of mine that will be swiftly corrected.

"Furthermore, Mimsee will no longer be in the house's service, but in yours, Oliver. She will remain your chaperone, and help you in any way she can. You're the man of the house, as is Tom while he's with you. Mimsee, as always, is your equal in my eyes. The three of you will work together. The sovereigns you earn will be shared."

Tom quivered a smile. "Sovereigns, hey? Never been paid in them. Only in pennies and the occasional shilling, if I'm real lucky."

"Where will Tom be staying?" I asked, even though I already knew the answer. What else could the trunk be for if it didn't contain Tom's belongings?

Now it was William's turn to speak up. "My son will be staying in here with you…Oliver." He said my name like it was something he'd scraped off the bottom of his shoe so a tanning boy could buy it for softening animal hides for the leather trade.

"That's wonderful news indeed." Butterflies fluttered inside me. I was to be with Tom more permanently. I couldn't be happier. As such, I tried to sit up again. My head pounded for my effort. I touched the place of my pain, my hand finding a bandage. "Ow," I hissed.

"Stay still, or you won't get better," Lady Penelope snapped.

"His Ma thinks it's wonderful as well," William said, his voice thick with disdain. "I have my reservations on the matter but, as Lady Penelope has assured me, my Tom will be well looked after. Even if what he's doing is unnatural, if you ask me."

Lady Penelope retorted, "Utter nonsense, William. As I've already told you." Her glare could have frightened away a raging bull.

William backed down by lowering his head. I had a feeling the argument had already run a previous course and he'd lost then as well. He was foolish to try it again so soon. I felt sorry for him in a way.

She returned her attention to me. "Oliver, you are to remain in bed for a few days while you recover." I caught a faint smile curling the corner of her lips. A smile of victory when it came to William, I imagined. "Tom and Mimsee will make sure of it."

"I'm 'ere to make sure you don't go crackers," Mimsee announced.

With Tom living in my chamber with me, I doubted I would ever get bored.

"How long was I unconscious?" I asked, changing the subject away from my aches and pains. "Because I'm hungry."

"I will get the house servants to bring up something to eat," Lady Penelope answered. "As for the rest of what's on your mind, I'll leave those sorts of questions for Mimsee and Tom to answer. You have your instruction from me, Oliver."

"Yes, Lady Penelope, ma'am," I said.

She smiled warmly. "Come, William, I do believe we haven't finished our words to each other yet."

"Yes, Madam."

"And don't call me Madam," she snapped. "I've disliked it from the beginning. It makes me sound like a cheap brothel mistress. What I charge here for one night, you wouldn't earn in a month of Sundays. Now, let's take our leave. I believe Oliver will be fine."

William wilted. "Yes, Lady Penelope." He held out the crook of his arm for her. She accepted it. Soon they were beyond my chamber's door, the house servants doing the same.

The door was closed.

"Oh, 'ave I got a story to tell you two, I have," Mimsee announced with a wicked grin.

Chapter Twenty-Three
The Demon Within

"What kind of story?" I asked.

Mimsee's smile became even more salacious. "The story I promised you, Oliver. Now it's time I told it, seein' as I don't do that no more."

"Your first time?" I questioned.

I knew the real reason she chose now to tell her tale. She felt like being a tease, wanting to make Tom blush. Somehow, I had a feeling that wouldn't be so difficult.

Tom asked, "First time…for what?"

"The first time, lovely, that I was flat on my back, legs up near my ears, and me thinkin' of England, o' course."

No, it wasn't difficult. Not at all. Tom's cheeks had already become a rosy stain. "Oh," he said. But his eyes widened. I knew he wanted to hear the story, as did I.

"Then tell it," I said. "We're waiting."

"'Ere, don't get your drawers in a tangle, Oliver. I'm gettin' there." She was enjoying herself. She had a captive audience; me laid up in bed and Tom eager to know more about the scandalous world he had unexpectedly found himself within. "Well, the first man I got shillin's out of was as pretty as a picture, 'e was. But he 'ad tackle that could be mistaken for the monster from the Loch, it was that big. It near on gave me a fright when 'e let it out 'is trousers for a bit of air."

Tom's mouth dropped open. "You mean…he had a tallywacker bigger than what Oliver's got?"

I appreciated how Tom saw me. I felt my cheeks burn. "I don't think mine's that big."

"No one's got one as big as our Oliver's, that's a fact." Mimsee giggled. "'Specially when it's 'ard. I wager you come over all queer, Oliver, it needs that much blood to bring it to full mast."

Tom laughed, squeezing my hand and giving me a wink. "Oliver's magnificent, no doubt."

"As are you, Tom." I laughed, too. Doing so hurt my ribs but I couldn't help it. My Lord Almighty, Mimsee was a tease and Tom was wonderful.

Tom had blushed into deeper red. Surprisingly, he said, "Do go on, Miss. I'm dying to hear what happens in your story."

She did so without hesitation. "See, the first thing 'e asked me to do when 'e was all free and easy, was to bagpipe him. Now, me bein' new to it all, I did know one thing for certain: 'e didn't have a Scottish accent."

I laughed even more, as did Mimsee. It hurt again. Tom looked confused.

"I don't get it," Tom said.

After Mimsee explained to him that the gentleman required the services of her mouth upon his beastly bits, an act known in certain parts as bagpiping, we spent the rest of the afternoon laughing and talking like that. Aside from my aches and pains and a throbbing head that pierced me behind my eyes, there were two things that hurt me the most.

The first: that Tom and I didn't catch the Skilamalink Man. Something that would come to haunt us later, I was certain. The second, and most important, was that I wouldn't be here with him and my best friend right now if chance hadn't favoured us. That thought stewed in my mind for a while as I considered it. I could have died. I would have no longer been able to see Tom. Or Mimsee. Or the Captain.

I had to process those thoughts for a moment. When I did, my stomach turned in a way I knew was profound. It lightened me. With all my soul I knew I wanted to be with Tom for as long as I could hold breath in my lungs.

I squeezed his hand, for he hadn't let me go.

Mimsee continued to tell salacious stories, while Tom, as gentle as he was beautiful, kept glancing at me knowingly between blushing. I understood from that he counted his lucky stars as well. We had a close call, and the next time we encountered the Skilamalink Man we would not be so easily defeated.

That was my promise to myself.

To Tom.

To Mimsee.

To my Captain.

During our rumbustious and sometimes very saucy conversation that made Tom turn redder than his hair, with lots of knowing titters and glances, I discovered that I was unconscious for only a short time. Mimsee was the one who had changed me into my nightshirt—as I should have guessed. While she attended me, Lady Penelope and William argued about Tom's decision to stay in the house with me.

Tom had said with finality, "Don't anyone want to know how I feel about this or what I want? I want to be with Oliver, and that's the end of it. You hear me, Pa?"

Lady Penelope had agreed. Tom was old enough to make his own decisions, and as such, it was his choice. Although, from what I could understand, it was Lady Penelope's offer that Tom could share the coin from my earnings that finally persuaded his father.

Money always convinced even the most self-righteous, in my experience.

Soon, a house servant knocked on the chamber door and

Mimsee answered. A trolley of food was presented. We all ate heartily from what Cook had prepared: a tasty dinner of handmade pies, pasties, and sweetmeats. Even beer in tall glasses was provided. I enjoyed that.

After dinner I slept, feeling drained and weary, but lightened by my company.

I didn't wake up until the next morning. What woke me was the familiar drawing of the drapes by Mimsee, sunlight streaming into the room to reveal motes of dust dancing in the rays, happy as I was for the new day. The only difference was an extra portion of sweetmeat treats on my nightstand and Tom curled up beside me, snoring gently.

He was wonderfully warm.

"'Ow do you feel, lovely?" Mimsee asked me.

I was still stiff and a little sore in places I couldn't put my finger on, but I knew they were internal. It felt like a demon lived within me, and even though the Skilamalink Man's Talent hadn't killed me, it sure lingered to cripple me.

"I think I'm fine," I lied.

I couldn't sit up unassisted, so Mimsee helped me. She also adjusted the pillows, so I was propped up with more support.

Tom stirred, yawned, and turned to me. His hair was more of a mess than usual. He looked a fright. "Morning, handsome." He then kissed me, right on my lips and sweeter than the sweetmeats I normally looked forward to.

"Good morning indeed, beautiful."

I could most certainly get used to such an awakening from him. His warmth surrounded me, and I smiled contently.

Later that day, I was still in my bed and unable to move.

Mimsee said, "'Ere now, Tom. It's time for you to practice."

Tom was sitting on the bed, holding my hand. He hadn't left my side all day. He was dressed in his afternoon attire, a suit more refined than his morning one.

At Mimsee's words, he looked at me, and I raised an eyebrow at him. I liked the idea of watching someone else do what I did. I didn't hesitate to mention that, of course.

Tom blushed, as was becoming common.

"Now, the thing to remember," she continued, as he stood, "is you ain't takin' off your clothin', but revealing more of yourself. You got to get 'em all worked up 'cause that loosens their purses, it does."

Tom let go of my hand to unbutton his jacket. "Like this?"

If Mimsee could have flown across the room and smacked his hands, she would have done so. "No! You're not undressin' to get into bed for a good night's sleep. I told you that."

Tom nodded feebly. I tried to suppress a smile but failed.

"Take your 'andkerchief out first," she instructed. "Then take off your gloves and the other bits of fancy you're wearing. Don't hurry, or it'll be over too quickly. Then 'e might want somethin' more from you for 'is coin, if you get my meanin'. You've got to give 'em time to take you all in. Move a bit as well. Like this."

She did a slow hip sway and used her hands across herself at the same time. "See? Got it, now?"

Tom's hip swayed. Unfortunately, he looked like he had weights attached to his elbows and knees. Only his midriff moved, even if as stiff as I'd ever seen. He would need a lot of lessons.

Mimsee sighed. "I can tell you're a peeler's son. You ain't got no grace about you, Tom. Not even an ounce." She helped correct his movement by coming behind him, placing her hands on his waist.

Tom spluttered, "There ain't much call for this sort of thing down at the peeler house, Miss. It would cause a riot if I did this sort of thing in there, I know it."

"Well, let's 'ope we can make somethin' of you soon. Otherwise, the only thing you'll arouse is laughter."

"He more than makes up for things with his looks, though," I supplied.

"Ta, Oliver."

"And a good thing, too, I say." Mimsee laughed. Even Tom managed a nervous smile, because I could see the sheer concentration on his face as he was trying to do as asked under Mimsee's assistance.

The poor blighter.

An hour or so later, Mimsee had helped Tom enough so he didn't look as rigid as one of those dress forms Lady Penelope used to help create her outfits.

"Now we can see 'ow it looks without your clothin' on," she said.

That was the part I had been looking forward to.

Chapter Twenty-Four
The Exorcism Begins

By the time Tom stood in front of me without a stitch on, looking as pleased as punch, I was aroused. Although, much to my dismay, my gentlemanly assets couldn't rise to the spirit of the occasion because of the sickness residing within me.

"What did you think of that, Oliver?" Tom asked, proudly.

Sure, Tom was inexperienced, nervous, and unpractised with his movements as he got down to his nakedness, but when he had, even the most critical would forgive his failings.

"I think you're beautiful," I replied. My breathing became difficult and my heart thumped against the back of my ribs to worry me.

But all that was forgotten for a moment.

I was in the presence of an angel. Tom's skin and hair glowed as daylight streamed across his body. His eyes glistened. The sight of him like that would remain with me forever.

Once Tom was dressed, weariness overwhelmed me.

I dreamed of him.

When I woke, Mimsee was preparing a plate of food from a trolley sent up by Cook. Tom was nowhere to be seen.

"Where's Tom?" I asked worriedly.

"'E's taken 'is leave to go spend a penny. Poor blighter. By the time I convinced 'im it'd be all right to leave you, 'e was near on cross-eyed 'e'd been holdin' on so long."

Why hadn't Tom used the chamber pot? Perhaps he wanted

fresh air, even though Mimsee always insisted my window was opened a crack to keep out the "smells boys make" as she put it.

I had to take her word for it; Tom smelt divine to me.

By the time Mimsee handed me a plate piled high with cold meats, knobs of sourdough bread, and cheeses both soft and hard, Tom returned. He was delighted I was awake.

"How are you feeling, Oliver?" He fussed over me, fixed pillows and bedclothes, and kissed me tenderly on my forehead to show his concern.

"Not good, I'm afraid."

I was not only weak, but I was tired and hurting all over—my insides most of all. The demon who'd taken up residence within me had called upon its brethren to join it. I felt no better than I did yesterday.

Worse, in fact.

Most of my time was spent sleeping, with only brief moments of lucidity, such as when Tom was taught to dance and disrobe teasingly. Other than that, I didn't get much respite from the pain.

"Right, that fixes it then," Mimsee said. "I'm takin' you to see Mister Okinawa. 'E'll know what to do, Oliver. Seein' as you've 'ad an unnatural fright."

"What I've had is the Skilamalink Man's Talent infect me," I said vacantly, not meaning to sound dismissive.

Tom pulled back the duvet, and instantly I felt cold. "I've called the coach that'll take us to the Limehouse district, Oliver. Just as Miss asked me to." He then helped me get out of bed.

So that was the reason Tom hadn't used the chamber pot. They had a plan, the sneaky weasels. I quivered a smile. "What's he going to do to me, this Mister Okinawa?"

Before I received an answer, a shudder of pain went through me to make me hiss through my teeth. Tom and Mimsee were either side of me, holding one of my arms each. Their concern was palpable; my pain was consuming. The reason for my sudden agony was most concerning. The demon and its friends inside me were awake and they didn't like the fact I was standing.

I didn't like it either.

Mimsee let me stay in my nightshirt, and Tom wrapped me in a woollen, navy blue frock coat that went past my knees to keep me both decent and warm in public. He also helped me into my shoes, because I couldn't bend over without losing my balance.

"Why in tarnation did it do this to me?" I complained bitterly.

Tom's eyes reflected his worry. "Cause you took it all—the dirty bastard's Talent—that's why."

"Tom!" Mimsee glared at him.

I knew she did so because of his uncouth language in front of her. But a knowing glint of her eye spoke volumes that she agreed with him. As did I. The Skilamalink Man was a bastard, and not the kind who came into this world illegitimately either.

Tom blushed. "Sorry, Miss, but it's true, an' all."

The coach was waiting for us, as Tom said. It was mid-afternoon. The sun was desperately trying to break through the gloom so common in Autumn. The leaves of the trees along the streets were yellowing. Soon they would be bare, a sign winter and the dirty snow would follow.

To get to the Limehouse district, the coachman had to take us over the Thames on one of the stone bridges used to get to the East End of the city. I caught glimpses of the river's black, oily shore at low tide. A group of mudlark boys were knee-deep in its filth, scavenging for anything of value to make a living. I blessed my stars, knowing I was fortunate I'd been adopted by Lady Penelope.

The streets narrowed the further we ventured into the East End. The buildings and houses seemed more run-down and certainly dirtier than other parts of the city. Lines of clothing were strung across the streets above, while below, children played in the dirt, sometimes reaching up with their grubby hands to beg for coins as we passed.

The driver used his coach whip often to ensure the horses didn't slow. I also blessed the foresight the man had for using running dogs—Dalmatians, I believed—to escort us on our journey. The panhandlers and vagabonds of the area avoided dogs, especially their teeth.

The coach stopped outside a section of the East End that accommodated London's Chinatown: laundries, curiosity shoppes, low class brothels, and places selling and administering ancient Chinese medicines were abundant.

There was even a theatre.

I hadn't been to a Chinese theatre. I'd like to take Tom to a show one day. I heard they were rather good. A poster plastered to a dirty brick wall told of a magician performing soon.

A magic show would be most amusing indeed.

The coachman opened the carriage door for us. The first thing that struck me was the smell of excrement and all the other unspeakable things open cesspits and the Thames contained in abundance.

The dogs never stopped barking, warning those who came too close to do so at their own peril.

"I'll wait here for you, Miss O'Donnell," the coachman said, bowing his head.

"That'll be fine," Mimsee said.

I was assisted into a Chinese apothecary-cum-pharmacy shoppe by Mimsee and Tom. My weakness was getting worse. Once inside, I couldn't help but become overwhelmed by the rancid, thick cloud of opium that didn't seem to dissipate. My nostrils burned from it. I coughed, as did Tom.

Mimsee didn't seem bothered.

Emerging from the cloud as if he were an apparition coming

into corporeal existence, the owner of the establishment came to greet us.

I assumed the man was Mister Okinawa.

"Good day to you, Miss O'Donnell. Back so soon? And who are these two gentlemen who accompany you today?" Whatever image I had in my mind about what a man of medicine should look and talk like, Mister Okinawa was the furthest from it.

He was shorter than me but very distinguished. Also, he was dressed in his finery, like that of a gentleman prepared for the evening: silken bowtie, clean-pressed white shirt, waistcoat, gold fob watch and chain, and trousers darker dyed but appropriate for the time of day. He didn't wear gloves or a jacket or coat, which was acceptable for a gentleman remaining indoors. His voice matched the clothing; clean and debonair.

I liked Mister Okinawa already.

"This 'ere is my brother, Oliver Merritt, Mister Okinawa." She gestured to each of us in turn. "And this 'ere 'andsome fellow is 'is companion Tom Arkwright."

Mister Okinawa bowed his head slightly. The man's hair was platted to a ponytail at the back of his head, tied with red and gold-patterned ribbon on the end.

"Ah yes, I believe you spoke of them last time you were here." But I saw no question or judgement in Mister Okinawa's eyes about Tom and I being introduced as two men who were together. "Your brother is the one who has been attacked by the Talent?"

"That's right, it is."

"Very good. Follow me, please."

Mister Okinawa led us to the back of the pharmacy. The shelves were cram-packed with hundreds of medicine bottles in all shapes and sizes, as well as bags of powders and all the other accoutrements of the trade. I didn't know how the man found anything.

We entered a small, dimly-lit private consultation room. Books, manuscripts, objects I could gather no function or purpose of, and a myriad of other things including taxidermized animals and sculptures of human body parts and genitalia, filled the room. As if it wasn't lacking space enough, several well-worn leather chairs were nestled amongst the clutter.

Tom and Mimsee helped me into one of them.

When I was settled, but wincing in pain, Mister Okinawa asked me the strangest questions. "Tell me, Master Merritt, is your mouth dry?" I admitted it was. "What colour is your urine?" I answered that it was about the same colour as it usually was. Mimsee confirmed that. "Does it flow freely?" I told him it hurt inside when I did do it, but as far as I could tell it came out just fine. "What about dizziness or vomiting?" No, I hadn't vomited, but was dizzy. And finally, he asked, "Do you have a rapid heartbeat?" I told him that only happened when I looked and thought of Tom, which was every waking moment as well as when I dreamed.

Tom blushed. "Same with me about you, Oliver."

"Love is its own disease." Mister Okinawa flashed a knowing grin. "If one is fortunate, however, one will never be cured of it at all."

I nodded in agreement. "What can you do for me?"

"What can be done will be a process, but you can be cured." He gestured to an examination table. One I'd only just noticed amongst all the other clutter. "The one who has used the Talent against you created a many-headed beast inside you. Fortunately, your heaven is warm, and the sun is still bright within. Unfortunately, your mountain breath stills. Because of this, your blood has become stagnant, slowing the flow of your qi. That is why you are weak, Master Merritt. However, the still blood can be drained so the qi can move freely once more. Hopefully then, the Talent's energy of your attacker will leave you. Hopefully then."

I didn't understand one word of what he said.

As he spoke, he retrieved a case containing more than a dozen large, bulbous glass cups, a candle, a bottle of fluid, and a knife shaped somewhat like a physician's scalpel. "Please, Miss O'Donnell, Master Arkwright, assist Master Merritt onto my table. He will need to have his back exposed for me to be able to do my work. I will be cupping and then cutting him so his qi will flow again."

I didn't think I liked the sound of that.

Chapter Twenty-Five
The Linkboy's Omen

Suffice it to say, having only been dressed hastily into a coat over my nightshirt, I wasn't wearing my drawers. I was soon without a stitch on, lying prone, my face in a convenient hole in the table. Mister Okinawa draped a towel over my bare backside.

"For your dignity," the man explained.

Mimsee said with a laugh, "Oliver ain't got no dignity."

"And ain't we all glad for that," Tom offered.

I lifted my head to see Mister Okinawa light the candle and set it onto a stand. He retrieved a bottle from a cabinet, this one large and filled with viscous oil. When he opened the corked lid, the smell of cinnamon and menthol wafted to my nose. He pressed his hand gently against my head, to get me to place my face into the hole proper. When I'd done so, with the oil lathering his hands, he began massaging my back.

I'd heard about people massaging others. Sometimes it happened in the rooms of the first floor of the house, usually as a precursor to other pleasures of the flesh—or as Mimsee put it, until the beast with two backs reared up to take over a couple's passion.

Thinking of that, I became concerned I'd lose my Talent's abilities. Would a massage vanquish it from my body, its touch deemed by my magic to be more intimate than holding hands or kissing?

I squirmed, about to voice my protest, when Mister Okinawa said, "I know what I'm doing, Master Merritt." He spoke that sentence with such authority and professionalism, I immediately calmed.

I breathed in deeply.

"What do you know of the Talent, Mister Okinawa?" I asked.

"In time, I will tell you. For now, let me work *my* magic."

I had to admit, once I relaxed, the massage felt good. More so when Mister Okinawa began working deeper to reach the knotted muscles between my shoulders. What he did and how it made me feel was a skill, and he was a master at it.

He then stopped. My weakened muscles missed his expert hands immediately. "This next part will feel strange to you. Once again, Master Merritt, please do not be alarmed."

I looked up briefly again, flushing concern. I saw him with one of the bulbous glass cups in one hand and a tool that held fast a lit wadding of cotton in the other; he'd ignited it from the candle's flame.

Again, Mister Okinawa moved with practiced ease. He placed the flame into the inside of the cup, expelling the air within it. An instant later, that cup was placed onto my back at the top of my right shoulder.

To say it was strange feeling was an understatement.

It felt like nothing I had ever experienced before, and as such I couldn't quantify it in any proper way. I could only say it felt like a strong draw upon my skin, as if it no longer wanted to be a part of me.

All ten of the cups, once vacuumed by the flame, were placed onto my back. After the initial pinch of each one, I began to relax. My back felt tight upon me.

Mimsee had obviously seen cupping being done before, or even had it done on herself, because she didn't seem to be overly concerned when I ventured a glance at her. Tom, on the other hand, looked as though he was watching a horror show, the kind one of those modern Magic Lanterns projected to scare folks for a penny a head.

After a time, Mister Okinawa began removing the cups. An odd sucking sound, one for each cup, filled the room as the air returned to the glass. If it felt strange with them going on, I certainly knew how to quantify how it was when he took them off.

Relief. Pure and simple.

"Ah, just as I suspected," Mister Okinawa said, whether to himself or to me, I couldn't tell.

With the knife he pricked at my skin where he'd placed the cups. Little stings, like that of bees, filled my senses. Again, uncomfortable, but not concerning. Which was unusual, because someone with a blade at the back of me would have ordinarily sent me into fits. Perhaps it was Mister Okinawa himself, his calm demeanour and his encouraging touch, that calmed me in ways I couldn't fathom.

Then, the cups were returned to my skin. I took it my blood flowed into the glass as their suction drew out the demon from my body.

I stole another glance toward Mimsee and Tom.

If it were at all possible, Tom's skin had paled even more, highlighting further his freckles. His eyes were wide, mouth agape. Mimsee held a smile, no doubt contented I was being looked after.

"I'm almost done." Mister Okinawa touched the back of my head to remind me to stop moving and to put my face back into the hole.

"What does it look like?" I questioned to no one in particular.

"It looks...I can't believe it even though I seen it with my own eyes," Tom began. I could hear him shift uncomfortably in his chair. He added, "There's a blue light coming out of you where there should be your blood!"

Mimsee was more considerate. "Now, Tom, don't you fret. It's just Mister Okinawa's magic drawin' out the Skilamalink Man's Talent from our Oliver, that's all."

When Mister Okinawa had removed the cups and cleaned where the foreign Talent had been exorcised from my body with something that stung and smelt of alcohol, he proceeded to rub a strong and spicy smelling balm over my back.

When that was massaged into my back, he used the towel that "covered my dignity", as he put it earlier, to wipe away any excess liniment from my skin.

"You may dress now, Master Merritt, please."

I expected Mimsee and Tom to attend me. Or at least help me off the examination table. Mister Okinawa gestured for them to remain seated. I got up slowly, expecting to still be weak. I felt light-headed, but the demons weren't inside me anymore.

Had the Skilamalink Man's Talent truly been vanquished?

My whole body came to life as I moved; muscles, ligaments, sinews, and bones, all working as they should. Tom handed me my nightshirt. I was able to go to him and take it without concern. He kissed me on my cheek as my reward, his warm lips welcome.

I sighed relief. I was cured of the Skilamalink Man's evil.

Mimsee clapped her hands in delight at the result of my treatment. Mister Okinawa held a proud smile and a glint in his eye that told me what he'd done for me would cost me plenty of coin. I was happy and gracious to pay him whatever he wanted.

Upon leaving the apothecary-cum-pharmacy, Mister Okinawa said rather enigmatically, "Remember, my friends, the Talent requires the flow of your qi, your most vital life force, to be effective. You do not want to be like the Skilamalink Man, only drawing on what gives gratification without the consideration of balance. Otherwise, your qi will stagnate, and you expose a weakness."

Was he trying to tell us the Skilamalink Man was vulnerable, that we had a chance against him? I didn't get much time to question him further; Mimsee was already out the door, urging us to hurry. Why the sudden rush, Lord Almighty only knew?

"Thank you, Mister Okinawa," was all I could offer, as did Tom.

"I will see you very soon, the both of you," Mister Okinawa called before shutting the shoppe's door.

Outside, the air was strikingly cold. It was also getting dark. The normally grey sky was blushing to black as the struggling London sun couldn't cope with lighting the town anymore.

Streetlights were being lit by a dishevelled old woman who shuffled terribly when she walked. She mumbled a conversation to a linkboy who walked ahead of her. The boy, scruffy and small, held a torch of burning pitch and tow, illuminating their path against the creeping night. I assumed they were related.

I didn't get time to ponder such things, because I soon understood Mimsee's reason for her haste. The coach, coachman, horses, and running dogs, were nowhere to be seen.

Chapter Twenty-Six
The Dogs of War

"Where the 'ellfire and damnation 'as the coachman got to?" Mimsee swore. "'E promised 'e'd wait here, didn't 'e?" Her hands were planted firmly on her hips in disgust.

Neither Tom nor I dared say anything about her use of colourful language, even though she was usually the one to point it out to us when we spoke profanely.

"I don't like the look of this," Tom offered.

I was about to suggest we hail another coach to take us home, when the sound of horse's hooves against the cobblestones drew our attention toward the far end of the street.

"There 'e is!" Mimsee proclaimed. When the coach was in front of us, she spat, "Where you been?"

"I apologise, Miss O'Donnell. I had a spot of bother a moment ago." The coachman was sweating, even in the cold. A look of fright was etched onto his wide-eyed stare. He glanced nervously behind the coach many times, as if expecting something. "I do suggest we hurry, though. There's some foul folk about these parts."

At that moment, with the neighing of horses and cracking of whips that rent the air, another coach came with blinding speed from around the street corner like the Devil himself had possessed its driver.

"Quickly!" the coachman shouted at us. "We must go!"

Mimsee didn't hesitate, she entered the coach's cabin before another word could be spoken. Tom urged me inside, too. With his hands upon my posterior, I was helped up the carriage's steps. If it were any other time, I would have been flattered by his freshness.

When we were all inside, I rapped on the cabin's roof and shouted up to the coachman, "We're secure!"

With Tom locking the latch to the door, the coach lurched forward with enough force to send me off balance. I careened into Tom. He yelped in surprise, because soon the both of us were sprawled out on the plush seat, limbs tangled, and our faces pressed close.

He chuckled. "Good thing we're into each other, ain't it?"

I kissed him on the end of his nose. "Good thing, too."

My concern, however, wasn't Tom. It was outside. Who was giving chase to us? And more importantly, why?

The hurried ride while being pursued by our mysterious hunters through the streets of the East End was uncomfortable to say the least, the cobblestones not as smooth as other parts of London. Many times, I believed the other carriage struck ours in an attempt to halt us. Whoever they were, they were determined. I'll give them that. Were they highwaymen after our coin? Or was it something more sinister?

I suspected the latter.

"What do they want with us?" Mimsee cried, reiterating my thoughts.

The coach was struck many more times; the jolts that resulted were wood-shatteringly worrying. If the pursuit lasted any longer, I feared our coach wouldn't.

What's more, we were going as fast as the horses could pull us. To me, the view outside the cabin's windows was a blur of gaslights and dirty buildings in macabre alternation.

Our coachman cracked his whip, as if he were mad. To say we were being thrown around inside the cabin like clothing shed by an overeager Corinthian man bedding the first available woman was an understatement. More than once, I banged my head against the cabin's roof, holding the top of my crown in protest. The coachman didn't ease up. His whip continued to crack. He was unrelenting, regardless of whether the coach—or even us—could cope with the torture of such haste.

I leaned over Tom to open the window. Or more accurately, Tom held me as best he could while I tried to see who our pursuers were.

To my dread, sitting next to their coachman in his box was my greatest fear. A man with a shadowed face, cloaked body, and blue glowing hands.

The Skilamalink Man.

He sent forth his Talent. Not in waves of ethereal energy as he'd done previously, but in bolts. It was as if the very lightning was plucked from the sky and was his to command. I was scared out of my wits as it struck our coach with a loud bang, searing and burning the back of it. We jolted. Our horses neighed with fear, and the running dogs barked in warning.

I ducked my head back into the cabin. "The Skilamalink Man is attacking us!" I shouted, spittle flying from my lips to wet my chin. I wiped it with my sleeve.

Tom jumped up. "The bastard!" His hands glowed. He scrambled to the opposite window, using his Talent to create an ethereal spider that spun a defensive webbed shield across his side of our coach.

Why hadn't I thought of that?

I didn't have time to ponder such things any further.

What I witnessed next would stay with me the rest of my days. I remember the coachman yelling "Up! Up!" as the Skilamalink Man sent more Talent-laden bolts toward us.

That time, as the Talent seared through the air thick with the London Particular, each Dalmatian leaped up from full sprint to block the energy from striking, bearing its brunt.

There were yelps of excruciating pain from the animals. I'd never heard such a thing. That was followed by the sickening sound of dull thuds against the cobblestones.

The dogs had been silenced.

Mimsee screamed.

"Lawks!" Tom cried.

The dogs' sacrifice halted the attack on the coach long enough so our coachman could evade and then escape our tormentor.

"Yar! Yar!" the coachman screamed, encouraging the horses to the last ounce of their strength.

But we hadn't evaded the Skilamalink Man for long, for he was as determined as we were. Without any running dogs acting as living shields, more bolts of Talent-energy struck us. The window next to me was shattered, the shock of it sending me off balance as broken glass covered me.

I fell backward. Thankfully, Mimsee stopped my fall, holding me tightly. "You get that right dastardly bastard, Oliver. You, too, I say, Tom!" she spat. "I'm 'ere to 'old you—the both of you."

She became our support, both morally and physically for what we did next.

I used my Talent to protect the coach as best I could, as did Tom. While I drew more and more Talent from within me, my thoughts on Tom to keep me positive, my hardness raged. I tried to block that discomfort as best I could. No easy ask.

A couple of times, Tom had to take a break.

I knew why.

As was my fear, our bodies defied us.

It was also Lady Penelope's warning. How we had to learn to control ourselves when we used our Talent. Easier said than done in the heat of the moment. I wished there was a way where we would be able to use our Talent without the side-effects that came with it.

Perhaps Mister Okinawa knew.

As I bundled all those thoughts to the back of my mind, returning to the moment, the coach was struck again. That time, one of the back wheels wobbled dangerously, smoke whirling off it.

The chilling laughter of the Skilamalink Man echoed through the streets as he continued his barrage against us. I moved my Talent-shield to cover the rear of the coach as best I could. Tom did the same. Almost immediately, our magical defences were tested.

Thankfully, no damage resulted.

For the moment, we were safe. The Skilamalink Man's Talent was deflected. It was an effort, but with Mimsee between us, we didn't fall or lose concentration no matter how much the coach was buffeted and rocked. My hardness became unbearably painful, though.

"It's working!" Tom shouted. "We're stopping his attack."

"Don't get too cocksure, Tom," I said, wincing because of my gentlemanly failings. "The lickspittler's still behind us!"

I didn't want to refer to our enemy as the Skilamalink Man anymore. That was too kind. He was no longer a man of shadow in my mind, but a manifestation of someone who perverted the Talent. The Talent should be beautiful and wondrous, like how Tom and I used it. It shouldn't be a tool to destroy or to murder.

"You're right, Oliver, you are." Mimsee was the brace between Tom and I, keeping us as stable as possible. "'E's sick, 'e is. Went and killed 'em poor dogs, 'e did. Just like that."

"I wish we knew how to attack with our Talent," Tom noted, also grimacing. "I'd like to give the bastard a taste of his own medicine."

We managed to hold out while our coachman did his best

to lose our evil pursuer. Many times, I thought we'd achieved it, only to have more bolts of Talent-energy strike against our defensive web of magic. The lickspittler was determined. I hated him with every fibre of my being.

Then the unthinkable happened.

Chapter Twenty-Seven
Constable William's Warning

Our enemy's Talent struck one of our horses.

The poor animal brayed the loudest, ear-splitting noise I'd ever heard. Moments later, the horse was stone dead. It had dropped onto the cobblestones in a tangle of reins, breast-harness, collar, and limbs.

Everything that followed happened within a blink of my unbelieving eyes. It was a chain reaction, if I was to describe it. The other horses fell, pulled down with the first. They neighed in panic but they too were quickly silenced as the coach's carriage ran over them.

I braced myself, holding onto the leather grab-handles for dear life. "Hold on!" I screamed at Tom and Mimsee.

In the instant I managed to secure my grip, there was a shuddering jolt that shredded my nerves as much as the coach's wooden structure. Our coachman was catapulted from his box. With a sickening thud and a spray of blood, he smashed into a nearby stone wall.

We were now trapped in an out of control, runaway coach.

My world suddenly became a terrible, strange kaleidoscope of colour and form. I didn't have the strength to hold onto the grab-handle any longer. Tom and Mimsee collided into me many times, as I them.

Seconds later, the cabin's roof was its floor.

We had come to a screeching halt, scraping against the cobblestones. The smell of tortured wood filled my nostrils. I moaned and touched my temple; my fingers were slicked with blood.

After an eternity, Mimsee came over me. "Are you all right, Oliver?"

"How's Tom?" I asked. "I'm fine," I added hopefully.

"I'm here, and I'm all good," Tom said. I sighed relief.

The sound of his voice was a good sign he wasn't badly injured. Thank the Lord Almighty.

The door latches hadn't held fast from the forces placed upon it during our unplanned horseless journey down the fog-laden street. I moved my legs, which were under Tom's. Nothing hurt too much. Only my head pounded. A small consolation as we'd lost a man, four horses, and three running dogs.

The Skilamalink Man, the lickspittler who disgusted me to the very depths of my soul, had a lot to answer for.

"Oliver, you're bleeding!" Tom's cheeks were red, but that time for a different reason than his usual embarrassment. He looked angry, reflecting my thoughts perfectly.

He offered me his handkerchief and we all helped each other clamber out of the ruined coach.

When outside in the bracing London Particular, the inappropriateness of only wearing a nightshirt and coat became apparent. Cold air clawed up my legs to my gentlemanly region. I shivered.

Tom held me. "Are you all right, handsome?"

"I am. Thank you, beautiful." I wanted to kiss him.

Mimsee yelled, "Lord Almighty, 'e's 'ere!" She stood in front of me and Tom, arms outstretched to protect us.

"Mimsee, move!" I ordered.

"No one's touchin' my boys, they ain't. Not while I 'old breath in my lungs."

I didn't get time to argue. With a clatter of debris kicked

aside, the Skilamalink Man emerged through the fog, hands aglow.

"That was a bit of a lark, wasn't it, Master Merritt?" he said, as sinister and acidic as if it dripped from the maw of the darkest demon from Hell. "I did enjoy that. Didn't you?"

"You'll pay for that, you hear me?" Tom shouted, scowling to bare his teeth.

The Skilamalink Man shrugged. "And here is your companion acting like he's your knight in shining armour once more, Master Merritt. How quaint. Tell me, young man. What's your name?"

"Tom," Tom spat with disgust at our enemy. "Tom Arkwright, that's who I am. And I'll protect my Oliver with everything I have—just you watch me."

"Ah, the peeler's son. How wonderful. You've chosen well, Oliver. He is a handsome one. Shame you'll both die together very soon."

"'Ow'd you find us?" Mimsee demanded.

"No." The Skilamalink Man's voice changed in timbre to one of annoyance, if only for a moment. "You don't get to speak to me, *whore*."

I became angered by that. "She can and she has, lickspittler. Now answer her. Why is it you torment us? Are you not satisfied you murdered my parents and all the others?"

"Such language. It doesn't become you, Master Merritt." Tendrils of Talent flowed from his fingers, beginning their journey toward us.

Tom drew upon his own, as did I. The cobblestones at our feet were now lit up by our magic, glowing blue. We were ready to defend ourselves yet again.

The Skilamalink Man pressed, "Don't you know the reason? If I can't have what you've got, then no one will have it. But I can assure you, I will get it all. You mark my words, Master Merritt."

I was momentarily stunned by what he'd said. "What are you talking about? I don't have anything of value to you."

"Don't be stupid, *Oliver*," the Skilamalink Man spat, his calm façade cracking for the first time. He hadn't even called me Master Merritt; he must have been rattled. He continued, "Fate may have put you where you are, no thanks to your father's gambling debts, but that house should be mine. Damnation to Lady Penelope, for if she could have recognised the child she bore out of wedlock to my father, then all this would have been unnecessary. So unnecessary. Alas, it wasn't to be. Now you and the whore are her heirs, and I must take what is mine by rights."

"Who are you?" I asked, suddenly feeling like a fly caught in a spider's web, one of intrigue as much as anything. "Lady Penelope didn't tell me she had a son, illegitimate or otherwise."

"Be that as it may, Lady Penelope was led to believe I died not long after my birth. But my plan, twenty-one years in the making, with enemies placed as close as friends around her, is now coming to a head. The woman who didn't want my father even though he put me inside her to give her an heir will pay her dues. I only have to remove you and the whore, and I can stake my claim."

When he spoke of his age, it rang a bell at the back of my mind. For the moment, I couldn't place why. Not yet. Too much was buzzing around in my thoughts to consider it clearly.

Instead, I decided to goad him. "Tell us who your father is then, seeing as you are content with the sound of your own voice at the moment."

Mimsee snarled. The Skilamalink Man glared at her. Tom remained steadfast, moving closer to me.

As I knew he wouldn't, the Skilamalink Man didn't take the bait. "That's for you to discover, Oliver. Life has to have a little mystery."

As soon as he said that, I knew he wouldn't kill us. Not yet anyway. Hurt us? Most definitely. He was the type who wanted to savour his victory for another, sweeter time. Perhaps once we discovered who he really was, then he would enact the final act of his devious plan for revenge.

And discover who he was, I would. With Tom and Mimsee's help, of course. Because, I was convinced there was a link to him through one of my clients. The smell of the Talent, so unique to each person with its nuances, and perhaps their kin as well, was the tenuous thread of connection. How else could he have remained so enlightened as to the goings on of Lady Penelope's house if someone of his knowing wasn't a regular there?

My determination to find that person solidified.

All of a sudden, the strong, fetid stench of pipe smoke leeching off the Skilamalink Man reached my nostrils. Tom gagged from it. I urged him silently to steady. As Tom calmed, we prepared our defences. Our ethereal spiders created our shields.

We were ready.

Mimsee retreated behind us.

I braced myself for the second time that night. The Skilamalink Man's Talent came closer, I could feel the tendrils push aside the thick air. Yet somewhat unexpectedly, it dissipated. The threat of his Talent was soon a distant memory clambering for recognition. I looked around, somewhat bewildered.

What had happened?

I quickly discovered my answer.

A voice pierced the fog. It was like the singing of an angel, the sound of our saviour emerging from the gloom. "There they be, guv'nor!"

I turned toward the voice. To my surprise the linkboy, holding his torch up high, was guiding a group of peelers to our aid. With them, the sound of clattering rattles rang out through the streets, calling for assistance.

"Over here, lads!" a voice of authority said.

"This one's dead, sir," another said, over by the coachman's body.

"Look at the state of it." A peeler examined the ruined coach. "Never seen such a thing in all my days."

The Skilamalink Man, the *son* of Lady Penelope, said, "Looks like you get another chance, Oliver. You as well, Tom. How nice." With a swish of his coachman's cloak, he withdrew his Talent completely and sank into the deeper shadows between the alleyways.

The linkboy was guiding William and his company of men, I could see that now.

"Hellfire and damnation, what the deuce happened here, Tom?" William grabbed his son, inspecting his frame and face, obviously ensuring there was no harm done to him. "Tell me…what happened?" His voice held venom, for he'd glanced over to me.

"We've *all*'ad a fright, 'aven't we?" Mimsee declared.

William seemed to be of his own mind about matters. "You could have got yourself killed, Tom. *He* could have got you killed."

Tom scowled at his father, shrugging off his hold. The next words he spoke were stained with his disagreement to his father's intent, "Pa, I'm all right. Besides, Oliver protected us, just as I did. Without him things could have been a lot worse."

"There's too much trouble around him, Tom."

"What're you saying, Pa?"

There was unbearable silence between them for the longest time. Only the continued sound of the rattles and the voices of disbelief from the other peelers arriving at the scene found my ears. Ears that were burning. I didn't like where this was heading.

I couldn't lose Tom.

Not now.

"I'm ordering you to come back home, this instant," William said with finality, grabbing Tom by the arm.

Chapter Twenty-Eight
Oliver's Father

At that moment, as if the Lord Almighty Himself had His hand in the turn of fate that happened next—as many who knew better than I supposed He always had throughout history eternal—a coach came to a halt not far from us, horses nickering. Lady Penelope was escorted out of the cabin by the coachman. She didn't need to be told what had transpired. She would have known. Like the linkboy, she came to my rescue with her words.

"William," she began, "how nice to see you here ensuring our children are all right. I knew the constabulary were useful, and once more it is proving to be the case."

William was taken aback. I could see the surprise drawn on his expression. But he'd pulled Tom further away from my side, the man's intentions plain for all to understand.

Tom struggled within his father's grasp. "Pa, let me stay with Oliver...*please*! I'm my own man now; it's my decision."

I wanted to go to Tom, take him away from his father and hold him in my arms. But there was that turn of fate I'd mentioned, one that now involved a determined juggernaut that couldn't be stopped. Not even by me.

Lady Penelope calmly placed her gloved hand in front of me, halting any advance I might have considered. It was her way of telling me I was to remain where I was.

She gave William a cursory glance before examining the street strewn with the remains of the carriage, its dead horses, dogs, and driver. "It is plain to me that Oliver and Tom will require more lessons on the Talent if they are to continue to aid us in ridding the streets of our fair city from the threat of the Skilamalink Man. Don't you agree, William?" Her tone was velvet, but the intention behind the softness had its foundation in steel.

"If our Tom wasn't involved with Oliver, then none of this would have happened, ma'am." The man's eyes were wild, his anger plain.

Anger toward me or anger that his precious son wasn't doing as he'd expected of him, I couldn't tell. I imagined it was probably both.

Lady Penelope, with gentle grace, offered her hand to Tom.

Tom took it without hesitation. As he did so he fixed his gaze, one of determination, upon his father. Next, Tom took my hand, showing his defiance without the use of words.

Warmth welled up inside me to relieve me of the cold I previously felt. A warmth that couldn't be mistaken as anything else within my mind and heart as that of love.

My love for Tom, and his for me.

As we held hands, a look of defeat spread over William.

Lady Penelope didn't relent. "You forgot to mention your prejudice, William. How you convinced yourself that it is my Oliver who is not only depraved because of the lifestyle he chooses to participate in with your son, but that he's also a bad influence on him. Am I correct in what I say?"

I loved her so much.

"Oh, I-I didn't mean it like that. I just worry about my boy, that's all," he stuttered, attempting to back-peddle, no doubt.

Lady Penelope was onto him. "I'm glad to hear it. Although, if I didn't know any better, I might be certain you were trying to take your Tom away from my Oliver. You must understand, William, with them both blessed with the Talent, they will never find another who understands each of them as well as they understand each other."

Mimsee interjected, "And they don't 'alf love one another, too. And no one can come between that, can they? Not when I'm livin' and breathin' and as I stand 'ere on God's green Earth, they can't."

"Well spoken, my daughter." Lady Penelope smiled. "Now come. There is work to do. Oh, and Oliver, I'm sure there is much you must tell me of tonight."

"There is, Lady Penelope, ma'am."

William, defeated once more by Lady Penelope's guile and logic, came to tentatively embrace his son. With two quick slaps on Tom's back, he then turned to merge into the gathered blue uniforms around us that were trying to make sense of what had happened. He barked orders at many of them. Angry orders. The peelers under his command snapped to it.

The little linkboy was still with us, his flaming light created dappling shadows around me. The boy couldn't have been older than six, if a day.

"I have to thank you for your help before we leave," I said to him. "If it wasn't for you gaining the attention of all those peelers, I don't know what would have happened to us. So, thank you." I reached into my frock's inner pocket with my free hand, feeling for my coins within my purse. They tinkled through my fingers. "What's your name, boy?"

"'Arry, mista magic man, sir," the boy replied, eyes brightening due to what his ears had perceived. "Name's 'Arry."

I retrieved a sovereign. It glinted in the torch's light. No doubt the coin wasn't as golden as the boy's hair. If he had attended the public baths and cleaned himself to reveal such a thing, that was.

"Well, Harry, this is for your assistance…and your silence about what happened here tonight. Understand?"

The boy nodded. "Ai, mista magic man, sir, I rightly do, I do." He took the coin, but not greedily. In fact, the smile upon his soot-stained face warmed my heart.

Mimsee sighed. "That was good of you, Oliver." Her satisfied agreement to my act of kindness bestowed upon the boy made her glow as much as the torch.

Tom held my hand once I pocketed my purse.

Lady Penelope, no doubt content with her victory against William, was being assisted back into her coach. She would require us to attend her promptly and I wouldn't delay any more than I had to; I didn't want to feel the sharp end of her tongue. Besides, another Talent lesson awaited. One desperately needed if recent events were any indication.

Before I could add another word, even to wish him well, Harry was at his grandmother's side, showing her my generosity. She beamed, waving her thanks at us with a crooked, arthritic hand.

Tom squeezed my hand, urging me to our duty.

During the coach ride back to the house, I told Lady Penelope everything the Skilamalink Man had divulged. She was as baffled as I was. As far as she was aware, the only child she was able to bear had died.

We all now understood that wasn't the case.

She also revealed that the man who had impregnated her to give her the child was an unknown—the arrangement purely a business transaction. One she paid handsomely for.

"Couldn't the Captain give you a child?" I asked.

"He was infertile, my dear boy." Lady Penelope touched her broach. "Hence, the arrangement was made. But such a thing never affected our love. As our love couldn't be hindered by restrictions of biology. As yours doesn't with Tom."

She also informed us she had wanted to adopt children ever

since she believed she'd lost her son. The Captain's death, however, came at a time before that could happen.

"After many years, I was finally able to adopt Mimsee."

Mimsee added, "I was abandoned just like that, little more than a street urchin until I found our Lady Penelope's door, I was."

Years later, and with Lady Penelope yearning for another to share her house and wealth, I was found crying beside my murdered mother.

"You are both gifts to me from the Lord Almighty," she said, fanning her face.

The feelings I had for Lady Penelope and my adopted sister suddenly overwhelmed me. I felt tears stinging my eyes. I loved them.

Lady Penelope, however, would never replace my mother. Nor did I believe she wanted to. She knew my mother lived in my heart, always. Even as I grew, my body maturing to adulthood, I had always held her hand when we were out together, as I was holding her hand that fateful night. Even though I was considered old enough to be my own man, my love for her was unconditional.

A part of me was ripped out of my soul when she was taken from my life. A hole that could never be filled.

But I had a thought.

Lady Penelope was special to me, that wasn't in doubt. "Lady Penelope?" I enquired at an appropriate pause during our discourse about the night's events. "May I call you my *father* from now on?"

Her expression reflected not only her understanding, but her approval. A tear rolled down her cheek. "That would be most appropriate, Oliver."

"That brings tears to my eyes as well, it does," Mimsee confessed.

Tom looked at me quizzically.

Lady Penelope—my Captain, my father—said, "It's a story you need to know, Tom. The choice you made before us all as witnesses earlier with your own father told me that you'll be my son's companion for as long as you hold breath. As such, you are family now, too."

She then explained how she was also the Captain, and why being called father by me was perfect.

Chapter Twenty-Nine
The Talent's Attack Aspect

Much later that evening, Tom and I reported to Lady Penelope's chamber. It was Tom's first Talent lesson.

"Just to warn you, this will be interesting," I said, as I rapped three times on her chamber door.

"What does that mean?"

"Oh, you wait and see, beautiful," I replied cheekily.

Tom looked worried, but I didn't add any more fuel to his concerns. We entered. My father was dressed in her evening attire, elegant but practical.

She didn't stand but got straight down to business. "I will now teach you both the art of Attack. As I'm sure you have realised the limitations your current knowledge of the Talent has caused you—along with Harvey, our coachman."

So that was his name, the brave man who tried as best he could to keep us from harm. I shall remember him for all my days. Harvey the coachman, his horses, and his Dalmatians.

I noticed there were large, pristine white dinner plates set out on stands all in a row along a fancily carved wooden credenza. It had been moved in front of her only window. Again, the drapes were left open, the darkness outside only tainted with the moon's slightest kiss before becoming new.

She continued, "As you are well aware, and as Mister Okinawa has informed you, the Talent draws on many things within you to manifest itself."

"Mister Okinawa said he'd tell us more about what he knows of the Talent, he did," Tom said eagerly.

But when my father gave him a narrow-lidded glare, a shoot of daggers almost, Tom lowered his head to look at a place somewhere by his feet. Roses blushed high on his cheeks.

Lady Penelope didn't like to be interrupted.

Now Tom knew that as well.

She cleared her throat. "He has informed me you must visit him again soon. Please ensure you do, as he has been a great help to me and this house over the years. To Mimsee especially, as she suffered with sickness when she was younger."

I nodded acknowledgement to her request. Tom did the same.

"As I have told you, Oliver," she said, "and as I'm sure you know as well, Tom, it is your positive thoughts that you draw upon so your Talent can be used to Defend yourself and others. This same process is used for it to Please and to give Sight—the aspects that you use upon each other during your intimacy."

Now I felt my cheeks heat.

Lady Penelope didn't seem concerned. "Which brings us to the other side of the equation." She paused, clearing her throat and taking in a deep breath. "To use the Attack aspect of your Talent, you must dwell in the negative thoughts that reside deep within the hidden cesspools of your emotions."

At an appropriate pause, one that wouldn't interrupt to cause her to chastise me, I asked, "Which negative emotion is the most powerful, Father?"

"Hate," she answered matter-of-factly. "Always hate. Then anger."

"Then that's easy," I said, frowning as I thought of *him*. "I hate that Licksp—" I cut myself off, not wanting to curse in my father's presence. She was a lady, and gentlemen didn't say such words in mixed company. Mimsee, of course, was the exception.

"I hate the Skilamalink Man with all the strength in my bones. What about you, Tom?"

"Hate is a strong word, it is," he replied, "but to be angry over someone, that's easier for me to come by. I'd have to say the strongest I feel in that way is 'cause of my sister Elizabeth. She's younger than me by a year but has always been my tormentor. She calls me a freak and takes every opportunity to humiliate me. All 'cause Pa dotes over me, seeing as I have the Talent and she don't. She thinks I took it all, being first born, an' all."

My father clapped her hands, obviously ready to proceed. "Then we are set. You know what to do next, Oliver."

I did. I disrobed, which didn't take as much effort as usual. I was in a fresh nightshirt and drawers, clothing Mimsee had fetched for me from the laundry room. I removed them quickly, for I could feel my body awakening as I began my breathing techniques.

Tom stood stock still, mouth agape for a moment. He looked at me, then at my father. He thumbed at his nightshirt's rounded collar, hesitant.

The moment I'd referred to earlier had arrived. Tom now knew full well the ramifications of my words, even though I'd spoken them cheekily.

"Too much Talent too quickly," Lady Penelope explained, "and the result will be as final as your manly blow, Tom. Your body won't be able to draw upon the Talent until you recover. You can't risk that happening if you're in battle with another. You must learn to control all your Talent's urges upon you, physically and emotionally. Your life, or even Oliver's, may depend on it."

Tom nodded, his cheeks reddened.

She added, "Being without attire during our lessons is one step to ensure I have a means to guide you. I believe you'll agree when I say it is far better to lose control here in my chamber, than out there where it will really matter."

Tom said shyly, "Yes, ma'am." He swallowed hard, his Adam's apple bobbing up and down his throat. But he got to it.

Soon we were both as my father expected, standing side by side and going through the routine needed to call forth the negative emotions that would power our Talent for the task ahead. I brought my mind back to that rainy, cold night as my mother's hand cooled within mine.

Tears stung my eyes. I was unable to help myself. I was swept away with grief once more. I felt each powerful wave of emotion crash against my insides, the Talent whipping up a storm within me, fuelling those thoughts.

My hands glowed and my gentlemanly asset immediately came to attention to bring me close to completion all too quickly. My stomach lurched and churned.

I panicked.

"Lawks, Oliver," Tom said, "You've got as big as I ever seen you. Quick as anything, too."

I had to control myself by regulating my breathing again. I managed to withdraw my Talent by not thinking about that night. It calmed the ocean of emotions that had welled up within me, enough so I had a window to gain control again.

Negative thoughts sure made the Talent potent. No wonder the Skilamalink Man used them to do his bidding.

"Go through your breathing techniques again, Oliver," my father suggested. "You must keep calm."

I understood then and there that my mother's death was too powerful to use. I was too inexperienced to control such strong feelings. I drew my thoughts to earlier that night. Of Harvey and what had happened to him.

I breathed.

I calmed.

I heard a loud bang as a plate shattered. It wasn't from my efforts. Tom had sent a bolt of his Talent to smash it to smithereens, a cloud of smoke mingled with bone china dust, the only evidence it was ever there.

But Tom only got one bolt into the lined-up plates.

"Calm yourself, Tom!" my father yelled at him. She was almost livid, flying out of her chair to get to him. "You're using too much Talent. Breathe! Calm yourself this instant!"

It was too late. No sooner had Tom's first attempt struck, he cried, "What the blazes—I can't!" His words became strangled as his whole body shuddered and ribbons of his conclusion found the floorboards.

Seconds later, Tom collapsed into a heap.

My father was at his side, offering her arm to him. Tom grabbed it, shaking. He was soon escorted to the nearest chair.

Tom gasped. "My Talent ripped right through me as though I was made of paper."

He was dripping with sweat, stomach rising and falling rapidly with his shallow breaths, and his permanently blushed cheeks were the most intense colour I'd ever seen. What's more, the end of his gentlemanly asset, exposed because his loose foreskin had retracted due to the intensity of his hardness, was a stark purplish hue.

"Now you know why it is important to remain calm and in control. You're useless now. The Skilamalink Man wouldn't hesitate to use that to his advantage." She scolded him, but her words weren't meant to be cutting, only a warning.

I'm sure Tom understood her meaning and what they taught him all too well. With his hands still trembling he took the offered glass of water, bringing it to his quivering lips.

I teased, "You're a one-shot wonder, you are, beautiful."

My cockiness, however, didn't last a minute longer. I didn't fare much better before my enthusiasm joined Tom's on the chamber's floorboards. At least I shot off two air-splitting blasts of lightning fuelled by my negative Talent before I crumpled into a useless ball.

One of my shots missed the plate. It burned a hole in the credenza's door, and the stench of scorched wood filled the chamber.

Tom didn't hesitate to point that out. "I'd say you're just as bad, you are, handsome." A glint of cheekiness sparked in his weary eyes.

I had to find a chair to sit in. I was exhausted by my exertion, both by my Talent and what my body released. Sweat dripped down my back and I trembled uncontrollably.

My father said, "I expect you both again for another lesson tomorrow evening. From what I've seen so far, there is a long way to go before I consider either of you even remotely ready for what may lie ahead. Good night, Oliver. Good night, Tom."

"Good night, Lady Penelope," Tom said, getting up gingerly to gather our clothes. He was still unsteady, shaking all over as if he was affected by some terrible disease, as was I.

"Good night, Father."

Chapter Thirty
The Gift from the Enemy

Tom and I went straight to bed once we'd managed to clamber back into our nightshirts. He kissed me on my lips sweetly, and I returned it, but I was still aching and numb. I remained so for the longest time, a couple of hours, if not more.

The negative Talent was powerful. It would take a while to control it…and myself…because of it. These thoughts saw me to sleep, along with dreams of the beautiful man breathing gently next to me.

The next morning, Mimsee performed her usual ritual, opening the drapes and my window, if only a crack because of the threatening weather outside. The clouds were as black as nightshade berries. She didn't supply us with the usual sweetmeat treats, though.

When I questioned it, she reasoned, "You're both sweet enough without needin' any more sugar." But her face was drawn with worry.

"You all right, Miss?" Tom asked before I could. "You look as though you've had a nasty fright."

He was right; Mimsee looked flushed, pale as winter's first kiss, even considering her beautiful tone of skin.

Before she could answer, a knock on my chamber door disturbed us. The house servants didn't usually bother me at this time of day. They knew Mimsee attended to my needs—Tom's as well now.

"Enter!" I called.

The house servant did so without hesitation after my command, bowing. Her voice was clear but supplicating. "Begging your pardon, Master Merritt, sir. Lady Penelope has news for you. She requires you attend her at your earliest convenience."

"Thank you. Tell her I will be with her as soon as I can." Which, knowing the etiquette of the house, meant I was to see her as soon as I was clean and well dressed. To attend her in my nightshirt was an impropriety that wouldn't be tolerated.

She would wait for me.

I looked once more at Mimsee, carefully, and she glanced away. I knew that face. She was aware of the news I was to be told. I held my tongue. I didn't want to impose upon her anything she didn't wish to reveal, and I also knew she'd want me to hear the news firsthand.

"Very good, Master Merritt," the house servant replied.

During this time, Tom had clambered out of our bed, using the chamber pot to relieve what had built up in his bladder overnight. The tinkle of his business was the only sound for a moment.

The house servant didn't leave my bed chamber, no doubt knowing that she would soon need to take away the chamber pot and empty it. As such, I urinated as well.

After we had bathed and dressed, all three of us went to the morning room. It was the traditional gathering place for the family, especially if news was to be imparted.

My father was already in attendance, as I knew she would be. She sipped freshly brewed tea from one of her favourite bone china cups. Beside her, on a stand, was a letter. It was face down, as if its contents were an affront. It didn't take me long to realise the news would be related to its contents.

Once we'd bowed and followed custom and courtesy, accepting tea and something to eat, namely toasted stone ground bread with butter and conserve spreads lavished over it to drip all over my fingers, my assumption was proved correct.

After I had wiped my hands clean of my breakfast, the letter was handed to me. I opened it. In neat handwriting, with flourishing loops and exaggerated curly serifs, done with the finest ink on expensive paper, were the words:

My dearest Messrs Merritt and Arkwright, seeing as we had so much enjoyment in each other's company last night, I have decided to leave you a little present as my gesture of my gratitude. You will find it outside and behind your house. Accept this gift also as warning of things to follow as my plan unfolds further. Your eternal nemesis, SM.

I looked up in horror as the words written sunk in. What sort of gift would such a depraved man leave me—leave us? Mimsee was clutching her chest. She was stricken with terror, the fright more than upon her.

Tom was as concerned and puzzled as I was, as he had been reading the note with me.

My father now looked pale. "I think you will need to see this with your own eyes, Oliver. You as well, Tom. But prepare yourself, the both of you."

"If it's all the same, I'll remain 'ere," Mimsee announced.

Had she already seen the gift? Or had she guessed as to what it might be? I knew I couldn't guess. My curiosity burned, but I grabbed Tom's hand. His strength would be mine.

I had a feeling I'd need it.

My father escorted us. I continued to hold Tom's hand, but my free arm was now locked within hers, as was expected when we were outside the house together.

At the entrance to the alleyway behind the house, she

stopped. "I will go no further, Oliver. I've seen more than enough."

I nodded my understanding.

What befell my eyes was a sight that would be eternally burned into my mind. Tom began to heave but didn't expel anything. I patted his back, comforting him as best I could. I couldn't blame him. My stomach turned terribly as well by what I witnessed.

"Oh, lawks, the poor blighters." Tom gasped and coughed, covering his nose and mouth with his hand.

Lying on the cold cobblestones, a sheen of dampness over them from an earlier drizzle, was the little linkboy Harry and his elderly grandmother. They'd been stripped and posed so I could see the terror of their final moments, their eyes lifeless within their grizzled faces. Not only that, the sovereign I had given the boy was still held tightly in his right hand. His other little hand was clutched within his grandmother's.

My stomach turned heavier. I fought back the taste of bile. Tom didn't have as much fortune; he finally let go of his breakfast, turning away in time so his vomit splashed against the nearest wall and not me.

I began to feel woozy and light-headed at that moment. The acrid stench of Tom's upheaval hung strong in the air. My father was well away from us, but she was fanning her face, keeping air flowing across her nose.

But their deaths weren't the worst of it.

Poor little Harry and his grandmother had been disembowelled. It had been done with deliberate and careful consideration as to the impact it would have on Tom and me. The hand that did it was skilled. Perhaps it had been done by the Talent, because not a nick of a knife or scalpel marred their flesh or viscera. All their insides had been placed with intent around them like a macabre halo.

I could smell pipe smoke, as dense and rank as the odour of Tom's spew. I could also smell the boy and his grandmother, their insides, and the release of their bowels upon death.

The light rain earlier had done nothing to wash away the dark pool of blood that had become their final bed. I lost my balance and my own stomach churned once more. I held it in. But only because I turned my gaze away in the nick of time.

The Skilamalink Man did that to them to warn us, to mock us, to goad us, and to unnerve us. He'd succeeded as far as I was concerned. I felt sick to my soul.

I couldn't contain myself. With a gut-wrenching heave, I stained the wall where Tom had earlier. When my stomach was emptied, I wiped my mouth with my handkerchief, bitter and vile were the after tastes that found my tongue.

It was Tom's turn to pat me on the back. "No man could look upon such a horror and not be affected."

"He…he did that to them before he…murdered them. To make them suffer," I managed. I didn't know that for a fact, but all I could hope was that they found death's release quickly.

"I know he did."

I looked up into Tom's tear-filled eyes through my own bleary vision. "We've got to get that lickspittler if it's the last thing we do, Tom." I found it burned within me more than ever to discover who the Skilamalink Man was—and tonight was the next lesson, one I would not fail. For Harry and his grandmother. For my mother and Nicole. For Harvey, his horses, and his dogs. For Harold.

I covered my mouth, no longer able to take in any more of the tragedy that lay before me. At that moment, William and a couple of peelers arrived at the scene. One covered the bodies with a cloth. They looked sombre and disturbed, as was natural upon discovering such a thing.

Tom went to his father and they embraced. "They didn't deserve it, they didn't," he cried.

I realised I was crying as well. I wiped my eyes with my sleeve. My father came to me, embracing me as well; her strong floral perfume masked the unpleasantness for a brief moment, settling my insides enough for me to be able to press on.

Tom's father said the most profound thing he'd ever spoken, more so seeing as it was in my company, "Tom, Oliver, I don't care how you do it, I want you to get that bastard. You hear me? I give you both my blessings, as I know you both mean a lot to each other now. I was foolish to think otherwise." He paused, composing himself, tugging on his uniform coat to straighten it. "I have...*faith*...in you both, as I know you will do what you must. You care for each other, so make that matter. Use your Talent together to get him." Through his teeth, and with words barely audible, clearly only meant for my ears and Tom's, he added, "Do what the deuce you must, but hellfire and damnation, get that lickspittler who calls himself the Skilamalink Man!"

I couldn't have agreed more.

Chapter Thirty-One
A Lady's Monosyllable

After I struggled with the midday dinner of this awful day, forking most of it around my plate because I couldn't stomach the thought of eating, I eventually excused myself and went up to my chamber.

Mimsee went with me.

Tom had decided to not attend the meal. He wanted to visit his Ma; seeing as things were now amicable between his father and myself, he believed the time was right to do so. I'd kissed him lovingly before he left. He promised to return as hastily as he could manage.

I already missed him.

Mimsee and I were left alone.

"He was…Harry…he was so young…and she was all he had," I said, still trying to quantify what had happened in my mind.

Every time I blinked, I could see the image of their defiled bodies burned into the back of my eyelids, adding to the growing list of those I would always see whenever I closed my eyes.

"I was beside myself by what I'd been told about it, I was," Mimsee said, coming close to me and resting her head on my shoulder. She smelt good, a fragrance as light and beautiful as she was. "I don't know 'ow you and Tom could 'ave looked at them poor wretches."

I didn't know either. But I'd thought about the incident too much and needed to get out of my stupor. It wasn't helping anyone dwelling on such horror, myself the most.

"Why do you look after me?" I asked, changing the subject. "Put up with me so, Mimsee?"

"'Cause you're my brother, silly."

"No. What I mean to say is—"

"You want to know why I do more than just attend you, don't you? Why I keep your chamber clean, bathe you, dress you, and do for you as the 'ouse servants should."

"Yes, I do."

She held my hand, her touch warm and soft. "It's because I love you, Oliver."

"I love you, too, Mimsee." I squeezed my hand within hers.

"No, you don't," she stated firmly. I was taken aback, but she offered a nervous half-giggle half-sigh. I took it she wanted to divulge what she had on her mind, so I waited. The next words she spoke hit me hard. "You don't love me like I do for you, you don't, Oliver. 'Cause the love I feel for you ain't like that of siblings, whether they've been adopted or not. My love is the kind that gets a lady all worked up down in 'er nether regions, deep within 'er monosyllable, if you catch my meanin'."

"I think I understand." I caught her meaning all too vividly: Mimsee *loved me* loved me. Everything I said next came out in a stuttering lump as I tried to convey as much as possible how I felt but without trying to offend her. I believe I failed. "But we can't be like that together. I've got the Talent. Besides, even if I didn't, we still couldn't...you and me. I'm a mandrake, as my father called me. And you know, it took me a long time to get over his taunts about my sexuality. I'm proud of who I am, and I have Tom now. I have you as my sister and best friend. I don't need anything else. So yes, I love you with all my heart, Mimsee."

I suddenly found it uncomfortably warm within my chamber, heat crawling up my neck to my cheeks. Her closeness became apparent. I shifted my weight. Not to get away from her, but to let her know the words we both spoke affected me, made me reach deep inside for feelings I thought had been locked away.

She didn't budge.

"I know that, don't I, lovely," she said with a sigh. "Never fear, I ain't going to do anythin' to you that's not right between us. Not like that, anyway. I care for you too much, Oliver. But that can't stop my feelings, can it? Besides, I'll do whatever it takes to protect you and Tom—no bastard's going to 'arm my beautiful boys."

It was my turn to sigh, but one of relief. How could I ever have doubted she'd be anything *but* my big sister, even though she had intimate feelings for me. I found that sad in a way. She shouldn't have to sacrifice her own life in the belief that she needed to provide, look after, and protect me. I wouldn't want that, not from anyone. "You're a wonder, you are, Mimsee. But there'll be someone out there for you one day, I know it."

"'Ere, good thing you're my brother. Otherwise, I'd give you such a wallop for sayin' that if you weren't."

"What do you mean?"

"I don't want anyone else, do I? You're my world. As is Tom now." Her voice was filled with conviction and had a finality to it. I was touched by her words.

No more needed to be said.

She no longer gave herself to men for money, her time spent looking after Tom and I. Mimsee had come to her own conclusions, and therefore had decided to live her life by them.

I had nothing but admiration for that.

"But monosyllable?" I questioned, cheekily.

Her cheeks reddened. Mimsee actually blushed, even considering the beautiful rich darkness of her skin. Usually that was Tom's honour. "It's a word us ladies use in proper company for our privates."

"Of all the words for…*it*…they're more than one syllable, aren't they?" I checked off the list in my mind: from the correct anatomical term, to those I'd heard many times on the first floor. Words such as "cloven inlet", "fairest flower", and "cock-lane."

I couldn't think of any single syllable terms.

Mimsee was more than obliging. "It's a polite way to say the 'c' word for it, ain't it?"

I then knew the word she was speaking of.

That word most certainly wasn't one to mention in mixed company, or even between friends. Unless one found themselves on the deck of a sailing ship heading around Cape Horn after months at sea. Then words like that were flung around so freely the air turned blue.

I, however, decided to keep playing our word game, if only to keep the rosy blush on her cheek a moment longer. "Cunny?"

She rolled her eyes to heaven. "The four letter one. Sometimes you're so silly for someone so smart, you are, Oliver."

But I was enjoying myself too much. "Cock?"

Her eyebrows raised, but she'd caught on to my game. A quiver of her wickedly cheeky smile caught her lips. "Most ladies o' this 'ouse don't 'ave those, not unless it's stuck in 'em, they don't."

"That's not what I heard. I heard a man downstairs talking the other day about the 'little surprise' he discovered on his chosen *lady* that evening."

"'E should 'ave paid extra then." She laughed and I joined her. "And I 'eard it weren't so little, near on as big as yours it was, Oliver. A right whopper."

"In that case, I'd say the man uttered words of more than one syllable when he discovered it dangling between her legs." I was almost in fits now, my sides hurting from laughter. Tears of joy welled.

I needed that.

Mimsee was brilliant.

She imitated the action she'd taught me with the courgette. "I 'eard it was more of a garble that 'e spoke, not many words at all." More riotous laughter. "See, this is why I 'ave to look after you, don't I?" Mimsee's tone turned serious. "You need me to keep you sane."

"Me? What about Tom?"

She giggled, wiping her eyes. "'E can look after himself. Besides, 'e's adorable and can get away with anythin' that boy. Not like you." Her sense of humour had twisted toward me. She was lashing it upon me, her next words proof of that. "But you ain't got nothin' other than that big white staff between your legs and a tight hole to rely on. Have you, Oliver?"

"Why you…" I released my hand from her grip, turning so I could push her onto the bed.

We laughed our lungs out.

As I wrestled her, Tom entered the chamber. "What'd I miss?"

"Mimsee being a know it all, that's what," I replied, struggling to keep her pinned down.

I hated to admit it, but she was stronger than me. That became fact when she wrenched herself up, flipped me over easily, and then sat on my chest.

She folded her arms in front of herself in victory.

"Do you yield, lovely?" she asked.

"I would if I were you, Oliver," Tom suggested. At the sight of me defeated, his exuberant smile made the spray of freckles across his nose become bright against his fair skin. "Anyway. Lady Penelope says she wants to see us. Best we go before Mimsee really hurts you."

He was right. I couldn't move.

"I yield! I yield!"

She slowly clambered off me, still holding her victorious expression at my downfall.

Tom offered me my jacket; I slipped into it with his help.

I knew why my father had requested Tom and I attend her. The next Talent lesson would not wait now that Tom had returned to the house.

Chapter Thirty-Two
The Cost of the New Science

Tom and I disrobed immediately once we were in my father's chamber proper, as was the required and expected etiquette for our Talent lessons.

My father was already in her night attire but wearing a brocade fabric dressing gown over her evening dress. She looked stunning. She was also dripping in silver and pearl-inlaid jewellery. The broach of the Captain's portrait adorned her outfit, as always.

I faced the plates set out as my targets with determination as I began going through my preparation exercises. We both knew what to expect as we drew upon our negative thoughts.

It didn't take long for the plates to meet their destiny.

I had destroyed six of them in quick succession. Tom blasted the rest into smithereens, the Talent-lightning from his fingers searing and terrifying. The air was thick with the smell of pipe smoke, ozone, and bone china dust. Tom's Talent scent still carried a sweet undertone; I was most certainly getting used to it. Very intoxicating and manly.

"That was for Harry and his grandmother," he spat.

When done, our Talent withdrew but our gentlemanly assets were as hard as peelers' truncheons. I was sweating profusely, and my bollocks ached with yearning for release. I could think of nothing else but my wanting for Tom. I needed him to Talent-touch me all over. Let him bring me to a satisfying conclusion to take away the immense pressure I now felt within myself. Oh, Lord Almighty, I couldn't wait.

As I quickly gathered up my clothing, trying my best to not think about the ache I endured, the want and *need* I had for Tom, my father said, "That was a lot better, the both of you. However, I can plainly see that you need to engage more control over yourselves."

"It's not...easy, ma'am," Tom stuttered, biting his bottom lip. I knew he felt the same as I did, his clothing also bundled up in his arms.

"Nothing worth doing ever is, Tom," she shot back. My father wasn't in a light mood. Something was on her mind. Something I would no doubt discover presently, which meant we wouldn't be excused so hastily, either.

I decided to try my luck anyway. "I think Tom and I should take our leave. To enable us to...recover from this lesson. We will return to attend to you again later if that is your wish, Father."

Her face hardened as if it was made from the ivory of the Captain's portrait pinned to her breast. "There is much to discuss between us, and it must be done straight away. I have work to do that requires my attention later. This house doesn't run on casual happenstance and delightful coincidences. I require you both to remain until what needs to be said is said and I dismiss you formally. Is that understood?"

I swallowed, hard. If words could cool a man's libido, those were close to it. I nodded my assent. "Yes, Father."

"Yes, ma'am." Tom groaned under his breath.

I had managed to get my drawers on. Thankfully, the touch of the fabric didn't prickle too sensually at my heated skin, even though I was still engorged.

Tom dressed as delicately as I did.

What seemed an eternity later, we were both fully attired and seated, sipping on tea that was a poor substitute for what I wanted to do to give me relief. My hands trembled and my whole body ached. I couldn't sit normally, always adjusting my pose to the least uncomfortable.

She produced the Skilamalink Man's letter from the top drawer of a Louis the XIV commode. "I have a dear friend who dabbles in graphology," she explained. "He said he would be more than delighted to analyse the handwriting from the letter and was hopeful that if there was a match to anyone who frequents our business from the signed receipts for services rendered, he'd find it."

"That sounds good," Tom offered. "Pa says science like that will one day help catch a lot of the criminals that lurk about. I mean, we can already tell the time of someone's death just by their body temperature. Who knows what we'll be able to do in the future?"

"Quite so, Tom," she said. I had a feeling this wasn't the end of the conversation. What she said next confirmed my suspicion. "Of course, naturally, payment for such a task would need to reflect the amount of work required to go through so many records." My father wasn't rich by being a spendthrift: every sovereign was accounted for.

I, however, had a feeling money wasn't the issue.

The penny dropped, so to speak.

I cleared my throat. "May I venture to guess that this dear friend of yours likes to look upon young men without any clothing on...men such as Tom and myself, perhaps?"

Tom shot me a glance. "Ah," he said, obviously coming to my understanding of what was underlying the discussion as well.

"You are quite sagacious, Oliver. You do me proud, as nothing gets past your keen mind, does it?"

"Except who the Skilamalink Man is," I grumbled. Tom placed his hand onto my thigh, his touch warm and tingling, refiring my desires instantly with his pressure. It was incredible the effect he had on me.

Tom asked, "When do you want Oliver and me to get all in the raw for your friend, then, ma'am?"

"My friend will be here shortly to begin the work. I would imagine tonight would be ideal, as he may take the rest of what he needs away with him."

A thought struck me. I blurted, "But tonight is when we are to entertain the weedy man, the one who smells of the Talent."

My father sipped on her tea, raising an eyebrow. Her face had softened. "Would you both be able to manage two performances this evening, then?"

"I'm game," Tom offered, "if you are, Oliver."

I sipped on my tea. It really didn't fortify me as much as it usually did, even though the brew was strong. "Only one way to find out, isn't there?"

"From what I hear Tom needs the practice." My father smiled. "My friend wouldn't be too fussy if the performance needed some ironing out, seeing as he doesn't have to reach into his purse to see you both in your natural beauty."

I tended to agree. Tom *did* need more practice, as we hadn't had the chance due to me only recently recovering from the illness the Skilamalink Man's Talent caused me. Then there were the events of this morning.

I promised, "We will use the opportunity to practice, as I know the weedy man will want a more polished performance."

"Very good," she agreed. "I shall inform my friend of the usual caveats, and that you are both indulging him for the benefit of polishing your act."

By that I knew she meant that she would make it plain to the man that he could only touch us with his eyes, and that Mimsee, our chaperone and bruiser, would be watching.

"May we be excused now, Father?" My body hadn't cooled

enough, my eagerness still pressed against my clothing rather painfully. Tom's touch upon my leg still sent shivers of delight up and down my spine. My mind began to cloud, yearning for the pleasures of his magic upon me.

"You are excused, Oliver, Tom," she waved her hand at us to reinforce her words. "I can plainly see you have other things on your minds. A good idea for you both to drain your bodies before your double performance this evening. Now go. You are excused."

I dashed up out of my chair, grabbing Tom's hand without ceremony. With sensual rapture drenching my voice, I mumbled, "Come on, Tom, I need you so badly it's killing me."

"Lawks, I need you too, Oliver. Don't I know it."

Chapter Thirty-Three
The Talent's Curse

In a matter of heartbeats, we had rushed hand-in-hand across the landing toward our chamber, footsteps thumping over the floorboards. Moments after the door was slammed shut, we shed our clothes.

My arousal hadn't eased, and Tom was beautifully engorged as well.

We hurriedly positioned ourselves on our bed so we could hold hands and kiss, but not touch each other's skin in any other way. My breathing deepened. The mental exercises I used to call upon my Talent took no time at all to manifest, happening faster than a hummingbird's wing beat.

More and more my Talent rose up, fuelled by desire, my needs, and my urges. I was writhing, moaning, and enraptured as Tom's Talent came to brush its ethereal fingers over my heated skin.

I did the same to him.

We explored each other with our magic, sensually, wonderfully, and beautifully. I cried out many times, my whole body enveloped with his Talent-touch. My lips trembled and I arched my back as Tom went deeper inside me. Completed me. Consumed me. I could sense his every want, as it mirrored mine. I could feel every nuance of his physical form; I was in wonder how my Talent-touch gave me so much intimate information about him, so that I could understand him on a level no other lover could.

It didn't take long for me to come to my conclusion in an explosion of all that had been pent up over the past hour, if not longer. So much so, my fluids reached my lips. The salt and bitterness of my release was as strong as my feelings for Tom.

Tom completed himself with me.

We lay there silent and still as our bodies cooled, holding hands, breathing hard, and staring into each other's eyes. I got lost within the blue pools of his, wonderfully so. When I was able to sit upright, even after my hunger had been satiated, I wanted more.

But my want that time was forbidden.

I don't know where it came from—a basic human need perhaps—but I wanted to touch him intimately with my own hand.

The more I thought about it, the more the urge increased. My breathing began to deepen again. I leaned over him, coming close to take in his smell—the tang of his Talent, sweet and smoky, the alkali of my magical efforts upon him, and his sweat drenched and musty manliness.

I became aroused once more.

Tom's eyes were closed. The more I studied his beautiful form, the way his conclusion had gathered within in the ripples of muscles across his stomach, I became enchanted. What would it be like to actually touch him? Could I run my fingers through the coarseness of his pubic hair, then venture down to explore him more intimately? Could I hold his manliness so I could feel its warmth and his awakening arousal as I did so?

My hand hovered over him.

Very close.

Did I dare? What would one little touch matter? I wanted to know what it would be like to feel Tom with my own hand. I licked my lips, feeling like Adam convinced to take that first bite of the forbidden apple.

I wanted Tom as other lovers had each other. The Talent-touch was magnificent, but actual touch...that would be something amazing, I was certain.

Why else would folks do it?

Suddenly, Tom grabbed my hand, knocking me from my reverie.

"Don't, Oliver!" His voice wasn't rough, but gentle and understanding; remnants of his own ecstasy still stained it to make it hoarse. "We can't. You know that."

"I want you more than anything," I confessed with a deep shuddering yearning, but also with frustration. "Why can't we touch each other and be with each other like proper lovers are? I want to be able to embrace you while we're like this in our bed, not just hold hands. I want to be with you, experience what it's like to have you inside me, skin on skin. Oh, by the Lord Almighty, Tom, I so want it."

"I know. I do as well." He breathed in deeply. "But we just... can't."

"I don't care." My frustration turned quickly to be spoiled by anger. "You're more important to me than my Talent."

"It's not about us, is it? It's about those affected by that lickspittler and who he's hurt. It's about who he's taken from us. Taken from you."

I sighed and thought of my mother. He was right. "Damnation to my Talent." I took away my hand. With it, I reached for the handkerchiefs on the bedside nightstand. I offered one to Tom. We cleaned ourselves up.

"Can I at least get a kiss from you then?" I asked.

He quivered a wanting smile. "I thought you'd never ask."

We decided to spend the rest of the morning in our chamber sharing kisses and remaining unclothed, as free as two people could be who were both cursed and gifted by the Talent.

It was small consolation, but one I came to cherish.

"I never expected to see that, I didn't," Mimsee said when she entered our chamber, not bothering to announce herself by knocking. She was staring at our nakedness while she pushed the trolley filled with the bounty of our midday meal Cook had prepared.

"Did you want us to dress, Miss?" Tom offered.

The wonderful thing about Mimsee was that she could read situations with a depth of perception most could never achieve. "Not at all. You can't do anythin' but look at each other and press lips, can you? It's not for me to take that away, is it? Oh, and, Tom, my lovely, you can stop callin' me Miss. I'm Mimsee to you."

"Right-o, then. Mimsee, it is."

Once Mimsee removed the cloches that had covered our dinner, I realised I was starving. Using the Talent took a lot more from me than my ability to be intimate with Tom; it drained my energy as well.

I devoured the varied meats, smoked and otherwise, as well as the vegetables, roasted and tasty. I mopped up all the gravy with the freshly baked Yorkshire puddings Cook was renowned for.

While we were eating, Mimsee said, "I 'ear you've both got to dance for that science-y man, all mister fancy pants, he is."

"You've heard correctly, Mimsee, as I know you always do in this house."

She ignored my jibe. "Well, 'e's 'ere now. Lady Penelope says 'e's ready when you are. 'E's waiting in the smokin' room, as keen as a schoolboy told he can go out and play in the snow, that one."

"Aren't they all," I stated matter-of-factly.

Tom swallowed his last mouthful of food with a loud gulp. "It's time. Now?"

I pecked him on his cheek. "Sure is, Tom. It's time to waggle your truncheon about for the cause."

"Oh." Once more, his cheeks blushed to familiar redness. He turned his gaze toward his navel, his expression reserved as he came to contemplation. Was he doubting himself?

"Don't worry. I'll be there with you," I said, giving him a reassuring touch on his freckled shoulder.

He trembled a nervous smile.

"And I'll be watchin' to make sure mister fancy pants don't try nothin' to you both, or 'e'll get a wallop about the 'ead from me, if not worse."

Tom's reservations were justified when we attended the man in question.

Chapter Thirty-Four
The Graphologist's Findings

To say Tom was wooden was a gross understatement. More like he was cast from iron straight out of the foundry, strong and unyielding. He couldn't be stiffer—and not in the way the portly gentleman, all sweating moon-like face and attired in his brash, almost inappropriate clothing, would have enjoyed, either.

Everything was rather stilted and somewhat desperate by the time Tom and I had got down to our shirts and drawers. He really couldn't take clothing off seductively. There was no doubt in my mind he saw such a thing as a means to an end, no matter how much Mimsee instructed him otherwise.

It would take a lot of time for him to change that mindset.

Time we didn't have.

Tom couldn't help it; he was brought up in a house where they had to share their bath and beds, being poorer than most middle-class folks as the family of a peeler. Taking off his clothing would have been about getting it over and done with, not about anything else.

Before our shirts were unbuttoned, I decided to take over for the both of us. "Just stay still," I whispered to Tom; my instruction wouldn't have been difficult for him.

He nodded mechanically.

The graphologist asked, "Everything all right, gentlemen?"

"All good, sir," I returned.

I began to take off Tom's clothes, incorporating the action into my part of the act. I had no choice. When he disrobed, he was all thumbs, about as erotic as flatulence in a confined space. I, however, danced around him, using him like a support, a pole I suppose.

My revised routine worked well, I believed…and hoped.

By the time we were giving the graphologist an eyeful, wearing nothing but smiles, the rotund man was drooling with pleasure. He wiped his wet jowls with his handkerchief, unable to tear his gaze away from what was revealed before him.

He said, "You are both incredibly fit and fine young men, I must say."

"Thank you, sir," I said politely.

Tom didn't return the gratitude so freely, as was the etiquette when given a compliment by a client. I nudged him gently. "Yes…thank you…sir," he stumbled.

The graphologist was a nice man, with a soft and gentle demeanour. Sure, he looked as unattractive and bloated as a fly-blown pig's carcass, but I liked him. I could see why he was a friend of my father's, as she wouldn't put up with boorishness or bravado from anyone, men particularly.

"Would you like us to kiss each other for your enjoyment, sir?" I said, my purpose not just for his entertainment.

If the man's teeth weren't rooted into his jaw, I'm sure he would have spat them out. "Oh…my. Why, yes. I'd like that very…much."

Tom looked at me, eyes wide. I winked. "For the cause," I whispered.

But here I had to be careful. We had to make sure we didn't touch each other in any unintentional way, especially our gentlemanly assets. To get around such an obstacle, because by now our obstacles were impressive, I had Tom sit down. I pushed his legs as close together as his comfort would allow, him being well endowed.

I leaned over Tom, my hands on his knees. When ready, we

kissed. It was a slow and sensual act, our tongues dancing together far better than our bodies could. My insides fluttered.

I became lost in Tom once more.

The noises we made were enough to fill the room with our intent.

I believed the graphologist relieved himself into his dribble soaked and sweat stained handkerchief. All I knew was by the time I had finished kissing Tom, the man was tucking the thing away in his trousers' pocket. He was flushed, and even more sweat beaded his ample brow.

I was aroused to aching.

Tom's gentlemanly asset was just as awake, and all I wanted to do was take him back into our chamber and Talent-touch with him again.

Unfortunately, I had to think of other things to cool myself, cast my mind back to our purpose. Not as easy as I first thought, because Tom held onto me as if I were still his support. His hand was clammy in mine, but his touch was as sensual as ever, even if unintentional. I decided the only way to keep myself distracted was to get on with proceedings.

"We're still working on our act together," I said apologetically. "Did you enjoy what we had so far to show, sir?"

"You've shown me more than enough to delight a perverted old man. It was wonderful," he said, cheerfully.

"Would you like us to get dressed or remain unclothed for you, sir?"

He waved his hand dismissively. "Oh no, please attire yourselves. There is now business to discuss and my curiosity has been more than satiated."

At that moment, Mimsee and my father entered through the velvet curtain. They were in their afternoon finery, fitting for ladies hosting a guest. Their tiered dresses were dazzling and made of the most expensive fabrics of fashion, no doubt.

Mimsee didn't need to say a word. I knew what she was thinking; our performance had been woeful. She put her hand to her mouth to hide her mocking smile. I shrugged. All things considered, I believed Tom and I did all right for our first time together.

When dressed into our working suits, the graphologist produced a pile of papers from a leather folder bound in twine he had by his side all that time.

"I have matched two possible links from the letter to the receipts Lady Penelope has provided me already."

"That was quick," I said. I'm sure he'd only been in the house a few hours.

He looked at me with almost loving eyes. "The thought of my reward for steadfastness on the matter spurred me on."

"Oh, right," I said.

Tom finally spoke. What he said got him a stern look from my father and almost made Mimsee lose her composure. "It's amazing what can be achieved when there's the promise of a couple of gentleman sausages to gander at as a reward, ain't it…sir?"

Mimsee then chuckled. She must have remembered herself and the situation and turned away without another peep.

I suppressed a smile.

"Indeed, it is, young man," the graphologist replied, seemingly unfazed by the comment. "And the sight of yours, Master Arkwright, was extremely satisfying. You are perfectly proportioned and delectably handsome, I must say. You as well, Master Merritt, even if yours is more intimidating. In a good way, of course."

Tom, suffice it to say, did as he always did: his cheeks reddened. I was used to such talk and thanked the man for his compliment.

My father remained expressionless and composed, as she

always was. With a hint of impatience, however, she said, "What is it you have to reveal from your study, Mister Trafford?"

"Well, as you may or may not know, the belief is that the style and form of handwriting can be passed down because of genetics. The way we hold a quill is from the structure of our hands, something we can get from our family lineage. As such, I believe I have two possible candidates."

He pulled out a receipt from the pile to show it to us.

"This example here. See, its loops and flourishes are strikingly similar to those in the letter."

He retrieved another.

"And this one, it clearly shows where the pressure and form is remarkably similar as well."

I asked, "And who do they belong to, these two promising candidates?"

"The first is penned by Lady Penelope's lawyer, Mister Bannister."

My mind went into so much of a spin, I felt giddy. How could I have missed that? Here I was delving through the list of my clients, when all the while I was looking in the wrong place.

I blurted, "Mister Bannister was the other man I smelt the pipe smoke on, I'm certain of it." I had to cast my thoughts back to the time the lawyer had come into my chamber with the finalised papers of my adoption to Lady Penelope and the Captain, only a few short weeks after my parents had been murdered.

Had he done it?

He couldn't have, could be?

My father raised her eyebrows. "I can assure you, I've never been involved with Mister Bannister. And certainly not in a way that would have produced this mystery son who now plagues our fair city. As I have already informed you, my suitor was anonymous and the arrangement purely one of business."

"I wasn't questioning your integrity, my dearest friend," Mister Trafford said reassuringly. "As I made you aware, it's the belief that some handwriting traits can be hereditary. I therefore believe there is a link to the letter and Mister Bannister in some way. Perhaps a family member of his is responsible. A brother, perhaps."

"I find that difficult to believe as well," my father said pragmatically. "I'm sure Mister Bannister would have cooed from the highest steeple if I had been with any of his kin. He's always been keen on improving his financial situation and social standing."

The last sentence struck a chime in the back of my mind, the words she spoke almost the same as those told to us by the Skilamalink Man the night we returned from Mister Okinawa's.

I didn't get a chance to add my thought to the discussion when Tom interjected, "But what if he didn't tell you a brother of his was the one who knocked you up, ma'am? It was kept a secret from you that the child had lived, weren't it?"

"Perhaps," she said unconvincingly, eyeing Tom after his vulgar description of what had transpired. I'm sure if anyone got close enough to Lady Penelope, "knocking her up" wouldn't be the etiquette. "It would mean I will need to call upon the services of your father, Tom, to investigate such matters."

Tom nodded.

"'Ere, it's all cloak and dagger stuff, ain't it?" Mimsee said.

"It usually is when money is involved," the graphologist replied.

My father began to look concerned; I couldn't blame her. The Skilamalink Man said enemies were as close as friends in the house. Perhaps Mister Bannister was the person to whom he was referring. I shivered, one that ran the course of my spine. It was as though someone had just walked over my grave.

In my mind I believed we had a viable lead. Finally.

"Who's the other one belong to then?" Mimsee questioned.
"The other is by the gentleman you all know as Arthur."

Chapter Thirty-Five
Tom's Enthusiasm

"I haven't smelt the pipe smoke on Arthur," I admitted. I also had to admit I could never imagine Arthur being the Skilamalink Man, even if he was the same age as him at twenty-one.

Mimsee offered, "Doesn't Arthur smoke cheroots? Couldn't that mask the Talent's scent? You know, sort of like 'ow rotten fish can mess with a dog's sense of smell?"

She could be onto something. "Perhaps it might, but I don't know."

Tom said, "Looks like we've got our two suspects, then."

He seemed confident in Mister Trafford's efforts. I wasn't so sure. Analysing handwriting wasn't an exact science, if one at all. There was still another man I needed to consider: the weedy man.

"It wouldn't hurt to investigate the client who I smelt the pipe smoke on, though would it?" I said to reinforce my thoughts.

"Speaking of which," my father said, standing. "He's waiting for you both outside in the foyer. I will tell him you'll be ready for him shortly. Mister Trafford, please attend me for supper. Mimsee, remain here with Oliver and Tom in your usual capacity. I will speak with you all afterward about going forward from here."

My father escorted Mister Trafford from the smoking room.

"Time to get to work again," Mimsee said.

"Although, Tom, you need to relax," I said. "You've got what they want, just let them salivate for a while before they see it. Loosen up a little."

"I did all right, didn't I?" Tom questioned, looking hurt. "That Mister Trafford ain't got no complaints. You heard him gush about me, didn't you?"

Mimsee cut in, "That may be so, but this next one's payin' and 'e don't want to see a dick on a dead donkey." I noticed that was one of the first times Mimsee used a more correct term for what Tom had between his legs. She really was warming up to him.

"I weren't dead, was I, Oliver?"

I kissed him. "Not to me, you aren't, beautiful. But do relax, all right?"

Mimsee rolled her eyes. "I'll be watchin' from my usual place, lovelies, but don't forget these 'ere." Out of her clutch bag she produced a black, silk blindfold and two pairs of leather gloves in the same colour.

I had almost forgotten about my idea of using the Talent on the weedy man to reveal any connection to our enemy. After what Mister Trafford had told us about what he'd discovered, however, the chance of our client being linked in any way to the Skilamalink Man seemed remote. I held a firm belief that Mister Bannister was a better lead than any we'd had so far.

But we had a job to do and coin to earn.

Two things went well during our performance for the weedy man, and two things not so well. The first, Tom relaxed enough to enjoy performing for an audience. No longer was he as rigid as a cadaver at the morgue or having the look of fright upon him.

I know he liked the kissing part of our hastily cobbled together routine as much as I did. The weedy man certainly did.

He slathered his lips often, keeping them moist, making more noise than we did. He was strange and gentle, I supposed, but definitely creepy.

The other thing that went well was the idea of the "game" we suggested when we got down to what the weedy man had paid for. I know he enjoyed seeing me without a stitch on, having Tom the same was more than a bonus for him. As such, he accepted the blindfold without complaint after only a few encouraging words by us.

"It'll be fun, an' all," Tom said, sealing the deal with a polite, "sir."

Before the weedy man put the blindfold on, he was to enjoy the spectacle of Tom and I enjoying ourselves for him, as agreed. With him putting on the blindfold, we'd then do the same to him.

"But only with our hands, sir," I reinforced.

The weedy man nodded agreement.

I could plainly see him beginning his journey toward ecstasy, the pupils of his wonder-filled eyes dilating. He continued to wet his lips while unbuttoning his trousers in preparation, bringing out his tackle without a care. Being of an upper-class upbringing, he was circumcised. His looked dry at the end of it, but no less interesting than any other gentlemanly asset I'd seen since dancing for men.

Tom's was the only one I wanted, anyway.

Which brought proceedings to the things that didn't go so well.

Tom, even though seated far enough away so any attempt by the weedy man to touch him could be avoided, didn't account for the distance his youthful exuberance could achieve.

Instead of Tom's fluids finding his own stomach, it shot up to splatter sticky pearls over the weedy man's rather expensive double breasted, silk-lined evening jacket.

"Lawks!" Tom cried, as we both grabbed handkerchiefs. "I'm so sorry, I am, sir." His face was bright red from both completion and embarrassment, no doubt.

I was still feeling the effects of my efforts. My mind was hazy, my body slow to its commands. Somehow, I managed to obtain water from the one of the many vases of flowers scattered around the smoking room.

After wetting the handkerchief enough so the suspicious droplets across the front of the weedy man's suit could be better removed, not just smeared into the material, I breathed relief.

"There. All gone, sir," I offered weakly.

Tom was still apologising.

The weedy man didn't seem angered. Thank goodness; I'd heard many stories from the first floor where any damage to a client's belongings would need to be paid for—most times out of the girls' payment.

If the man had done it over himself, that was his fault and he'd have to deal with it. In this case, it was Tom's doing. If Tom was going to be charged for a new jacket, then so be it.

But I had a feeling the weedy man appreciated my quick thinking. Besides, he had two young men to enjoy for the price of one. It all evened out in my reckoning.

The man licked his lips. By that, I knew the wanted us to continue, Tom's indiscretion already forgotten. And that's the other thing that didn't go so well.

Chapter Thirty-Six
The Suspects Narrow

Tom and I couldn't draw upon our Talent.

It's not that it had disappeared, far from it. I could feel it bubbling and seething deep inside me. The problem, and I hadn't thought of this when I invented the game to try and investigate whether a client had the Talent or not, was that I'd just relieved myself, as had Tom.

My Talent was indeed linked inexorably to my libido, meaning that when I was spent, it would take time to recover if I wasn't sufficiently aroused. Thanks to the incident with the man's jacket, I had no urges. Even with every positive thought I could dredge up from the deepest recesses of my mind, I couldn't call my Talent forth.

Not yet, anyway.

"What're we going to do?" Tom whispered through his teeth. "I can't use my Talent...not yet."

For the longest time we stood there stock still, gawking at the weedy man's arousal while it looked back at us one-eyed, waiting for action. The man, now blindfolded, writhed in anticipation. He groaned. His tongue working to keep his lips wet.

"I don't know," I hissed back as quietly as I could manage, considering panic had struck me.

Just as I was about to tell the client the show was unfortunately over and offer him a refund, Mimsee, thank the Lord Almighty, came to our rescue.

She entered the smoking room as stealthily as a cat, expertly took the situation into hand, so to speak, and gave the weedy man what he wanted without so much as a bat of an eyelid. When done, she winked at us then scurried back to her spy hole behind the portrait before the man was any the wiser.

Tom had the look upon him of witnessing a marvel.

I couldn't blame him.

He then nudged me, nodding his head to draw attention to something he'd seen. Sure enough, as the weedy man removed the blindfold, I could plainly see what Tom wanted me to notice: a tobacco stain on the pad of his right thumb.

The weedy man didn't harbour the Talent at all.

The next morning, as was family tradition recently, we were summoned to the morning room. William was waiting for us, and he embraced Tom. Surprisingly, he also embraced me, if only briefly and with a single slap on my back. I supposed for him, it was a beginning to his reconciliation.

Mimsee and my father were already in attendance, enjoying breakfast. I was starving, so I tucked in after I performed the required formalities of etiquette. Tom did the same.

"By God, I hear you've made progress and you've got a lead," William said through a mouthful of cured ham and poached egg on stone ground toasted bread.

I didn't believe much more needed to be said on the matter. I was certain my father or Mimsee had informed William about Mister Trafford's findings. I agreed, "Yes, we have, sir."

William must have also agreed, because he said, "I'd like you both to come with me while I pay a visit to our friend, Mister Bannister. Just in case things get a little interesting and I need your Talent abilities. Lady Penelope has so kindly supplied the address from the house records."

My father nodded graciously at being mentioned.

Mister Bannister was the only other man I smelt the pipe smoke on. If he was anything like the Skilamalink Man in Talent power, he could be a problem if things turned nasty. Would we be ready for him?

"Sure, Pa," Tom said, making the decision for us.

I acquiesced. At that I got a polite nod from my father in approval, her expression one of pride upon her owlish façade.

"I'm comin' along as well," Mimsee announced.

No one argued with her.

After a pleasant coach ride deep into the exclusive boroughs of London, we arrived at an elegant middle-terrace townhouse nestled within a tidy tree-lined mews. I couldn't help but notice that no matter how much coin folks earned, the thick London Particular covered us all equally.

"You won't see no shivering Jemmies around here," Tom whistled when we alighted from the coach and were all standing on the porch to Mister Bannister's stately looking home.

"I'd say the beggars in these parts would wear better suits than we do," I laughed.

Tom chuckled as well.

"Probably given more coin in a day than we earn in a week, they are," Mimsee offered.

William used the doorknocker with enough determination to announce to Mister Bannister that he had visitors of importance at such an early hour of the morning. An hour that could almost be considered uncivilised; well before seven o'clock, if not a minute. The man was probably in his bath.

There was no answer.

Tom's father knocked again. That time with even more tenacity, if possible. After another long moment of no reply, William tried the ornate, gilt handle. Naturally, the door was locked.

"It's locked," William stated obviously.

"Can't you just break in, being a peeler?" I questioned. "What I mean to say is, wouldn't you have the authority to do that in the course of investigating a suspect?"

He looked at me as though I was speaking a foreign language. "What the deuce? No, no, that wouldn't be wise, Oliver. Us peelers are about as popular as mouth sores on a six-penny bunter, we are. If there's no crime committed, we don't have much say on matters when it comes down to it. Not someone at my level, anyway."

Tom suggested, "Why don't we use our Talent to open the lock, Pa? You can't be blamed then for no wrongdoing. No one ain't gonna understand how it was unlocked." He winked. "Not our fault the door was open when we got here."

William's lips crawled to an acknowledging smile. "I'd say you'd be right, Tom, my boy. This door *was* open when we got here, plain as day."

"Did you want the honours, Tom?" I asked. Tom nodded. "But only draw upon the smallest amount. We might need you for other dangerous matters very soon if Mister Bannister gets upset with our intrusion."

"Got it." Tom closed his eyes. His hands soon glowed with blue gaslight. A blink of an eye after that, the fingers of the Sense side of his Talent were twisting ethereally into the door handle's locking mechanism. A tense moment followed. A bead of sweat formed on his brow. Then, a click. "Done," he announced triumphantly.

"Well done, lovely!" Mimsee said, almost cooing.

William opened the door.

"Are you all right?" I asked Tom. There were more beads of sweat at his temples. Even using a small amount of Talent clearly had an effect on him.

"Just give me a moment or two and I'll be as right as rain. At least I only had a little movement down there in my beastly bits that time, Oliver. Must be gettin' used to it, I say."

I accepted his answer, patting him on his shoulder in reassurance and congratulations.

We found ourselves in a marble-tiled entrance way, one filled with expensive furniture. Even the ostentatiously-wallpapered walls were plastered with oil paintings of sweeping landscapes and portraits of people, obviously his family.

When Tom caught his breath back, we followed William and Mimsee into the house.

The drapes were all drawn, the house dark and quiet. Perhaps the man was still in bed. No house servants could be seen either. That was strange. A weird feeling of dread began to well up to tickle at the back of my consciousness as we crept cautiously through the lavishly appointed house.

Then we saw Mister Bannister.

My first theory was correct.

Mister Bannister *was* in his bath. Although, he wasn't getting out of it in too much of a hurry.

He was dead.

Murdered.

William held his handkerchief over his mouth. "Goodness, may the Lord Almighty have mercy on his soul, the poor blighter."

The rotting stench of flesh well into putrefaction hit me hard. I gagged. Tom and Mimsee did the same. With our noses and mouths covered, we stood stock still for a moment, transfixed by what we'd discovered.

Mister Bannister was soaking in water contaminated with his own blood, tongue lolling, face a bloated mask of horror, his internal organs floating around him like they were ingredients in a macabre stew. It would be another sight that'd be burned into my mind forever.

I suppressed another retch.

"Lawks, you wouldn't serve that up with onions," Tom said gasping.

I'd seen enough and I went out to the landing to get some fresh air. Tom and Mimsee joined me. They both had the look of the fright upon them. No doubt I looked the same. We didn't say a word to each other for the longest time.

What needed to be said anyway after such a discovery?

William came out soon after, white as a sheet. He held a note. "I found this in there. It's for you, our Oliver. You, too, my dear boy."

"What does it say?" I asked.

William answered, "I think you should just read it."

Chapter Thirty-Seven
The Dragon Master

What the note had written on it left no doubt in my mind that the Skilamalink Man not only knew we were close with our investigation, but he was also enjoying the hunt.

My dearest Messrs Merritt and Arkwright, my uncle has just been dying for you to arrive and find him. I do believe you can now literally smell how close you are. Isn't this such fun? Yours, your eternal nemesis, SM.

I read the note many times.

The man was not only a lickspittler, he was insane as well; murdering his own kin for the enjoyment of the "chase", as he obviously perceived it? Was it all a game to him?

If it were, the stakes were too high for too many people. I swallowed hard. Tom looked peaky, his concerns reflected in his baby blue eyes.

Mimsee read the note after I'd finished with it.

"He's admitting he's related to Mister Bannister," I finally said. "The graphologist, Mister Trafford, was right."

I surprised myself with that admission. Perhaps there was something to the science of analysing handwriting after all. Or perhaps it was just a very good guess on Mister Trafford's part; I suspected the latter.

William said, "I've got a good friend who can go through the Parish Register of the local church. He can find out who Mister Bannister's brother is and if he's had any children. Boys born in thirty-three is what we're looking for."

"Ain't 'e that Bishop Oxbridge fellow you talkin' 'bout?" Mimsee asked.

"That's right, the very same," William replied. "Do you know him, lass?"

"I know 'im all right," she said surreptitiously. "Just 'cause 'e wears a collar don't mean 'is tackle don't want for 'im to go fishin'. I'll go talk to 'im and 'elp 'im look in the Register's records, all unofficially like. Besides, 'e owes me a few favours and I want to get out of this house. It's givin' me the horrors standing 'ere beside myself, it is."

The stink off poor Mister Bannister was wafting into the landing area. Aside from agreeing with Mimsee about needing to take our leave, I also thought it was a brilliant idea for her to check the Parish Registers while William did what would be required of him at the scene of the crime. I didn't need any imagination to know it would be a dreadful task cleaning up our grim discovery.

Mimsee left. She had a way with folks that would give us an advantage. As for Tom and me, I had an idea that was important in my mind. Something I knew couldn't wait, thanks to the reminder earlier when he picked the lock with his Talent.

"This place wasn't half bad 'til we found it came with a stinkin' dead body," Tom said with dripping sarcasm.

The colour had returned to his cheeks once we were downstairs and away from the horror of a man marinating in his own blood. I couldn't have agreed more. I placed the Skilamalink Man's ghastly note into my coat's inner pocket.

When outside, Tom and I caught a Hansom Safety Cab to the East End—a nimble journey thanks to the driver's knowledge of the streets and the carriage's sleek two-wheeled design. That and the fact only one horse was needed to pull it.

Mister Okinawa's apothecary-cum-pharmacy beckoned, and we were soon engulfed in remnants of opium smoke and the many fragrances of the medicines and other exotic substances within his establishment.

The man greeted us without surprise and a courteous bow.

"I believe it's time we were told everything about the Talent, Mister Okinawa," I said after the formalities of greeting. I reached into my pocket to hand him the note. "Too many good people have been murdered. It's got to come to a halt."

"You believe you are the ones who will stop this man, Master Merritt? Master Arkwright?"

"We do," Tom stated straightforwardly.

Mister Okinawa showed no sign of emotion. "Then I believe it is time. Follow me, please."

He led Tom and I beyond the back of his private chamber where he'd treated me the other night. We came to a secret door concealed by an ornate, well-woven tapestry of a strange battle of flatulence between warriors, women, and even horses. I believed I noted a depiction of a cat farting among the weave's artwork as well.

"That's a bit different, ain't it?" Tom offered, staring at the tapestry.

"I see you admire the reproduction I had done of the *He-Gassen* scrolls. I found them amusing, so I had a good friend of mine weave me one for my private collection. It fits into this space rather well, don't you think?"

I wasn't so sure. "Does it mean something that it depicts folks passing wind on each other?" I asked.

"Oh, yes, indeed it does."

"Then do tell us," Tom said.

Mister Okinawa offered a grin that went beyond his lips. "I believe it means that laughter is just as good a medicine as what comes out of a bottle in most cases. Never forget that."

I thought about his words for a moment. It was true;

Mimsee and Tom made me laugh often. As such, I always felt better when I was around them.

Nevertheless, I didn't get too much time to contemplate life's abstractions. Mister Okinawa pushed his way through the tapestry's representation of what could only be described as a flatulence war to guide us into a long, darkened hallway.

The further we went along the hallway, music from a harp or similar instrument being plucked grew louder. Many rooms led out from either side, and I wondered where they went. I couldn't give much thought to my curiosity, because Mister Okinawa's pace quickened.

He took Tom and I to the end of the hallway, removing a Persian rug to reveal a trapdoor. We were led silently down to a basement, the stairs lit by strange, red candles that cast dancing spider-like shadows across the stone walls.

We stopped at a thick, wooden door reinforced by wrought iron.

"Please, be respectful and remove your shoes before entering." Mister Okinawa gestured to a place to leave our shoes. "Master Xun Xiuying requires the utmost in traditional formality. Also, please do as I do until invited otherwise. It is most important."

"Of course, Mister Okinawa," I said, my curiosity burning.

I removed my shoes without question, as did Tom.

Mister Okinawa pushed open the door. He uttered something in his own language; a greeting perhaps. His voice was soft and velvety, as welcoming as I'd ever heard it. I assumed he was talking to this Master Xun Xiuying fellow. I couldn't see the man.

Like the stairs, the room was darkened. There was a rice paper screen blocking the view to half the room. Only a few lanterns burned.

Mister Okinawa entered deeper once a cold voice spoke,

again in their own language. He had placed one fist into the palm of his other hand, bowing as he proceeded.

I did as he'd instructed and copied the gesture.

Tom looked at me quizzically but followed suit.

Much to my amazement and interest, and once my eyes became adjusted to the dimly lit room, I discovered that the basement was an art gallery of some sort. Many paintings, drawings, etchings, and woodcut prints adorned the stone walls. There were countless more stacked in rows, scattered about the room.

The harp music was more noticeable, but I couldn't see the instrument that produced the pleasant sound, or even the musician who strummed its strings. Incense burned strong. Beyond the rice paper screen was an artist's desk.

Here, there was a lantern illuminating a man sitting at the desk. He was in his twenties, if a day. He inked a large, long-bristled sable brush with careful patience. With it, he gracefully wrote strange characters across a clean sheet of paper, right to left.

Had all the artwork been done by this man?

"My Great Master, may I introduce you to our honourable guests, Master Oliver Merritt, and his beloved companion, Master Tom Arkwright." Mister Okinawa bowed once more, again with the same hand gesture.

I did the same, but again didn't offer any words. I simply didn't know the social etiquette here other than Mister Okinawa telling us to copy his movements.

Tom remained silent, too.

The stool the young man was perched upon creaked as he turned around. I supposed he could be considered handsome in the sense that he was striking. His features were harsh upon him beneath his thick eyebrows. Even though he looked young, his dark, strange eyes seemed to hold eternity.

He looked us up and down.

Finally, after what seemed a glacial amount of time, he said, "Nǐ hǎo. I have been waiting a thousand years to meet you both."

Chapter Thirty-Eight
The Dragon Symbols

"Oh. Pleased to meet you as well, sir," Tom said, still bowing.

I wasn't sure whether or not Tom understood the full ramifications of Master Xun Xiuying's greeting. The man said he'd been waiting a thousand years to meet us. *A thousand years!* I never proclaimed to know everything, but I believed I knew he certainly couldn't be that old.

Could he?

But I bowed and offered my reply. "Pleased to meet you as well, Master Xun Xiuying." I did my best to get my inexperienced tongue around his name. I hoped I hadn't butchered the nuances of it and insulted him.

He didn't indicate I'd done so.

Master Xun Xiuying stood. "My honoured guests, I understand you are having troubles of late." His accent was thick, not as clean as Mister Okinawa's. I was able to understand him without strain to my unaccustomed ears at such inflections of heritage, though.

Tom said, "We sure have been having troubles. There's been this bastard who calls himself the—"

Master Xun Xiuying raised his hand, cutting Tom off mid-sentence. "You misunderstand, my friend. My meaning was that you are both having trouble with your Talent. From what my humble servant, Mister Okinawa has informed me, it has been considered that you both have too much Yang. Something that needs to be corrected if you are to continue on your path."

Tom shrugged. "It's Oliver here who is better endowed with the Yang than I am. His is a right eye waterer, it's that big."

I gave a quick belly chuckle. I couldn't help it. Mister Okinawa smiled. "Good medicine," he said with a wink.

"Ah, yes, the humour of youth and their ribald comments that amuse them. Most entertaining indeed." Master Xun Xiuying turned to address Mister Okinawa. "I would be grateful if you'd prepare an area for us, so I can then instruct our honourable guests."

Mister Okinawa immediately bowed. He then began folding down the rice paper screen and clearing an area at the centre of the basement. Strange Chinese symbols had been painted on the brickwork floor in thick, black paint.

Now back to us, Master Xun Xiuying said, "Tom, you are to stand on the Dragon Symbol of Strength. Over there." He gestured to where he wanted Tom to go. My companion obeyed. To me, the man said, "And, Oliver, you are to stand on the Dragon for Control." I did so.

Rather oddly, I felt warmth inch up through me from the ground once I was on the symbol proper. Was that the reason why we had to remove our shoes? I didn't get time to contemplate such matters, as was common of late. Master Xun Xiuying hadn't finished his instructions. "Call upon your Talents. Prepare to defend yourselves. Now, please!"

What happened next was a blur. I wouldn't have believed it if I hadn't participated in it.

Not only did Master Xun Xiuying possess the Talent—the strong smell of incense masking the familiar pipe smoke of someone who had it—he was a deft hand at using it as well. He also moved like a graceful tiger, quickly but with as much precision as he required for his art.

The result was devastating for Tom and me.

Just in time, my ethereal spider cast its web of Talent,

springing forth from my fingertips as soon as the man sent his Talent-lightning toward me.

I was stunned and stepped back from the force of his strike. As soon as I came off the Dragon Symbol for Control, my loins stirred as my Talent raged to keep up my defences. I quickly stepped back onto the symbol.

Immediately, my body calmed, and my arousal softened. I took a moment to contemplate that revelation.

Tom was now the Master's target.

He shot Talent-lightning toward Tom.

"Lawks!" But Tom defended himself well, even managing to shoot a lightning bolt back to Master Xun Xiuying.

It struck the wall, dislodging a painting in a cloud of stone dust. It was a marvel that Tom had been able to accomplish such a thing, I thought, admiring him.

I certainly couldn't defend and attack so quickly.

Within the blink of an eye, I was once more targeted.

Over and over the man took turns attacking us with his Talent, randomly firing at either of us as he saw fit. Soon my whole body ached, and I was sweating profusely. I began breathing heavily, but to my utter surprise, I remained in control of my body.

I couldn't believe it.

An eternity later, the room was no longer overpowered by the scent of incense, but the intense pungency of pipe smoke derived from so much Talent use. I had fired many times at Master Xun Xiuying, and he'd returned it in equal measure. His grace and poise never faltered; he was like watching a seasoned dancer perform at the Theatre Royal.

"Defend again, Oliver, please!" he ordered. That time, he used both of his hands together, joined at their wrists, to send Talent-lightning at me.

I was stunned by the sheer force of it once it slammed into

my protective shield, my ethereal spider's web of protection instantly dissipating. I was thrown off the Dragon Symbol to land flat on my buttocks near a stack of calligraphic prints.

The very moment I came off the symbol, and with my Talent still engaged and surrounding me in a tangled web, my gentlemanly asset instantly became engorged. I yelped as I tried to get up. However, my body finally defeated me. I shuddered, folding like a drunken sailor punched in his breadbasket during a rowdy tavern brawl. My groin burned hot, sweat stung my eyes, and my diaphragm convulsed. I even hiccoughed while curling into the foetal position.

Master Xun Xiuying came over me, his face in shadow. I was reminded of the Skilamalink Man. I started, raising my arm over my face in reflexive defence.

Once I realised it wasn't my enemy over me, the pipe smoke smell different from the man I hated with all my being, the Master said gently, "You are defeated now, I believe."

"I sure am," I replied with another shudder as my gentlemanly asset passed more of my conclusion into my drawers. I turned to see that Tom was in the same predicament. He was quivering, rolled up as I was, knees pressed to his chest.

"What have we learned here today? Please, tell me."

"That I can't step off the Dragon Symbol unless I want to get killed," I offered weakly.

I knew it was a silly answer because there was no way any enemy would let me remain on a painted symbol on the ground while they attacked me. But I couldn't help but notice how effective it was to be protected by the dragon.

My head began to throb as much as my gentlemanly assets.

The Master tutted. "No, Oliver. The symbol means nothing. It just gave your mind something to concentrate on while you used your Talent. What you should have learned is that you must create your own Dragon Symbol if you are to succeed.

Your body is your temple, but your mind is the god within it. Distract the god by giving him something to think about so you can accomplish the task at hand, and your body will not let you down. Sometimes we worry about too much, and I believe it is so with you and Tom."

Tom groaned. "So how do we find our own Dragon Symbols, then?"

The Master smiled. "That is the real question here, isn't it, Tom?"

Chapter Thirty-Nine
The Honourable Ones

Mister Okinawa served us a yellowish-brown fluid in tiny cups that he called Oolong tea while our clothing was laundered and dried. The brew was sweet and fragrant, but not as fortifying for me as my father's Earl Grey blends.

For the moment, Tom and I were attired in silken robes depicting mountain scenes and peasant farmers on rice fields. Master Xun Xiuying was inking Dragon Symbols on small squares of rice paper.

"For you to wear about your person," he stated as he handed Tom and I a few of them once the ink had dried.

"Which one of these do we use, then?" Tom asked, thumbing through the small stack of symbols he'd been gifted. I wondered that myself.

"That is what we shall need to discover. I have drawn all the Dragon Symbols, one on each card. You will need to go through each of them in turn to know which one works best to distract the god within your temple so you can concentrate on the direction and flow of your Talent. Then your Yang and Ying will be in balance. You will be ready."

I believed I understood what he was saying but decided to change the course of the conversation. "Are you really a thousand years old, Master Xun Xiuying?"

For the first time, he smiled at me, those deep eyes spanning the depth of heaven and the stars within it. "I didn't say I was a thousand years old, Oliver. I said I'd been waiting for you and

Tom for that long. My story is far longer, for when I was younger my form was not what you see before you, but that of a beautiful dragon."

He shifted his weight, the stool creaking.

He continued, "In my youth and when I was a dragon, I was arrogant and filled with lust. I believed I could do as I pleased. I thought my powers made me invincible, with no one able to tell me otherwise."

"You would be powerful as a dragon," I offered.

He chuckled. "Not so. In the haze of my own foolishness, I raped the woman who would become my mother, because as my seed within her grew, my dragon form faded away. I was to learn that this was my punishment from the gods themselves. I'd angered them with my contempt to others and to myself."

"That's messed up, ain't it?" Tom breathed.

"We all tread paths meant for us," the Master replied. "My path meant that when the woman gave birth to me as a human, my dragon self had died. My sentence for such a horrific act against a woman of virtue and fairness was to live immortal, to know intimately every endless moment from my birth, remembering with horrifying clarity what I'd done."

I didn't have words. His story was incredible.

"She was my shame because of what I did to her. And she was my love because she was my mother. She always told me, until she breathed her last mortal breath, that I would one day meet two who had as much power as I. They would need my help. She told me these two would be different, as they'd be two men who were each other's heart and soul."

Tom sat wide-eyed, clearly amazed by the immortal Xun Xiuying's story. As was I. His story reminded me in a way of the Ouroboros, the father of his own self.

"If I understand this correctly, you're going to continue to teach us more about the Talent?" I asked.

"Indeed," the immortal said, re-inking his brush carefully, "but all in good time, Oliver."

"I have to say, I'm chuffed about that news," Tom said. "I mean, if it weren't for you, Master...Dragon," as Tom called Master Xun Xiuying that name, the immortal smiled, "we'd still be paralysed by our own Talent."

Mister Okinawa said, "That was just the first step of a great journey for you both. Now, please, we must proceed with the task at hand. Finding your Dragon Symbol is most important."

For the next hour or so, if not more, we tested out each of the Dragon Symbols in turn. Being in loose robes, it was easy to see which ones were more effective than others. Master Xun Xiuying found our hardening fleshly gauges most amusing if a symbol we used didn't work.

"That particular dragon does not serve your temple, Tom," the immortal observed laughing. "You look like a three-legged crane!"

Tom, of course, burned red at his cheeks.

I laughed.

Mister Okinawa joined in, chuckling in his gentlemanly way. I really did understand what he'd meant about laughter being good medicine.

Finally, by the time our clothing had been returned to us, I had settled on the Dragon of Prosperity for my symbol. Tom had chosen the Dragon of Protection. The symbol's influence on me wasn't all encompassing, but I knew I could easily deal with a mild stirring in my gentlemanly asset when I used my Talent now.

Far better than being without it.

Once dressed, we thanked Master Xun Xiuying, and he returned to his art without another word. I swore he had changed from the first time we'd been introduced. His eyes were different, now flecked with gold. I dismissed the thought.

All too soon, Mister Okinawa escorted us back through the tapestry depicting the amusing flatulence war. When in his apothecary-come-pharmacy shoppe proper, he said, "I will have my sons return you to your home, Master Merritt, Master Arkwright. But you must visit again very soon; the Great Dragon Master will insist it be so."

"Does Master Xun Xiuying have much more to teach us?" I inquired.

"Teaching is like laughter. There can never be too much."

After Mister Okinawa undertook a conversation with someone behind a closed door, and we were outside his establishment in the usual London weather, I soon found out what he meant by his sons taking us home. What I saw amazed me: two strapping young lads, no older than twelve, if a day, came up the narrow cobblestone street together, pulling a brightly coloured rickshaw. They were twins, identical and strikingly so. They introduced themselves as Hao and Tan.

"Honourable sirs, you have met our great ancestor the Dragon Master then?" Hao asked.

"Sure did, an' all," Tom replied.

Tan, with a hushed reverence, said, "Then you are the two he has always spoken of?"

I answered, "He believes so."

Tan and Hao looked at each other, sharing a look only they understood. Perhaps because they were twins, they could communicate on a level no one without the gift of being in a womb together could understand.

Finally, Hao said, "Whenever you need help, ask any of our kin and we will be there to aid you, honourable ones."

"Thank you," was all I could humbly reply.

After a rather enjoyable rickshaw ride through London from the East End to our home, my father greeted us in the terrazzo tiled foyer. She had changed into her afternoon attire already, wearing a full emerald-coloured dress with a flowing V-line bodice, collapsed sleeves, and plunging neckline.

The Captain's portrait brooch was pinned above her breast, close to her heart, as always. A teardrop diamond hung on a gold necklace around her neck. To me it symbolised her sorrow for the loss of her man more than any other piece of jewellery she owned.

"Tell me, was your visit with the Dragon Master enlightening?"

I nodded. "We believe so, Father."

At that moment, Mimsee came through the double front entrance doors, sending natural light into the foyer as best as London could manage for the time of the year. She was holding in her hand a roll of parchments, beaming a smile triumphantly.

"I found 'em!" she announced. "Mister Bannister's brother and 'is son!"

Chapter Forty
A Shocking Realisation

The moment after Mimsee announced her news, my father immediately shepherded all of us into the morning room. She ordered a summoned house servant to provide us with fresh tea, scones, crumpets, and pancakes.

Cook would be busy.

"How did you find the records of them so quickly?" I asked.

Quite honestly, I would have imagined going through the Parish Registry a greater task than most would wish to undertake. Most churches didn't have reliable recordkeeping. If they did, the majority weren't in any retrievable order or transcribed by the churchwarden without errors.

She unrolled the first parchment scroll onto the nearest table, flattening it out with her hands as best she could; the crinkle of the paper seemed loud in the silence of anticipation.

My father offered a couple of candlesticks to use as paperweights.

When satisfied the scroll was readable, she pointed to a handwritten entry in flowing script. "Well, see 'ere. Bishop Octopus says—"

"Don't you mean Bishop Oxbridge, Mimsee?" Tom cut in.

She let out a snort. "Oh, my lovely, what little you know. When a pretty girl goes visitin' a lonely ol' bishop in a stuffy ol' church, he quickly becomes all hands, don't 'e? 'E's Bishop Octopus, and that's that."

I found an opportunity too good to waste. "What did you

have to do to keep his hands from distracting you from your purpose?"

"'Ere, you're such a tease, Oliver, you are."

"I was taught by the best."

She offered me a knowing, cheeky smile. "Well, to give you your answer, let's just say I know firsthand 'e's been sneakin' too many snifters from the sacramental wine. That blow of 'is tasted very bitter. Like the Devil's breath itself, it was."

Tom almost choked on his own tongue. I had to pat him on his back. "You put his di—crozier staff in your mouth to get what you needed?"

"All for the cause," she said proudly. "And besides, you couldn't do it, could you? Not havin' the Talent, I was the best person for the job. Those Register records were a state. Only with his 'elp could I make 'ead or tail of it all. And 'e wasn't 'elping me without some carnal persuasion either, no matter how many favours 'e owed me, was 'e?"

I became sombre. "You needn't have done what you didn't want to, no matter how much is at stake here, Mimsee."

"Was nothin'. You know I'd do anything for you, Oliver. You, too, Tom. Now, don't you worry your pretty 'eads about it. I got what we needed, didn't I?"

After a long silence, the house servant arrived with our pre-dinner refreshments.

My father, who had seemed most amused by our conversation, said, "Please, Mimsee, tell us what you found."

She got on with it. "Well, our Mister Bannister was the youngest child of five brothers. But with 'im permanently in the bath now, there are none of 'em left. They're all dead."

She pointed to the relevant sections within the written lines on the extract that noted their dates of death. My father dished out tea and plates of food to each of us.

Mimsee explained, "I thought that was the end of it, until

Bishop Octopus told me to check the Marriage Register, not that Births and Deaths one. Well, you could've knocked me over with a feather, you could. It turns out Mister Bannister's mother remarried, didn't she? Caused all the fuss back in the day. A right scandal. But from that union, there was a child. A boy."

"Let me guess," Tom said. "Mister Bannister's half-brother was the one who gave Lady Penelope a son by their arrangement, but for reasons of his own choosing, he told her the baby had been born dead?"

I added, "And this dead child is now twenty-one and seeking my father's fortune."

"Right you all are," Mimsee said.

I noticed my father remained silent, studying the parchment. I sipped on my tea—a far better brew than Oolong, I had to admit.

Tom offered, "So that graphologist fellow was kind of right then, wasn't he? The Skilamalink Man's writing is similar to Mister Bannister's, because they do indeed share blood."

Again, I hated to admit it, but graphology had proved its value. Then again, after finding out there's a man who was once a dragon but is also his own father, I imagined Mister Trafford's dabbling would be considered an evidence-based science in comparison.

My father asked coolly, "What is the boy's name, Mimsee?"

Mimsee audibly swallowed. "Reginald 'Arthur' Drummond, Mother. The 'igh and mighty Lord, 'imself, it is."

The room spun. My body wanted to do many things in that instant, but most of all I felt sickened to my very soul. My emotions then welled. I almost fainted. My mind burst with the ramifications of what Mimsee had said, from the murder of my parents by this man, to me performing for him, believing him to even be a friend…and then more than that.

We smoked together.

Laughed together.

He even asked me on a supper date.

I retched dryly, needing to get fresh air into my lungs. I tried to stand, but my hate for that lickspittler seethed like violent lava flows inside me. I stumbled. Tom came to hold me.

What would my mother have thought of me? I got naked for that man. I enjoyed myself for his viewing pleasure. All the while, he had the blood of her and all the rest on his hands.

I hated myself with everything I had for being so narrow sighted. The man, my enemy, just sat there, cool and calm, watching me while I performed for him. How could I have been so blind? So stupid? His charm and his money and his cheroot smoke that hid the scent of his Talent made me naïve to who he really was.

I couldn't help myself; I began to cry as my emotions overwhelmed me.

Tom embraced me proper, kissing the hot, bitter tears off my cheeks. "We'll get the bastard, we will," he said with all the anger I'd ever heard from him. "Now that we know who it is, we'll get him!"

I felt as though I was really going to faint from the shock of it all, getting the vapours. "It...*can't*...be him," I stuttered, straining to get the words out.

My shoulders heaved, and Tom rubbed my back with more purpose.

Lady Penelope stood. I could see her tears through my own blurry vision. We both cried tears of betrayal.

She, unlike me, held her composure. "It is rather convenient that this evening we are due to pay Arthur a visit, isn't it?"

"Begging your pardon, ma'am?" Tom questioned.

I couldn't speak yet, only able to mouth a whimper as my emotions continued to vie for control over me. Tom held me tighter. His warmth my only comfort.

My father dabbed away the tears that had welled in her eyes with her handkerchief; Mimsee was holding her hand. "This evening is the night of the supper Oliver promised to attend."

Again, I couldn't speak. I couldn't believe any of this. It was worse than a nightmare. But I didn't know how I could have done things differently, which was the problem.

The Skilamalink Man integrated himself into our lives to accomplish the most devastating effect upon us he could. No doubt the supper was really an invitation to get rid of me and Mimsee and everyone else that stood in the way of his inheritance.

I even ventured to wager he'd arranged for his uncle, Mister Bannister, to set up the legal paperwork to ensure his inheritance once we'd been disposed of. I felt for the lawyer; he would have had no idea he was also a target once his usefulness had run its course.

"Then I've got to get my Pa and a couple of the lads to come with us," Tom suggested.

"Most prudent," my father agreed. She gave her attention to Mimsee. "Can you please see to it, my daughter, that Tom and Oliver are wearing appropriate attire for this evening. We may be about to face the one who desires to take everything from us, but we will not do it defeated or with our standards lowered because of him. We are strong, we are family, and by the Lord Almighty as witness, this murdering scoundrel has crossed the wrong people!"

Chapter Forty-One
The Beggar Boy's Secret

It took me a dragon's age to calm.

Tom was with me as my support, as was Mimsee. As if to stab at my conscience and mock me, the weather outside became unusually clear. Sunlight even broke through the clouds and smog, with enough blue in the sky to mend a pair of sailor's trousers, as they say when there was a shred of hope amongst the gloom.

The sight of it made me feel worse.

We were walking down the High Street. Mimsee was between us, one arm offered for each. Both Tom and I obliged her. We were perusing various fashion shoppes with the intention of purchasing this evening's attire, shillings in her purse from the house coffers.

She had insisted we go with her, get some fresh air and clear our heads before we went to Arthur's house later that evening. I tended to agree, even though it really did little to ease the overwhelming feelings of doubt, anger, and hatred I felt for both myself and Arthur.

"We'll get 'im, we will," Mimsee reminded me often.

Tom had already made his father aware of what had transpired. William would be attending, along with a couple of his best men. Somehow, that didn't instil me with much confidence. The Skilamalink Man had been playing me—playing us—all along.

We entered a high-end tailor's shoppe in the more exclusive

section of the street. The bell that hung above the door tinkled to announce our entrance.

A comely middle-aged man swooped across the richly carpeted floor to greet us. "Good afternoon, sirs and madam," he said fluently and with practised ease. "How is it I can help you this fine day?"

I still wasn't ready to speak. Thankfully, Mimsee was well versed in dealing with shoppe attendants. "Good day to you," she began with the best formality she could muster. "We want two suits. One for my brother, Oliver. The other for 'is companion, Tom. But it's got to be off the peg. It's for this evenin' so there's no time for custom."

The attendant's eyebrows shot up faster than the crinoline skirts on the first floor on a busy Saturday evening. "Off the peg?" After his initial shock, the man seemed to calm. "Do they know their measurements?"

"I know my brother's," Mimsee offered, "but not Tom's. 'E'll need to be measured."

"I see." The man pulled out his roll of measuring tape and chalk from his jacket's front pocket. He gestured for Tom to go to the triptych of ornately framed mirrors near the fitting room. When there, the attendant got down onto his knees. "Which side do you dress, sir?"

"Hey?" Tom asked suspiciously. I realised he'd never had a suit measured for him, off the peg or tailored, in his life. Before I could warn him of what was going to happen next with the tape measure about to be thrust up against his inside leg, he jumped away, yelling, "Oi, watch it, an' all. You near on touched my truncheon."

The man sighed. "I did ask you which side you dressed, sir."

"I didn't know what that meant, did I?"

"'E dresses to the left," Mimsee said, the curl of her lip

unmistakable as to her intent. She was in one of her mischievous moods.

Tom looked at her. "How'd you know that?"

"Seen enough of you to know which way you put it in your drawers, 'aven't I?" She giggled.

Again, it was Tom and Mimsee who lightened my mood. I managed a brief smile, even if guilt prickled at the nape of my neck as a result of it.

When Tom was measured, the man selected two matching midnight blue crushed velvet dinner jackets, as Mimsee insisted we look the same. They also had lovely satin facings in a darker shade. The trousers complimented the jackets as did the bow ties.

Mimsee paid for them and asked the attendant to box them up and deliver them to our house by five o'clock, and not a minute later. The attendant assured us he'd have his best delivery boy do so.

Outside once more, the sky had returned to the drab, depressing grey of expectation. A young boy, attired in dirty rags that barely clung to him, bumped into Mimsee as he rushed past.

I believed it was deliberate.

Now, I knew she was wise to the way of street pick-pockets—or dippers, as Tom called them—so her purse would have been secure about her person. What she did reveal knocked me back to the reality of our situation.

"That beggar boy gave me a note, 'e did."

I finally spoke, compelled to do so by some strange force rising within me. "What does it say, Mimsee?"

She opened it. After an agonising pause while she read, she announced, "It says we've got to follow 'im."

Tom took the note off her. "She's right."

Mimsee snatched it back. "Now why would I lie about somethin' like that, Tom?" He shrugged and she frowned at him before turning back to me. "What do you think it all means, Oliver?"

"There's only one way to find out," I said. "We've got to follow the boy."

As luck would have it, the beggar boy was waiting for us at the entrance to an alleyway that led off the High Street. He was gesturing for us to go down into it. Now, I knew of many folks of ill repute or little morals who would lead ladies and gentlemen down into darkened alleyways to rob them of their coins. I didn't believe that was the case here, because the boy went with us. Most would have run away by now, collecting their pennies for a job well done from an accomplice at a safe distance.

What confronted us amongst the filth and debris, nestled within the stench of cesspits and rat holes, was a dirty, soot-stained beggar. The man was too poorly to be anywhere else but in this awful situation. He was also huddled up as if the weight of his circumstance was too much to bear. He hacked a wheezing cough many times.

I winced.

The poor blighter.

The boy went to him, sitting close and comforting him. There was an obvious attachment between them. Perhaps they were father and son.

When the man lifted his head, made aware of our presence by the beggar boy, his identity became apparent. In a million years, and even if Master Xun Xiuying had told me himself who to expect, I would have never believed it.

"Arthur!" Mimsee cried out.

My Talent ignited instantly over my hands, its ethereal blue light ready to strike at my command. Tom's did the same. He came close to me.

Together we'd do what was needed.

What was necessary.

Yet, for the longest time, I stood there unable to bring myself to strike at Arthur in cold blood. He didn't offer any sign that he would defend himself. He didn't even draw upon his own Talent.

Something wasn't right.

Why was Arthur amongst the garbage in the back streets of London? Why wasn't he trying to attack us? He had the perfect opportunity, the best chance he'd get.

Also, who was the boy who cared for him?

I eased my Talent's power.

My mind began to focus on what was presented before me, no longer drawing from my emotional state that seemed to be a whirlwind of late. Tom didn't seem to share my logic, his hands still glowed brightly.

Mimsee, however, was attending Arthur. She wiped his dirty face and broken, blood-stained lips with her laced handkerchief.

I placed my hand on Tom's shoulder. He finally calmed, his Talent withdrawing as mine had.

"It's time for the truth, Arthur," I stated with as much authority as I could muster.

Arthur looked me in the eye. With his voice as coarse as gravel, he replied, "I didn't know it before, because I never knew he'd go this far, but it's my brother Thaddeus who is responsible for all this. He's the one you must seek, Oliver."

Chapter Forty-Two
The Unreliable Records

"Begging your pardon," Tom said, "but what the blazes are you talking about? You're the Skilamalink Man, you are. Admit it!"

Arthur coughed. "I'm no more that evil man than you are…and who are *you*, by the way?"

I realised Arthur hadn't met Tom. "He's my beautiful companion, Tom Arkwright," I said proudly as I held Tom's hand. "And I wouldn't have it any other way, no word of a lie."

Tom squeezed my hand, reinforcing my words as truth.

Arthur looked between us. If I wasn't mistaken, a flash of jealousy flickered over his stare. "You are a very lucky man, Tom, to be with someone as wonderful and caring as Oliver."

Tom was about to answer, but I didn't have time for compliments or even the dance of conversation. I interjected, "We'll take Arthur with us to the house. The beggar boy can come as well. It's high time we got some answers to this puzzle."

I wanted to know more than anything what was going on, but I didn't want to do such a thing in the back alleyways of London. There were always lurkers and opportunists about.

No one argued with me.

If there was a word more powerful than relief at what we'd just discovered, I was at a loss to name it. Arthur wasn't the Skilamalink Man. In response, my Talent returned to its reservoir, resting within me like a beast contented.

For now…

When we were back home, I asked a house servant to fetch

my father and to have her attend us in the study. In Arthur and the beggar boy's state of unkemptness, I didn't think it was appropriate we conferred in the morning room.

Mimsee organised refreshments for our unexpected guests. They both ate what was offered with gusto; not bothering with etiquette, they used their fingers to shovel the food into their hungry mouths. Most of it went down their fronts because of their haste. I ventured to wager it had been a while since either of them had eaten something wholesome, if leftover cold meats, heels of bread, and rinds of cheese from dinner could be considered as such.

A short time later, William burst through the door, my father in tow. Both looked somewhat bewildered by the turn of events, standing stock still by what confronted them.

I knew exactly how they felt.

"What in the hellfire and damnation is going on here?" William spat.

"I beg your pardon, William!" my father snapped, a tone that made him perfectly aware of his language in such mixed company, the boys' presence included in that. William offered his apology.

My father then said, "Tell us this instant, Arthur. What is the meaning of all this?"

Arthur told us his story.

I had to commend him: he didn't falter, even under our keenest scrutiny from numerous prying questions. He kept calm and dignified, as I had known him to be, while he explained to us how his father, the half-brother of Mister Bannister, had two sons.

One from the arrangement between himself and Lady Penelope, the other to a whore with whom the man fell in love with. Both sons were born only ten months apart, but it was

Arthur who was always favoured. He told us that he was the hope of the family, the one who would inherit the wealth.

Thaddeus—the whore's boy as he came to be known—raged with jealousy all throughout his childhood. He was also gifted with the Talent, as strong as ever and able to wield it to his will after teaching himself how to control it. Thaddeus also taught himself how to kill others with his Talent. At first starting with insects, then cats and dogs, and then finally people; folks who he thought had done him wrong or he didn't need anymore.

As Thaddeus grew beyond his childhood years, he planned and planned. While Arthur was given a good education, all the money spent on him to help secure his position and gain favour in higher circles, Thaddeus grew ever darker within his thoughts. One night, in a fit of rage, he murdered their father and his mother, the whore, in their bed.

It seemed to me that things came to a head when he murdered my parents for a debt my father couldn't pay back to him, and I found myself adopted by Lady Penelope through his own uncle's doing.

Thaddeus felt betrayed because I was taken in by Arthur's mother, something he had always wanted.

As such, Thaddeus began to take measures so he could take over Arthur's life. Seek the ultimate revenge to gain what he believed was rightfully his. Arthur told us that the night he returned home after he'd asked me to supper was when Thaddeus seized his moment and revealed to Arthur his plans.

Up until that point, Arthur assured us he'd been told his mother had died after his birth, as Lady Penelope had been told he'd died. It was then Arthur knew of Thaddeus's plan—to gain everything.

Arthur escaped his brother's Talent-lightning by a hair's breadth, jumping out of the window and fleeing to the point of exhaustion. He was found the next morning by the beggar boy; a boy who, for some reason, looked after Arthur.

"Why didn't the Parish record Thaddeus' birth?" I asked.

I already knew the answer, though. As I had suspected, the churchwarden could have easily been bribed to omit certain details. Or threatened with death, which was more likely. Arthur confirmed my suspicions. The original account of his birth had been burned, probably by Thaddeus' Talent. The copy that was given to the Bishop, as was expected and required by Easter week each year, had the omission within it.

No one would know of Thaddeus; Arthur would be the one they would blame if an investigation was undertaken. As we'd blamed him once we discovered the link.

A link I now knew was in error, thank goodness.

"I believe you have spoken enough, Arthur," my father stated politely. "I would like you to stay here as our guest, and the boy who helped you as well. I'll get the house servants to show you to a bath and attend you both. Fresh clothing and a meal will also be my honour to provide. You have been a good friend to me over the years, Arthur. I have gained much this day from what I thought was devastation. I have another son, and for that I am grateful."

Arthur looked relieved. "With your adoption to Lady Penelope, it seems to me we are some strange measure of a family, Oliver."

"Strange or not, family is about people who care for one another in a way that transcends their status of birth or their circumstances," I told him.

Arthur smiled. I could plainly see the cuts across his forehead and nose where he'd smashed through his window to escape Thaddeus. "I suppose if that's the case, you won't be dancing for me anymore."

I didn't know whether that was a jest or not, considering the revelation I just spoke and what had happened between us in the past. With careful consideration, I uttered, "No, I won't be."

Before that course of conversation could continue to its fullest conclusion, the beggar boy spoke through a mouthful of bread, "Name's Oscar."

I turned my full attention to the beggar boy, smiling. "Tell me, Oscar. Most folks of the street would have robbed Arthur and left him for dead. Why didn't you?"

The boy shrugged, "'Cause I didn't."

And that was the truth of the boy's heart. He had nothing, yet still gave to another for the simplest reason: to offer a helping hand to someone in greater need than himself. That was the courage of a Saint as far as I was concerned, especially for someone who lived on the streets.

Mimsee went to hug Oscar. "'E's just adorable. I could eat 'im all up, I could." For a moment Oscar looked horrified, until he must have realised Mimsee's words were nothing more than the clucking of someone enamoured by a good-natured soul.

Once the house servants had escorted Arthur and Oscar from the study, to help clean them up and attire them in fresh clothes as instructed, William said, "I suppose this Thaddeus fellow is the real Skilamalink Man, and he's the one waiting in Arthur's house for us this evening. Like a spider waiting to catch his flies within his web, I'd say."

I glanced at the mantle clock.

It was almost five. Because of the supper that had been arranged, there wasn't a client for Tom and me to entertain that evening. We had the night off. I considered that supper was usually served any time between six and eight, so we had a lot to do and not much time to do it in.

I took Tom's hand, we excused ourselves, and together we

retired to our chamber. We had to prepare for what lay ahead of us. Mimsee attended us, as she always did.

Thaddeus would soon have a lot to answer for.

Chapter Forty-Three
Oliver's Inheritance

The journey to Arthur's detached bungalow on the outskirts of the housing boroughs of London was a sombre affair. It was raining. It was also painfully cold. Our new dinner jackets required us to wear thick overcoats to stay warm.

Tom shuffled close to me.

To my other side, Mimsee sat. In the carriage seat opposite, were William, my father, and Arthur. The other peelers rode in a separate coach.

The beggar boy, Oscar, remained at the house. I was told Cook took an instant shine to him. Which of course had nothing to do with the flurry of compliments the boy gave to her cooking as he wolfed down everything offered. My father promised him a job within the household…as an errand and house boy.

I smiled at that.

"You never had the Talent, Arthur?" Tom asked, breaking the silence—one which thankfully wasn't strained.

Arthur replied, "I did have it long ago, but it was only very weak. It was lost to me soon after I married, and we had a child together. But, as you've no doubt been informed, it was a waste for all of us, because my Talent was taken away from me as they were taken by Scarlett Fever. I now have nothing."

"I didn't know that," Tom said. "I'm sorry, truly I am, to hear such a thing."

I put my hand on Tom's knee to reassure him; it wasn't his

fault he hadn't been told. He placed his hand over mine, warming me.

Arthur half-frowned, half-smiled. "You're a good man, Tom. Look after Oliver."

"That's my intention for the rest of my days, it is."

When we arrived at our destination, to say it was an anti-climax would have been an understatement. The house was dark. No one was in attendance. I noticed the smashed window off the drawing room. Arthur went inside his home with William and the other peelers.

My father, Mimsee, and Tom remained with me outside under the protection of the porch. The rain hadn't eased.

Pinned to the front door was a note. *My dearest Messrs Merritt and Arkwright, the chase is not yet over, and the game is about to change. Keep your peckers up, because you'll need it. Yours, your eternal nemesis, Thaddeus Drummond, aka, SM.*

"He mocks us!" I shouted with frustration and consternation. "The lickspittler of a man mocks us!"

I gave Tom the note. His words were a little bit more colourful than mine once he'd read it. "Lawks and damnation to my blood. That bastard with his bollocks hung so low on him, his tackle has probably shrivelled up to nothin' but a nub. A right bloody rantallion he is, I wager!"

"Gentlemen! Watch your language," my father said scoldingly. "He's our enemy, that much is certain, but there's no use cursing at him until the Devil can hear. We must remain civilised, as to be anything else would be to stoop to his level. And we will not be like that under any circumstances."

I apologised, as did Tom. But I burned inside. Thaddeus was playing with us, goading us, and trying to keep us off-balance.

What's more, he was succeeding.

Every time we seemed to get close to him, he was one step ahead. That burn became anger. Anger for him and all he'd done.

"Tom's right, though," Mimsee said bringing me back from my reverie. "Bet 'e's got small tackle on him. That one's a right nutter, more than likely 'cause of his inadequacies, I'd say."

My father shot Mimsee a glance of daggers. Mimsee shut her mouth instantly, adding no more to her words. At that moment Arthur, William, and the three peelers emerged from within the house.

"No one's in there," William said, stating the obvious.

I had a thought. "Arthur, who's the one who'll benefit by inheriting all your wealth…if something happens to you, that is?"

Arthur seemed to hesitate, probably to gather his own thoughts. "It all just seems so silly now but I felt lost for such a long time without really understanding why. It's hard to describe, but I knew a piece of me was missing. I was never told you were my mother, Lady Penelope." His voice began to break under the weight of twenty-one years of emotion.

Lady Penelope, my father, embraced Arthur. They stood together, her arm in his, as true mother and son. With her other arm, see took in Mimsee, Tom and I. We were all her family, the relief upon her face plain to see even in the darkness of early evening.

The rain eased.

We returned to our coach.

Arthur hadn't answered my question, but I had a feeling that once we were in the privacy of the coach's cabin proper, he would talk.

My suspicion was correct, as always.

He took a breath. "It is easy to judge with the benefit of hindsight, but I believe my father was haunted by his decision. There was no doubt he wanted your wealth, Mother, as well as his own. He spoke to my uncle about it often. I didn't understand the connection until recently, but I now know that was why my uncle became your lawyer—to set things into place. But my father also wanted to forget about what had happened. Bury the bitter past forever, as it were. Perhaps it was his guilt as to why he asked my uncle to draw up the documents that would ensure Oliver and Mimsee would inherit your wealth once they had been adopted by you."

"You may be right," my father offered.

Arthur continued, "However, the past wouldn't remain buried. As Thaddeus grew, it became clear my brother inherited my father's greed. He wanted everything my father was too afraid to give him, no matter the cost. There had been hurdles set before him, thanks to my father's change of conscience. But that wouldn't matter. My brother likes a challenge, as you all well know."

"Let me get this straight," William said. "If Thaddeus gets rid of you, he gains the wealth of two families?"

"It's not quite that simple. You see, my wealth was my own through my own hard work. And it certainly wasn't my doing that Thaddeus murdered our father and I was his sole heir."

My father, always quick to assess any situation, said, "In your kindness to me, you had your uncle draw up the documents that would have you bequeath all of your wealth and all your worth to Oliver and Mimsee, didn't you?"

Arthur nodded. "It was the only way I could make amends for my father's treachery against you once I discovered it. Treachery that also deprived me of being with you for all those years as well."

Tom said, "What you're saying is that Thaddeus has to get rid of us all to get anything because of what you did, Arthur. Sounds like motive to me, it does."

"Oh, it certainly does," William agreed.

It was arranged that Arthur would stay with us in the house's guest suite. He said he didn't want to return to his home. Not yet.

Later that evening, Tom and I were getting ready for bed. We had been holding hands and kissing. Enjoying the only touch we could afford. As usual, my urges rose quickly because of it, and I suggested to him that we explore each other with our Talent once more. Tom agreed enthusiastically with more kisses.

We were about to remove each other's nightshirts, when there was a knock at our chamber door.

"Enter." My frustration was tainted darkly in that one word.

Arthur came in. He must have seen our interest in each other as plainly as the noses on our faces, because he coughed into his hand. "I'm sorry, I didn't mean to intrude. I can see you in the morning, Oliver. When it's more convenient."

Tom said the most surprising thing I've ever heard him utter, voice tainted with lust and almost breathless. "If you're coming in, sit down and be quiet. Me and Oliver have got to get on with it now we've started."

Chapter Forty-Four
The Talent's Madness

After my initial shock, I didn't get much time to argue the point. Tom was obviously driven by his awakening carnal needs, and I couldn't blame him. He had grabbed the bottom of my long nightshirt and pulled it up over my head as quickly as you please. I was both surprised and aroused by him taking control of the situation.

Tom discarded my clothing onto the floor. My interest was apparent and getting more so as Tom disrobed himself. Arthur, now seated, gasped at the sight of him. He was clearly impressed by what he witnessed. The only thing Tom and I wore in Arthur's presence was our lust-filled smiles.

Mine for Tom; his for me.

In an instant, we were lying side by side on our bed. We kissed. I called forth my Talent, as did he. Soon, we were exploring each other with our magic. With plenty of groaning, my hands fisted and bunching sheets, I writhed and arched my back as my mouth fell agape with my ecstasy.

I was quivering all over. In raptures of bliss, of agony, aching and yearning, as we touched each other deeper and deeper. It wasn't the same as actual physical love, skin against skin, but I had come to accept that this was the best we could do for each other.

Acceptance that I let take me away.

After my reward came from me, and with sweat beading on

my brow, breathing hard, I reached for a handkerchief. There weren't any on the nightstand as per usual.

There was a moment of puzzlement. Had Mimsee forgotten to replace those we'd used earlier?

Arthur gave me one of his with a wink and a beaming smile. He'd already wiped himself. Surprisingly, before he buttoned up his trousers, I noticed he was uncircumcised.

Perhaps in the rush to hide him from Lady Penelope at his birth, such considerations of his status in society and the expectations of having him circumcised as a result were overlooked.

Tom must have noticed as well. "Your tackle's not cut, Arthur. I thought all the toffs got it done." His words held no malice.

"Why?" Arthur must have decided to accommodate Tom's uniqueness of observation. "Did you not like what you saw, Tom?"

Tom shrugged. "Oh, it's all right, if you've gotta know. Enough there to do what's needed of it, I'm sure. But I much prefer Oliver's."

"Glad to hear it."

I laughed. Tom was unique, I'll give him that. For making me smile, I kissed him. His warm, red lips were a pleasure against mine.

When done, and with Arthur's eyes wide at the sight of us sharing the only truly intimate contact we dared attempt, I decided to change the subject. "What did you think of the way we enjoy each other because we have the Talent?"

"I do believe that was one of the most beautiful things I have ever seen," Arthur replied.

At that moment, I could see the resemblance to his mother I had noticed when I'd first met him but at the time hadn't made the connection of family.

"It's also a curse," I stated.

Arthur tilted his head to show his understanding. "I know."

Tom asked, "Do you think that's why your brother's gone as mad as a hatter? Because he can never be loved—not unless he finds someone who has the Talent and he can do with them like how me and Oliver do it, I mean?"

"You may have a point, Tom. He never allowed me to show him any affection. Come to think of it, he never wanted it from his mother or my father either. He was a loner, always in his chamber plotting and mumbling to himself. You are right; I think he is mad…in a strange, depraved sort of way."

When we'd cooled enough and returned to our nightshirts, Tom, never one to keep from blurting out the questions that came to the forefront of his mind, asked, "Why is it you like the lads now, Arthur? I thought you said you were married and had a child?" The question wasn't said in any way to judge to my hearing. Tom never judged anyone, least of all those he liked. He must have liked Arthur to want to share with him what he'd allowed him to witness.

Arthur became reserved, but I knew etiquette demanded he must answer a question posed to him. "I believe one should fall in love with the person, not their gender. When I was younger, a girl stole my heart. Now she's gone, and my heart is available once more. If fortune finds me, be they a man or a woman, then it will not matter. I will love them for who they are."

It was through his words that I realised Arthur really had loved me, and his intention was to court me for his affection. The supper invitation was the beginnings of that journey. If Tom hadn't arrived to sweep me off my feet, then things could have gotten very complicated. Arthur might not be related to me in any possible way, but due to circumstances of fate, he was inevitably part of my family now.

I said solemnly, "You mean much more to me now than

what I believed possible, Arthur. But now it's different. We can't linger in the past if we are to make a better future for ourselves."

"I tend to agree," Arthur said.

I had a feeling that from then on, he wouldn't want to watch Tom and I again when we were intimate. At that moment, everything changed. It was for the best, for all of us.

Tom and I talked with him for another hour or so, if not more. Finally, after Arthur left us, I kissed Tom goodnight. We held hands while I dove into the depths of sleep, my dreams filled with how fortune had turned to give us back Arthur.

As I came to the edge of unconsciousness, a voice pierced my mind. It was like the shrill cry of a distant kestrel searching for prey. It sounded its warning to me. Tomorrow, I knew within my bones but couldn't venture a guess as to why, there would be the change in the game that Thaddeus had promised.

I hoped I was ready for it.

Chapter Forty-Five
Han and Tao's News

The next day, Mimsee wrinkled her nose up at the soiled handkerchiefs on the nightstand. "Boys!" she muttered as she drew the drapes and opened the window.

The dull, dreary light outside crept lazily into our chamber, as if it needed waking as we did.

"Mimsee, how early is it?" My mind was still a muddle from the Talent-touch love Tom and I shared last night.

She didn't answer straight away, still fussing about the chamber. She opened the window wider. "Oh, Lord Almighty, I can't 'alf smell that you've both been knockin' about with your Talent in 'ere. Best you both be gettin' out of that bed so I can strip it down. Those sheets'll need washin' as well."

Tom yawned, stretched, then smiled when he looked upon me. "What's going on, then?"

"We've been given our orders."

Tom looked at Mimsee. "Oh, right."

She was standing over us, hands planted firmly on her hips. "Say, there's three handkerchiefs dirtied by gushin's 'ere."

Not a lot got past Mimsee. After all, it was her keen eye and sharp mind that found the entry we required within the mess of those Parish Registers. Sure, she had to go down on the Bishop like we'd practised on those courgettes, but she wouldn't let anything stand in the way of achieving what she wanted.

Tom was relieving himself into the chamber pot, his flow

loud against the porcelain. "That'll be Arthur's mess, that would," he chimed in without turning around.

"Arthur came in 'ere last night?" Mimsee questioned, sounding scandalised. "Didn't take 'im long, did it? You watch him, Oliver. 'E's got the eye for you. You've got Tom now, and Arthur's got to know that."

I felt the need to explain, as I didn't want Mimsee to get any ideas. "It's all right, Mimsee. It's—"

"We gave him an eyeful of what we do." Tom now turned after completing his morning duty, shaking the dripping off his gentleman's asset. "Then we gave him his marching orders. It's all sorted, Mimsee."

After consideration, I don't think I could have said it better myself. Tom, like Mimsee, had a very special way of looking at the world. Lord Almighty, I loved them both so much.

Mimsee relaxed. "Arthur does love you, you know."

I looked her in the eye, they were dazzling hazel against her smooth, dark skin. "He's not the only one."

A wicked grin curled her lip. "Can't imagine for the life of me why I do, though. You'll only be pretty for so long, Oliver, you will. Then it'll be over between us. I only go for the ones with tight backsides and 'ard truncheons."

"I'll always be with you, Oliver." Tom was climbing into his morning suit's trousers. "No matter how flabby your buttocks get or soft your truncheon goes."

I didn't know whether to be offended or gracious. "I think there'll be a few more years yet before anything of mine goes flabby or soft."

Mimsee laughed. "'Ere, you're so easy to catch, you are."

Tom joined in with laughter as well.

After a hearty breakfast, with Arthur joining us but my father absent—which meant she was taking the guise of the Captain to attend to business—Hao and Tan were announced by our new errand-come-house boy, Oscar.

"Got guests!" was the actual announcement, as he burst through the doors of the morning room.

I knew the boy would need to be trained in the ways of etiquette and ceremony, but for now, his brusque delivery would have to suffice. I was pleased to see Hao and Tan so soon.

Until they delivered their news, that is.

After bowing and gesturing in the way that I came to know as the traditional greeting among friends, Hao said, "We know where the serpent's den lies, honourable ones." I knew he was addressing Tom and me. I felt "honoured" just by the mention of the word, let alone the ramifications as to the meaning of it.

"How?" was all I managed before Tan added, "Patience please, Oliver."

I blushed like Tom, but for a different reason.

Hao continued, "We know of the Skilamalink Man's whereabouts, because the Dragon Master took flight last night after he had a vision." I couldn't help but get the feeling that somehow the warning in my mind I'd experienced last night had some connection to what I was hearing now. "He discovered the den within the St. Giles Rookery."

"So that's where my brother has been hiding since he murdered my father and his mother," Arthur proclaimed.

"Easy enough to get lost in there," Tom contributed. "Pa says he only goes into the Rat's Castle if he's got ten men at his back and they're all within whistling distance of each other."

Mimsee added, "Most folks I know who go in there don't come out the same—if at all."

What they were all saying was interesting, but I wanted to know more specifics. Not only did I want to know *exactly* where the Dragon Master had seen the Skilamalink Man, but how did he accomplish such a thing? Did he really take flight and become a dragon?

Before I could question Hao, the Captain entered the morning room. In her disguise, I couldn't fault how good she looked as a man, even in daylight.

"That is good news," my father said. "Thank you, Master Hao. Thank you, Master Tan. You have served the Dragon Master and your father, Mister Okinawa, well with your attention to us." Even her voice was perfect, deep from her chest, not high in her throat. At the same time, it was fluent and practised, not sounding at all like someone putting on a deeper register deliberately.

Hao and Tan bowed.

At that moment, Oscar barged back into the morning room. "Got more guests! Seven of 'em." He turned quickly on his heels and ran back out of the morning room.

My father almost looked shocked by the boy's gross breach in protocol with his unceremonious announcement. I suppressed a smile; Oscar would fit in quite well here. After all, one former beggar boy living in a house filled with orphans, prostitutes, cross-dressers, and mandrakes wouldn't spoil the broth. In fact, I knew he'd add considerably to the dynamics of the house and give it more flavour.

William entered, taking off his tall, hard hat politely. He bowed to Mimsee, offered his hand out to Arthur, and embraced Tom and me. Finally, he came to my father. "Ah, Captain, so good to see you this fine morning. It's been a while."

"Too long," she answered, shaking William's hand, pumping it like a piston as gentlemen did when greeting each other.

Six peelers were behind William. Thankfully, they'd either decided to remain loitering in the foyer or had been ordered to do so. The morning room would have got rather crowded otherwise.

"It's getting like London Bridge Station during Canterbury week in here," Arthur proclaimed.

Mimsee chuckled but didn't speak. I could see her attention was drawn elsewhere. I followed her stare. Through the open door, one of the peelers was studying her, smiling bashfully. He was a blond-haired young man, fetching in his uniform and pleasant to behold.

I leaned over to her, and whispered, "I bet he's got a right big truncheon he'd like to show you." I lavished my words upon her, emulating what she'd spoken to me when I'd first seen Tom.

But Mimsee was always quick, both in wit and guile. "It's a fact a tongue is far better. And by the way 'e poked 'is out at me just then, I know deep in my burnin' shame that 'e can use it all over me."

She seemed to flutter then flush, bringing her hand up to her face to fan herself. I smiled. Good on her. Although, it had to be noted that Arthur was also admiring the young peeler, two high points of colour upon his cheeks.

My mind then went down a very risqué path.

The three of them?

Together?

My private amusement didn't last long.

William stated, "The reason we're here, Captain, is that…well, I think it'd be best if I showed you all. Damned well never seen such a thing in all my days. Scared the bejesus out o' me."

Chapter Forty-Six
The Rookery of the Enemy

Of course, it goes without saying that where William and his squadron of peelers took us was indeed within the rookeries of the East End, namely the St. Giles region.

I rode in a coach with Mimsee, Tom, Arthur, and a couple of peelers. The Captain and William went in the second coach with the rest of his men. He thought it wise we didn't ride without protection, hence the reason we were separated and escorted.

Much to my amusement, the blond-haired peeler found himself between Mimsee and Arthur. I sat, as always, with Tom. An elderly, more experienced peeler, one more interested in dozing off than attending to his duties, made up the third person on our seat.

"What's your name, lovely?" Mimsee cooed flirtatiously.

"Stirling, ma'am," the blond-haired peeler replied. "Stirling Jones."

"That's a very handsome and commanding name," Arthur chimed in, his voice as thick as treacle and smooth as velvet. No thanks to his previous experiences with me, Arthur was no longer a quiet or reserved man when it came to attracting the attention of other men. "Just like you, I feel."

"Yes, sir." Stirling began to fidget. Poor Stirling. I don't know if the lad enjoyed such attention, or he was so out of his league he didn't know what to do other than remain polite. I wanted to give him a gentle warning that he was a mouse being hunted by two cats.

Tom, however, must have seen things differently than me and was far more direct. "So, Stirling. Do you like to play backgammon or are you the type of lad who likes things a bit more traditional between the sheets?"

I witnessed the moment Tom's meaning dawned on Stirling's face. He glanced nervously between Mimsee and Arthur. Stuck between them, he had no way out. He began to perspire.

Rather diplomatically, but with his left leg fidgeting, Stirling uttered, "Begging your pardon, sir, but I can't answer personal questions. I'm on duty."

Arthur shrugged. "We'll just wait until you are off-duty for your answer then, handsome. Isn't that right, Mimsee?"

Mimsee agreed, adding, "When you off the clock then, lovely?"

"Yes, sir, we will. Six o'clock, ma'am."

A lurch of the carriage indicated that not only had we stopped, it also marked the end of our conversation. Seconds later, the coachman opened the door for us.

The terrible stench was the first thing that struck me. If Mimsee complained about how our chamber smelt musty when Tom and I released ourselves after we'd Talent-touched, then the putrid stink that found us was as if a rabid pack of hounds had been copulating with each other all night amongst the rubbish, excrement, mud, and filth of St. Giles. My eyes watered from it, and my mouth stung.

"Lord Almighty, that's more than ripe!" Arthur blanched.

Mimsee covered her mouth with her handkerchief; Tom and I did the same. It didn't really help. Stirling and the other peeler were the first to exit the cabin. I noted, rather gallantly, that he offered his hand to both Mimsee and Arthur in turn to assist them out of the carriage.

Tom assisted me.

To my ear, Tom said quietly, "I reckon peeler Stirling wants both Mimsee's kettle drums and Arthur's white staff together, don't you think?"

I'd say Tom was very observant.

While we clambered our way through the debris that littered the filthy streets, mudlark children, linkboys, urchins, petty criminals, vagabonds, bunters, and street sellers all gawked at us with their beady eyes. Most stares came from behind broken doors attached to dilapidated buildings or from behind crates, under lean-tos, and from inside the tents they called their homes.

The peelers began to whistle at each other as we picked our way through the slum, their signal to keep close. Tom and I did the same. I didn't want to get lost, not in this place.

If the East End was the backside of London, St. Giles was indeed the haemorrhoid-ridden, well used sphincter. Even the London Particular was nastier here, almost an acid yellow in places and as thick as if I were breathing the fumes from Satan's pit itself.

As we proceeded, a bedraggled young woman, wearing tatters and with a face as mucky as the inside of a chimney flue, waddled up to me. She grabbed my arm and I winced.

"Suck on your pipe for a shilling, I can, sweetie," she said with a terrible lisp. She had no teeth. Not at the front, anyway.

I was stunned, and for a moment I stared at her in disbelief. I shuddered. Thankfully, Peeler Stirling swept in and grabbed the poor wretch. "Come on, Miss. Move along. Nothing for you here."

"I'll even swallow your blow for no extra!" she yelled, as another peeler took over, making sure she didn't bother us anymore.

Finally, and with swear words more colourful than what I'd even heard from Tom's lips, she staggered away to melt back into the gloom, filth, and hovels of St. Giles. The Rat's Castle, as Tom referred to it.

"She had no teeth," I finally managed, still somewhat disbelieving as to what had transpired. My jacket's arm had her dirty handprint upon it.

"Don't worry yourself too much, Oliver. She's a blowsy," Peeler Stirling explained. "She probably lost a couple of teeth to circumstance, then chose to pull the rest out deliberately. Gets them more coin if they've got no teeth."

I nodded my understanding. I'd heard of those types of girls...and boys. Never thought I'd ever see one, though.

Peeler Stirling offered a reassuring smile.

Tom came closer. "You all right?" Again, I nodded. I wanted to hold his hand, but now wasn't the time or the appropriate place. Besides, William shouted impatiently for us to get a move on.

When we finally arrived at the scene—a rundown warehouse, to my knowing—I knew why William had never seen the likes of what confronted us, I had to agree wholeheartedly.

There had been a massacre.

Folks had been slaughtered, indiscriminately butchered to pieces.

There was blood. So much blood; legs, arms, heads, innards, everything, everywhere. Men, women, children. All unclothed. All fixed with the look of sheer fright upon their dead, gaunt faces.

I couldn't count how many of them there were, but it would have been more than a hundred, probably two. The stink of the Skilamalink Man's Talent, bitter and ripe and evil, hung in the air even more pervasively than the foulness of St. Giles. This was deliberate, calculated, mass murder. I couldn't think of any other way to quantify it. My mind reeled. I felt overwhelmed.

I lost everything in my stomach.

Mimsee was spared from the horror by not being allowed into the warehouse. The Captain stayed with her, as did the rest of the squadron. A few peelers, brave souls I'd say, stood guard at the entrance ways. None of them faced the carnage.

Tom also vomited. The heaving sound of his expulsion echoed through the warehouse to lend even more disgust to what we saw, if that was indeed possible. I patted him on his back even while my knees felt weak, and everything was becoming all too close. All I could see were the dead eyes of the victims staring up at me. Pleading. Judging me for not having done anything to prevent what had happened to them.

I began to feel claustrophobic despite the vastness of the old warehouse. My throat tightened and I gasped; Tom held me. Now was the most appropriate time for him to do so. His touch was reassuring, but didn't ease my disgust, anger, or disbelief.

"Sorry you had to see this." William came to reassure us both, he was affected, too. The man was quaking. How could anyone not be? "But we need to get the bastard, once and for all."

Tom spat, "We'll get him, Pa. We'll deucing well get him."

Arthur, even though as white as a sheet, must have had insides made of cast-iron because he didn't lose his breakfast. He only stared at what was before him in gaping horror, hand over his mouth. Eventually, he had to turn away.

We all did.

Peeler Stirling handed me a note. I knew the Skilamalink Man, the lickspittler, the murderer, the mad bastard, wouldn't be able to resist boasting about his handiwork.

I was right.

My dearest, Messrs Merritt and Arkwright, welcome to the end game. I hope you like the present I left you. They were a little upset by what I did to them, but they served their purpose. I do have a lot more fun in store for you both very, very soon. Prepare yourselves, gentlemen. Thaddeus Drummond, aka SM.

Prepare ourselves? How could we prepare ourselves if this was the sort of thing we were to face? I didn't get much of a chance to contemplate it any further, as was common lately. A terrible scream pierced the thick, dirty fog-laden air.

My heart sunk when I recognised the voice. Mimsee!

Chapter Forty-Seven
The Luck of the Irish

Tom and I dashed as fast as our legs could carry us out of the warehouse, William, Arthur, and Peeler Stirling in tow. My heart was pounding against the back of my ribs from my sudden burst of exertion.

When outside, my stomach turned with my worst fears. I couldn't see Mimsee or the Captain anywhere.

Once again, to my ever-growing horror of this whole terrible situation, the squadron of peelers who had accompanied us were scattered about the filthy ground. Talent-lightning marring their blue uniforms. All dead. I didn't doubt they'd been killed before they could even cry out in warning.

Then it dawned on me.

The massacre inside the warehouse had been a means to get us into the Skilamalink Man's domain and to serve as a diversion. His intention all along was to take one of us.

Tom gave me a frightful glance, the horror on his face reflecting perfectly how I felt. His hands glowed, as did mine.

"That quim-faced bastard's got Mimsee and the Captain!" The crude statement, spoken as only Tom could, was obvious but needed.

To hear it out loud brought it to vivid reality, bringing my mind into better focus.

William went to one of his men's bodies. It was the elderly peeler, the one who attended us on the way to St. Giles. He didn't look so peaceful now, his face a mask of terror. A note was pinned to his chest; William plucked it up, read it, snorted disdain, then handed it to me.

He didn't look so good.

Tom and I read it together. It contained no formality, just one sentence: *Shaftesbury Avenue, the abandoned flash-house.*

So, that was it, the final move of the game. The Skilamalink Man's lair, as it were.

William said, "Hellfire and damnation, there's no time to call for any more men. We've got to get to that deucing flash-house quick smart if the Captain and Mimsee are going to have any chance at all. Peeler Stirling, it's you and me with our Oliver and my Tom."

"Yes, sir!" Peeler Stirling saluted.

"You've got one more man than you think, Constable." Arthur came into view. He'd picked up a peelers' truncheon, tapping it into the palm of his hand. Determination had struck his steely eyes. Peeler Stirling gave Arthur a knowing smile. Arthur added, "I'm joining you." I caught that the last part was directed more to the young peeler than us.

William obviously wasn't one to refuse help when he required it. "Very well, good sir, you're with us," was his practical response.

I suddenly remembered something important. "Have you got your Dragon Symbol on you, Tom?"

"It's in my shoe," he replied.

Mine was in my shoe as well. Thank the Lord Almighty we'd had the foresight to place them about our person before we ventured out this morning.

"Then we're ready, William, sir," I said.

"Lead the way, Pa," Tom added.

It didn't take long to get to the flash-house on Shaftesbury Avenue. I could see why the building was abandoned; it must have suffered in a recent storm as part of the roof had collapsed to let in the weather. Normally, flash-houses were a hive of activity, mostly run by criminals who employed young boys and girls to expand their business which comprised of stealing anything that wasn't nailed down, including silken handkerchiefs. This one was eerily empty.

"Keep your peckers up, lads." William pushed open the door.

It creaked too loudly. I held my breath.

Inside, the flash-house had been stripped of everything of value long ago. Only crates and boxes remained, scattered about. But the lack of furniture or accommodation wasn't important or what took the very air from my lungs.

High above us, unconscious and surrounded by the blue ethereal haze of Talent, were the Captain and Mimsee. Tendrils of light, their eerie chain and rope, suspending them like they were living chandeliers.

I saw red.

My Talent ignited, stirring my loins despite the Dragon Symbol's controlling influence. I knew I had to calm if I was going to get everyone out of there alive, but my sense of duty to help Mimsee and the Captain was so great it overwhelmed me to the point of madness.

At that moment, I heard Tom gasp, as did Peeler Stirling and Arthur. William uttered his usual curse of hell and damning. They'd seen something I hadn't.

"Now, now, Master Merritt. If you free them they will fall and die," the voice of the Skilamalink Man said, echoing through the abandoned flash-house.

The disgusting evil lickspittler of a man, dressed in his coachman's cloak, the cowl pulled up to hide his face, sat on a chair at the far end of the room. He had one leg crossed over the other, giving the outward appearance of nonchalance. Of arrogance.

My abhorrence for him seethed as much as my Talent.

"Let them go, you rantallion bastard," Tom blurted.

Peeler Stirling produced his cudgel from off his belt's holster. Although, I didn't really expect him to believe such a puny weapon would have any effect here, I appreciated the gesture. William and Arthur came to flank Tom and me.

The Skilamalink Man—nay, Thaddeus Drummond—said, "I can assure you, young Master Arkwright, that I don't possess small tackle."

He stood, removing his cloak with a graceful flick of his wrist. Underneath it, he was dressed in a smart, black pin-striped suit that emphasised his thin frame.

He was Arthur's twin in image.

I had to look between them both to discern any noticeable differences. I found few of any worth, other than Thaddeus had a more prominently beaked nose.

Thaddeus continued, "So, welcome to the end game, gentlemen. And you as well, my dear *brother*. Although, I have yet to reveal my final strategy. Let's change all that shall we? Come in, lads; come say hello to our guests!"

I'd been told St. Giles had a large Irish population. From that, I believed most of its male citizenry swarmed around Thaddeus over the course of the next few heartbeats. To then say they were bruisers would be an understatement. Most were big, barrel-chested men, arms rippling with muscles that looked like horseshoes stuffed into sacks and holding weapons of any and all description from cudgels and maces, to axes and swords.

Many of them had fiery, wild beards, but most were skin-headed or had hair cropped to within an inch of their skull. All of them had scars, some of them still healing.

One bruiser at the front, the largest of them all, was missing an eye. The black hole of it went deep into its socket. I felt unnerved by the sight of them all standing beside our enemy. This wasn't going to be easy, if it ever was.

I swallowed.

"Lawks, they look as tough and ugly as a barrel full of bull's bollocks, that lot do!" Tom stated in his unique way of surmising a situation in a sentence.

Then, the one-eyed thug howled a war cry that shredded my flesh. He raised his cudgel high. At his command, the men surged forward like a strange tide of dirt, sweat, and muscle. Malevolent expressions of deranged delight struck on their faces and all of them yelled feverishly at the prospect of impending violence as they charged toward us.

Tom quickly kissed me on the cheek. "You Defend first, Oliver. I'll Attack. Now!"

As the saying goes: all hell broke loose.

Chapter Forty-Eight
Hell's Release

"Take cover!" Peeler Stirling screamed at the top of his lungs, grabbing Arthur and pulling him away so they were both behind the nearest packing crate.

William dashed to the other side, also finding cover.

Tom, the Lord Almighty above love him as much as I, shot the first volley of Talent-lightning into the oncoming storm. The sheets of it struck more than a dozen men. All those who were hit screamed in agony for a brief, final moment before collapsing onto the dusty floor like marionettes with their strings cut.

Smoke billowed from their chests where it struck. In stark juxtaposition, the stench of burnt clothing and flesh against the sweet smokiness of Tom's Talent was profound within my nostrils.

But Thaddeus' henchmen weren't deterred. They still came, like blind lemmings on a suicide run. Immediately, I called forth my Talent proper, sending up a large defensive web-like shield to protect Tom and me.

"Again, Tom!" I yelled. "Strike them again!"

Tom obliged. No sooner had his hands became aglow, his fingers shot forth more energy. More screams. More men fell. Thaddeus smiled malevolently at the carnage Tom had already created, clearly enjoying how his game was playing out.

A thought struck me.

Thaddeus was holding off; he hadn't struck back. My

stomach turned. I didn't like that. Tom glanced at me, his eyes reflecting my concern.

Tom, hands aflame with tendrils of Talent, goaded, "Come on, you bastard. Get on with it. I can take on any one of your bruisers, I can. If not all of them."

There was no response from Thaddeus, other than an almost imperceptible tilt of his head toward the one-eyed man. Our enemy remained controlled, even with Tom's continued and colourful language taunting him. My curiosity was piqued.

What did Thaddeus have in mind for us?

The one-eyed man raised his hand and yelled something I couldn't understand, but words that must have been a combination of his own tongue and the dialect of the area: St. Giles Greek, I believed it was known.

Tom must have understood the fellow. "Just you try it, you lickspittler!"

When those words were spoken, there was a pause in our battle. Thaddeus' men stood stock still. An eerie silence came over the warehouse like a suffocating blanket.

I took the opportunity to appraise our predicament. William had come to stand behind my Talent shield, brandishing his weapon. Peeler Stirling and Arthur were engaged in melee with four thugs. They seemed to have a handle on things for the moment, because, thankfully, the constabulary had been trained in hand-to-hand combat. Arthur was his capable backup. How long they could hold up, especially if more joined in the fight, I wouldn't venture a guess.

"Bring out the barrels, lads!" Thaddeus said, snapping me back to the moment.

From behind the wall of ugly muscle, there was movement. Seconds later, two burly men, uglier and larger than the one-eyed bastard—if that were at all possible—came to the front of the crowd carrying an oil barrel each. It seemed as easy for them to do as it was for me to carry my stovepipe hat.

The reason for the pause was revealed.

"Gentlemen, it is rather unfortunate for you the Dragon Master didn't give you enough time to tattoo your protective symbol onto your skin." Thaddeus rolled up his sleeve, doing so slowly and for dramatic effect. Tom was right; he really was a rantallion lickspittler. On Thaddeus' arm, inked permanently onto his skin, were Chinese characters. His Dragon Symbol was the Dragon of Change, if I wasn't mistaken. He added, "Now, I do suggest that you both take off your shoes and remove your Dragon Symbols. Otherwise, I don't think things will go so well for you or your friends and family."

My thoughts went to the piece of paper wedged into the heel of my oxfords. My protection, now so revealed, suddenly seemed to be the weakest link in my chain of hope. Something I thought would protect me would not if it were taken away so soon.

William said, "Oi, what the deuce is going to stop you pouring the oil over the floor and igniting it anyway? Even if our Tom and Oliver do as you ask, *Thaddeus*."

To confirm where my train of thoughts were leading me, Thaddeus slowly looked up. Mimsee and the Captain were still wrapped in the cocoon of his Talent. I knew he literally held their fate in his hands. I seethed once more, my Talent burning, my shield's tendrils thickening as the ethereal spider spun more threads to protect us further.

Through my newly fortified web of magic, I saw Thaddeus draw his attention toward his own brother and Peeler Stirling. I followed his gaze and had a feeling the evil man was making his point. He smiled.

What struck me about his theatrics was startling but, considering we were so outnumbered, inevitable. I swallowed hard again. Thaddeus wanted me to know he was the one in control here.

And he was.

To my horror, Peeler Stirling was suddenly on his knees, defeated. A man with potato-sack arms held a knife to the young man's throat. Arthur fared no better: two men held him.

"I believe this is what we call checkmate, Master Merritt—Master Arkwright. How delicious the game was, and you did play rather well, I must say. I do thank you for that. Now, I won't ask you again. Do as I say, and everyone can go free."

"What'll happen to us if we do that?" Tom spat.

"What? No insults that time, Master Arkwright?" Thaddeus tutted. "How unlike you and your muckspout mouth to not speak such filth, now isn't it? However, to be a gentleman and answer your question, I'm going to kill you. And your lover, Master Merritt. And my brother. Although, not necessarily in that order. When that's all said and done, the Captain—or shall we say, Lady Penelope—will be forced to bequeath to me what is rightfully mine. All her wealth and all her fortune. Then I'll do as I promised. But only then."

Tom scowled.

"That's no incentive for us to do as you ask." I withdrew my Talent shield, wanting to strike at him instead. Thaddeus must have calculated my intention, for he gestured up toward Mimsee. The supporting Talent shroud that supported her in mid-air faltered.

She slipped.

By the Lord Almighty, my insides fell with her. If Mimsee was hurt, I don't know what I'd do. I gasped in horror, then cried, "Mimsee!"

At the exact moment of my doing so, Arthur gave a muffled yelp, punched by one of the bruisers in his breadbasket with a sickening blow; he doubled over in agony, coughing up his guts.

"You see, Master Merritt, it's so easy to control this situation. You are my puppet, and I am done with you and those who have hindered my ambitions. I weary of the game. You've lost, and now I want to see you suffer before I dispose of you once and for all." He nodded to the thick-set men who carried the oil barrels. "If they haven't done as I've asked in ten seconds, spill the oil and ignite it. Ten."

I knew he'd do as he'd said. Why wouldn't he? Thaddeus had proven time and time again he would do anything he thought was required to get what he wanted. Arthur was on the floor, spreadeagled; Peeler Stirling had a trickle of blood down the front of his neck; Mimsee and the Captain were taken higher up, the inevitable fall greater when the Talent that held them was released.

"Nine."

Tom blasted more Talent-lightning, but such a move must have been anticipated. The bruisers came to protect the oil bearers, taking the hit for them. More men hit the floor, stone cold dead.

But not those who mattered.

"Eight."

William cried, "You'll pay for this, Thaddeus." It was a rather pathetic, if valiant, attempt at trying to quantify in his own mind the adversity that encroached so heavily upon us all.

"Seven."

I seethed. I aimed my Talent at those before us, together with Tom.

"Six."

More men fell, their charred bodies piling up at the feet of those who quickly replaced them. More than two-hundred ruffians stood before us now.

"Five."

I screamed. "We won't go down easily!" From where that came from, I had no idea.

The stench of burnt flesh found my nostrils again as more and more of my Talent reached out and struck at our enemies' hearts.

"Four."

Tom faltered. He stopped using his Talent.

"Three."

I halted as well. Our efforts hadn't made the slightest impact on the insurmountable odds against us.

"Two."

I grabbed Tom's hand. If we were going to go, if this was the moment of our deaths, I wanted him to know I was with him. Always.

William put one hand gently on my shoulder, the other on his son's. It was his way to show us support. His way of telling us we did our best and that he not only understood, he forgave us as well.

"Time's up, gentlemen."

Chapter Forty-Nine
The Enemy's Depravity

"All right!" I held up my hands; Talent no longer coloured my skin. "I concede. We'll do it. Just give us a moment."

I felt overwhelmed and beaten. My heart had sunk down to the pits of my soul, and my skin crawled with both anger for myself and fear for what was to follow.

Not for me, but for Tom and the others.

"Then do as I ask!" Thaddeus boomed. "This instant!"

He seemed rattled. *Strange.* He'd won. A thought suddenly hit me as clearly as a grandfather clock striking the hour. I found Thaddeus' behaviour interesting. It told me he wanted—no, always needed—to be the one in complete control. If he should lose control…that could be his weakness.

My thoughts swam.

Tom squeezed my hand, bringing me back to the moment. With his simple gesture, I didn't feel like a failure anymore. Far from it. I felt empowered because of the one who stood by my side.

Because of Tom.

I ventured a quivering, nervous, emotion-filled smile, drawing from my companion's strength. "Let's give him what he wants—what he's missed out on all his life." I whispered to Tom.

I bent down, giving the impression I was to remove the Dragon Symbol from my shoe. Instead, I controlled my breathing, centred myself, and called upon the Pleasure and Sight aspects of my Talent.

Tom, as I knew he would, caught on, doing the same. Moments later, ethereal tendrils of our Talent crept their way across the flash-house's floor toward Thaddeus.

Thaddeus' hands ignited, sending sheets of Talent-lightning our way. Most of the energy struck his own men, including those holding the barrels of oil. There were more agonising screams and the warehouse filled with the familiar cries of those about to knock on death's door to go beyond the threshold to the never after.

To my dread, one of the barrels hit the floor with such force it split its contents, sending forth oil in a viscous tidal wave to slick over those unfortunate enough to be near it. That resulted in surprised shouts, something different to the ones of agony beforehand.

Panic began to take over.

Meanwhile, the bruisers in front of Tom and I were touched by our tendrils of Talent. There were gasps, before the men collapsed in euphoric agony as they were caught in that intense moment before coming to their agony of bliss.

They soon joined their fallen comrades who had met their fate against the lightning.

I could see into them with my Talent-touch, and even though they were as tough as brick outhouses, they still had all the urges every man had. I used that knowledge against them, ensuring they would remain incapacitated.

Moments later, my Talent touched Thaddeus.

At the same time as I accomplished my goal, the moment I could see into him to know everything about him, from the colour of his soul that was as dark as Satan's heart, to his carnal desires that were just as depraved, Tom was struck on the shoulder by Talent-lightning.

"Oliver!" he cried.

William rushed to his son's aid. Tom had fallen, but his

father broke his descent. They were both on the dusty floor moments later. William cradled Tom's head, bringing him close and embracing his son.

The senior constable looked up, eyes watery and bloodshot. "Do what you deucing well have to, Oliver! Get that rantallion bastard! I'll see to our Tom."

Tom didn't look good. His face was drained, eyes staring wildly. The jacket at the front of his shoulder had a dark and nasty wet mark upon it, getting larger. Wisps of smoke curling toxically around him.

Tom shuddered, his breathing laboured.

I wanted to go to him. My concentration wavered; I almost lost the thread of my Talent-touch.

Tom, hoarse and with lips quivering from his hurt, stuttered, "I love you, Oliver, I do. But if it's the last thing you do, get that bastard! Make him pay for all he's done, you hear me? Make him pay." He closed his eyes.

A wave of disbelief, anger, and sorrow rose up to strangle me.

I choked.

Tom seemed so helpless in his father's loving arms.

But he was breathing.

Arthur cried out, "Now's your chance, Oliver!" before he was silenced, kicked in the stomach by the men around him.

Peeler Stirling had trails of tears down his cheeks as the knife at his throat bit deeper. His horror plain for all to see.

Mimsee and the Captain were still unconscious and suspended. There was a lot to do, and only I had the opportunity to do it.

I steeled my resolve.

Besides, Tom had said that he loved me. He loved me. In the whole of creation, under the very heavens and across God's green Earth, those words from him meant everything to me.

"Time to change the game, Thaddeus," I growled, even if what I was about to do was the absolute last thing I wanted to do with our enemy. Talent-touch should only be about love, because that's all two people of the Talent can do together to show physical affection. I couldn't touch Tom like normal folks did, so we Talent-touched. That was our intimacy, the one thing that was special between us.

I didn't want to do such a thing with Thaddeus.

Swallowing hard, I steeled my resolve again. For my love of Tom, I had to do what was needed. Had to do what I knew could save us if it worked. My nerves struck me. I was going to Talent-touch with my enemy to see deeply into him, to know all his desires. But hopefully such a thing would weaken him, as it did when I was overwhelmed by the Sense and Pleasure aspects of the Talent.

Again, I swallowed.

This was it.

I gave my all, reaching down deep within the man to touch him where he'd kept himself hidden, secreted away his true urges so he could fuel his hate and ambition without hindrance. I could feel him stirring, become aroused, and I concentrated on that. It was like trying to throw a thimble-full of water into a raging furnace of hate to try and quell it, but I persisted. Determination was my strength now, pouring even more of my energy into my effort.

He hardened, as did I.

I became uncomfortable and hot. To be like that with my enemy, linked in a way I'd only been linked with Tom before, caught me off-guard by how potent it was. How unnerving it became as it shredded at my thoughts and emotions.

To know Thaddeus' desires intimately, to discover he'd been with his mother in an inappropriate manner—using his Talent to do so—sickened me. I was shocked by my discovery, unable to get out of my mind the image of them together.

I stalled.

Disgusted and feeling dirty, I almost lost my hold upon him again.

"You are a lickspittler, in every sense of the word!" With my determination to end him doubled, I didn't lose the connection, but gave him everything I had.

Thaddeus' eyes went wide with disbelief. He gasped. Just when I thought I almost had him to conclusion so I could attack, when I thought I could get him to lose complete control and render him useless, the hell that had broken loose previously got far worse.

As I myself came to full engorgement—my Dragon Symbol unable to calm me enough because of what I'd discovered—somehow the oil that had been spilled over ground and flesh alike was ignited.

A wall of flame whooshed up before me. I staggered back. Heat and ash and the stench of cooked flesh and the filthy clothing it was wrapped in suffocated me. I recoiled and coughed. There were more screams of agony.

A few of the bruisers stumbled out of the flames aimlessly, macabre in their death dance, like the Burning Man effigies set on fire during Guy Fawkes Night.

My Talent lost its hold.

Because of my failing, Thaddeus let Mimsee and the Captain fall.

Thaddeus immediately sent forth more of his lightning while I scrambled as best I could to both compose myself and try and save Mimsee and the Captain. I managed to dodge the Talent-lighting within an inch of its scorching touch, rolling onto the floor, my shoulder bursting with pain as I did so. I had no time to consider myself. I was only just able to cushion Mimsee's fall with the Sight aspect of my Talent, solidifying it so its tendrils became an extension of my hands to take her weight.

"Father!" I shrieked as she disappeared into the crowd of thugs, vagabonds, and rogues from the fall.

I was gutted, as if my whole insides had been ripped out of me. What made it worse was the fact I couldn't see if she was injured. It hurt me because I didn't know. Hurt me so deeply my soul was cut, scarred forever.

How could I have let this happen?

I didn't get time to contemplate my feelings or thoughts. Thaddeus sent more lightning toward me. I had to let go of Mimsee to avoid being struck.

She was still unconscious.

Many weren't as fortunate as I. More of his own men were felled like trees; screaming stilted cries of agony and disbelief before their eternal silence took hold. Those around the freshly fallen men went quickly from panic to anger. The crowd of thugs surged forward with a new determination, weapons brandished. The tide of muscle was once more heading toward me.

The enemy was at the advantage, for I was alone against them.

Chapter Fifty
The Failing of the Flesh

Alone or not, I had to prevail.

Again, Talent-lightning scorched everything around me, the stench of pipe smoke rife in the air and as thick as the London Particular. Through some miracle, I remained unscathed as I dodged it, using my Talent-shield as best I could. Also, through some miracle, and to my surprise, after I'd used so much Talent, I hadn't come to a sticky end.

Not yet anyway.

Unfortunately, I didn't get much time to assess how anyone else was faring. Not that I could anyway. My Talent-touch must have infuriated Thaddeus. He was striking out belligerently at me and anyone before him, my world a haze of destruction and a mist of blood. My enemy's face became a strange, twisted mask, taking on a macabre, sinister form like that of a Plague Doctor of old.

A few of Thaddeus' minions who'd escaped his wrath tried to grab me. I learned, very quickly, to use one hand to strike with my Talent-lightning, while the other kept up my shield. It was as if I were a knight from the days of yore, but instead of weapons of combat, traditional or otherwise, I wielded magic.

Sure, my hardness raged despite my Dragon Symbol, but I didn't have much time to consider such discomfort. A strange confidence empowered me. Perhaps I had a chance here.

I stood up defiantly.

By heaven, if I were to tackle Thaddeus' army on my own, then so be it. I was ready. I shored my footing, able to stand steady without too much discomfort, while keeping away those who got near at the same time.

Unfortunately, just as I gained an ounce of confidence, as it always happened, the game changed yet again.

More men of ill-breeding and little education in the queen's English, poured into the flash-house to replace the fallen. Once more, I was hopelessly outnumbered. I cursed under my very breath, as Tom would in the same pickle.

And a devil of a pickle it was, too.

Thaddeus must have considered his fresh recruits as nothing more than cannon fodder, for he continued to strike out with his Talent. Even more men screamed and died, creating a confusing cacophony of wails, yells, and screams with bodies going every which way, including into the air.

To my astonishment, even more men came into the flash-house.

This was going to be another massacre in the making.

I couldn't contemplate such matters, the scale of it too large to comprehend. I had to remove any thoughts that weren't important, those that only served as a distraction. I needed to get to those who mattered the most to me.

I turned away from the carnage, but not before placing a protective shield around Tom and his father. No one could get to them, with either magic, cudgel, or fist.

That comforted me.

Another comfort was that I had drawn everyone's attention.

I could no longer see Mimsee and my father as every bruiser charged toward me, wanting my blood. I presumed they were still unconscious, but there was too much going on for me to go help them just yet. I hated that but had no choice. Besides, my hope was that they would be left alone until I could get to them.

That left Arthur and Peeler Stirling.

I made my way over to them, dispensing with the man who

held the knife at Peeler Stirling's throat with a swift flick of my hand and strong command of my Talent. The man I struck dropped. Peeler Stirling gasped, grabbing his neck. Blood slicked his fingers, but he nodded his thanks and told me he was all right.

Together we set upon those holding Arthur.

The Talent-lightning from Thaddeus still stormed around us. Many times, it sizzled close to my ear. One time, while I attempted to dodge it, I tripped on a dead man. The lightning caught my shoe. I looked at my foot where it should have been.

Horror gripped me.

It was the shoe that held my Dragon Symbol. I could see the singed paper on the floor not more than a few feet away.

What Thaddeus couldn't get me to do before became a reality.

At that very moment, I knew my Talent use needed to be limited if I wanted to remain useful. "Stirling! Help Arthur. I've got to try and stop Thaddeus again so I can get to Mimsee and the Captain."

Peeler Stirling had picked up his cudgel and was smashing it into skulls. The sound of bone being splintered joined the soundscape of death all around me. That gave Arthur the chance to get up.

Once more, Peeler Stirling and Arthur were fighting together, standing back-to-back, working as a team. I knew they'd be all right.

I returned my attention to Thaddeus.

The man was irate. Bodies were piled at his feet, but he used more and more lightning to strike out. Again, I did my best to avoid it. I had no choice but to use my Talent to attack the men he sent to kill me. I hoped my body would last long enough even with my excessive Talent use.

As if to reinforce my fears, Thaddeus said, "You haven't the stamina nor the control of your body to keep going, Master

Merritt. Your training is incomplete. The Dragon Master failed. You've failed."

I closed my eyes for the briefest moment, coming to a decision. If I was going to fail, then I would let it be spectacular. I composed myself, gathering my Talent's strength. Once more, I sent out the Sight and Pleasure aspects of it toward Thaddeus. With every passing moment I used my Talent in such a way, I felt myself succumb to my own failings. My gentlemanly asset ached and pressed harder against my drawers. I groaned, feeling the weight of my inevitable conclusion consume me.

But I persisted.

My Talent almost reached Thaddeus...

I didn't last as long as I hoped.

With a frightful shudder that marked my ending, my ejaculate gushed forth, sending waves of both euphoria and dread surging through me. I buckled at my knees, collapsing into a tangle of post ecstatic uselessness.

My Talent withdrew.

Thaddeus had me.

His frenzy of lightning stopped. Moments later, through the muddle of my mind and blurred vision, he came over me. His cruel smile almost made me retch.

"Just make it quick," I begged.

"You're in no position to make requests of me, Master Merritt."

I groaned again. My bollocks ached unbelievably, as did everything else from one end of me to the other, including all my insides. The effect of all the Talent use once the Dragon Symbol no longer protected me had struck me all at once. I needed to recover. I wanted to sleep.

I was sure Thaddeus would make that permanent.

"Then do what you have to," I whispered, no longer capable of doing anything but utter those few words.

His hands began to glow. "It has been amusing, I must admit. But with you out of the way, there will be one less obstacle for me to overcome, and I'll be a step closer to fulfilling my plan. Good day, Master Merritt. Perhaps we'll meet in another place and time…"

Chapter Fifty-One
The End Game

"'Ere!" A familiar voice rang out, echoing through the flash-house to reverberate in my disbelieving ears. "You leave our Oliver alone, you damned muck-sniper!"

I managed to turn my head toward the voice. My eyes widened and my mood brightened. By the Lord Almighty, what I saw filled me with hope and ignited a small semblance of strength inside me.

Mimsee!

There she was, hands on her hips, the look of a freight train upon her. She stood at the entrance to the flash-house. Not only that, Hao and Tan, and more than one hundred of their Chinese friends were with her.

I'd never witnessed anything so wonderful.

"This can't be!" Thaddeus proclaimed, seemingly as startled by her sudden appearance as I was. "Get them, lads! Get them!" He called forth his Talent-lightning once more.

To say hell had broken loose before was incorrect and an error on my part. Now it was like every demon and cursed soul from the deepest pits of Satan's boudoir, their eternal damnation prior to this moment spent copulating in the most depraved ways unimaginable, had crawled up to seek revenge for what had condemned them. The flash-house exploded into a mess of limbs, weapons, fists, head-butts, kicks, swearing, and more terrible screams of the discontented.

Thaddeus' face twisted in anger as the Irish and the Chinese fought.

But that small spark of life Mimsee had gifted me, as she always did when I was at my lowest, gave me enough strength to do something I would have never dreamt of under ordinary circumstances.

I awkwardly heaved myself up to my feet, eventually becoming stable. Thankfully, my action wasn't noticed. Not until it was too late, anyway. While Thaddeus was busy killing folks indiscriminately with his lightning, I punched him right in his breadbasket, striking him as hard and true as I could possibly manage.

My fist burst with pain as my knuckles sunk deep into the spot just below his sternum. With a great exultation of air and shock, he doubled over.

His Talent was silenced.

"You didn't defend yourself properly, lickspittler," I spat. "We may not have tattoos like you, but the lessons we were taught by both the Dragon Master and Lady Penelope—*my father*—were to improvise if required."

I stood stock still, staring down at what I'd done with my physical self, something that my Talent couldn't have achieved.

How was that for lateral thinking? "Check mate," I added.

My father and Master Xun Xiuying would be proud.

Before Thaddeus was able to right himself, Arthur came to finish what I'd started. A couple of uppercuts later, his brother was spreadeagled on the floor, out cold.

Peeler Stirling handcuffed the bastard.

I was done. I felt weak once more now that I had spent absolutely everything within me, my gentlemanly parts in absolute agony and my body sore to my bones.

Arthur offered me his hand.

I accepted it just to keep myself upright.

All around us the Irish bruisers were scattering, charging out the exits as fast as their legs could carry them. The Chinese men who aided us had outclassed and outfought all who opposed them, using their rather stunning martial arts skills. Their moves were like watching a dangerous dance. I was glad they were on our side.

"Take me to Tom please, Arthur," I said, my voice as weak as the rest of me.

The shield I called upon for Tom to protect him and his father was gone, as was inevitable after I came to my gushing. William's emotions were running down his cheeks.

"I can't wake my Tom," he said, pain thick in his voice.

Hao and Tan rushed to my side, concern greater than I understood drawn across their brows. Hao said, "We must take the honourable Tom to my father. He will draw out the poisonous Talent of the enemy from within him."

I couldn't argue with that. I only hoped we weren't too late. Tom now looked worse by my reckoning; dark circles under his eyes, his lips blue, and his skin cold and clammy to my touch.

Tan uttered something in his language to a few of his friends close by. In an instant, Tom was lifted by many gentle hands.

Mimsee joined me, grabbing my other arm.

I didn't need her to do so but appreciated her gesture all the same. Mimsee was fantastic, she really was. The sight of Tom being carried away, so helpless and vulnerable, made my own concerns feel as if they were fog burnt away by the sun.

Besides, I was regaining my strength…slowly. "How did you…I thought you were unconscious, Mimsee? Where's Father?"

Mimsee replied, "I don't righty remember everythin', but I do know I woke up next to 'er. Then, blow me down, four of those bruiser boys 'elped us. It was a right shock, let me tell you. They were sayin' they caught Father, because you'd already caught me with your Talent. I've got to thank you for that, Oliver." She pecked me on my cheek, her touch as warm as her soul.

"You don't have to thank me." Her thanks were never expected; I'd do anything for her.

"Then those lovely boys made sure we weren't hurt while they 'elped us escape. Told us they didn't like Thaddeus. Scared of 'im, they were. 'E'd threatened to kill their families if they didn't do what 'e wanted. So, they escorted us back to the 'ouse like real gentlemen—Father might be tuckin' into a hot dinner as we speak if they got 'er a Hansom Safety Cab there."

"I take it you made some new friends, then."

She winked. "They make 'em big out 'ere in Rat's Castle, don't they? Those boys have arms as thick as lampposts. But I've got to say, one of 'ems not 'alf bad on the eye. Got 'air as dark as crow's feathers, just like yours. Right good looker as well." In a lower voice, she added, "Might even let 'im give me one if he plays 'is cards right. Those lads have right whoppers like yours, they do."

I couldn't help but smile. "Mimsee, you're one in a million."

We were escorted through the filthy streets to waiting coaches by Hao and Tan. A dozen or so peelers had arrived on the scene. Thaddeus, still unconscious, was being hauled away.

Soon the clip-clop of hooves against cobblestones indicated we were on our way to Mister Okinawa's apothecary-cum-pharmacy shoppe. And not a moment too soon.

Mister Okinawa was waiting for us, looking like a doting father. Tom had faded in and out of consciousness during our journey, moaning in pain through dry, cracked lips. He was carried into Mister Okinawa's private chamber, stripped down to his undergarments, and placed onto his back on the treatment table. With the extent of the Talent-lightning burn evident across his shoulder, still wet and oozing, the strange custom of cupping and blood release began.

Mister Okinawa, once he'd cut Tom, placed the final set of cups across Tom's chest and all down his abdomen, almost to his fiery red pubic hair that was visible above the waistline of his drawers. To experience a thing and to watch a thing were two different matters entirely. I stood amazed, holding Tom's hand firmly to let him know I was with him.

The cups began to fill with Thaddeus' foul Talent.

The evil that had poisoned Tom was slowly being drawn out.

William was by Tom's other side, and Mimsee next to me. I didn't know where Arthur and Peeler Stirling were, but I suspected they'd make sure Thaddeus was taken away without incident. I hope they'd keep the bastard in a straight-jacket and put him in a cell with no way out, not even by magic.

When Mister Okinawa was done, the cups removed to leave perfect red circular marks on his fair skin, Tom improved. He opened his eyes. My spirit lifted and I felt a great sense of relief wash over me.

"Did we win?" Tom croaked.

"We won," I replied.

"That's good. 'Cause if we hadn't, I might have been a bit miffed."

I laughed, leaning down to kiss him tenderly on his lips. "Lord Almighty, I love you so. You know that?"

"Good thing you do. I wouldn't let any ol' good-looking lad kiss me. Not right on my gob, anyway." Tom was brightening further. His skin gained colour and his cheeks reddened. Even the freckles across his nose and shoulders darkened to their usual healthy tint. "And I love you, an' all, Oliver. I know that with all my heart, I do."

"That's so sweet, that is," Mimsee said with a sniff.

"I'm proud of you, Tom. You as well, Oliver." William was holding Tom's other hand. He carried a strange expression, one that clouded his eyes.

I asked, "Are you all right, William, sir?"

He nodded, as if to shake off my question. "It's nothin', it ain't. Not my business now. You've done what was asked of you, and more. What happens now is between you and my son."

Tom must have caught on. "Pa, you've gotta know, I'd give up my Talent for Oliver. Just as you gave up yours for Ma." He then turned to look me in the eye, unconditional sincerity within them. "I'd give up everything for you, I would. Talent included. No lie."

Without any hesitation, I said, "In all my thoughts, waking and dreaming, I never imagined I would find someone who has completed me as much as you have, Tom. I'll do whatever it is you ask of me without question and until I take my very last breath."

My words held no doubts or regrets. I was honest with him as I was as honest with myself.

Mimsee now had tears in her eyes; William looked surprised but didn't protest either. I squeezed Tom's hand and kissed him again tenderly and slowly. When we parted, he smiled. A smile that filled me with hope for our future together. "Then we can be together as real lovers now, can't we? 'Cause, I don't need my Talent no more if I got you."

"We can," I replied. "And I need you, too. More than I need to breathe. I'll give up my Talent for you, Tom. Without question."

Mister Okinawa gave a polite cough into his hand. "That's not strictly true, honourable friends. Nothing has to be given up, especially when it comes to your Talent." He raised his hand to halt any enquiry. "The Dragon Master will speak with you about such matters, as it is his place to do so, not mine. When you're ready, of course."

Chapter Fifty-two
The Path of Patience

Of course, we were ready.

At our best haste, considering Tom wasn't fully recovered and I was still dealing with my own failings—uncomfortable in my clothing due to my Talent-induced release—we were ushered beyond the tapestry depicting the flatulence battle. Without another word, my anticipation building as to what Master Xun Xiuying would tell us, we were escorted down the corridor. We then descended the stairs that led to the Dragon Master's chamber and took off our shoes.

The smell of incense and the sound of harp music found me before I spied him. He wasn't at his artist's desk. Instead, he was getting dressed behind the rice paper screen. I was only able to see his silhouette.

When he appeared, I performed the traditional greeting we'd been taught by Mister Okinawa. Tom and the others did the same.

"Ah, Master Merritt. Master Arkwright, so glad to see you've prevailed. As I knew you would."

What the Dragon Master was wearing wasn't the surprise. In fact, considering his uncountable age, the black trousers, shoes most martial artists wore that were flat and made of black cloth, and adorned in a traditional tang-zhuang jacket—high collared with knot-work buttons and made of the finest silk—was to be expected. What astonished me was the fact he wasn't quite human anymore.

I couldn't quantify what I was looking at, but the best way I could describe it was to say he was human in form with two arms, two legs, and a head, but had the scales of a dragon upon him. Those scales were emerald green and gold tipped.

"What in heaven's name has happened to you, Master Xun Xiuying?" Again, I was probably being impolite, stepping on etiquette with my question. I couldn't help myself.

William gasped.

Tom, as always, was the realist. He was quicker than I to assess what we saw before us. "Lawks, you're changing back into a dragon, aren't you?"

Mimsee simply said, "You're beautiful, lovely."

Master Xun Xiuying didn't seem perturbed by the slip of my tongue, or anyone else's comments for that matter. "As I had informed you when we first met, Oliver and Tom, you are the two I am destined to help on your journey to greatness. As you can see," he gestured to himself from top to bottom, "when I do so, I will return to my true self. I thank you; it is through you both that I will be redeemed in the eyes of my gods for a centuries old crime I have lived with for so long."

I was pleased we could help him and had almost forgotten the real reason we'd come to visit him in his chamber. That was, until Mister Okinawa cleared his throat politely. "Dragon Master, our honourable guests will need to learn about the Path of Patience, don't you think?" He bowed. "Before they do anything rash."

"Yes, thank you my faithful servant. That will be all." Mister Okinawa bowed again, leaving the chamber without turning his back on the Dragon Master. "And my servant is right. You both must keep hold of your gifts. There is a long way to go yet, so much to learn and so many who will need your Talented assistance. It has been foretold as such, just as my destiny has been foretold that it intertwines with yours, Oliver—Tom."

"Tom and I would like to be with each other as normal folks can be," I blurted.

I didn't know whether the Dragon Master's motive for wanting us to hold onto our Talent was for himself, or for something far more ominous. I then thought better of it. He hadn't proven to be selfish; not to us, anyway.

His next words changed everything.

"There is a way you can keep your Talent and be together as you wish," he explained. "However, as Mister Okinawa has already alluded, it is a patient path you must tread to be able to have both. Care must be taken."

Tom looked at me, then addressed Master Xun Xiuying. "I'm willing to give it a go. To have both would be somethin'."

"Indeed," William agreed, sounding surprised.

"Please go on, Master Xun Xiuying," I added curiously.

He bowed, his emerald scales glinting as the change in his posture caught the lantern light. "You know that you can already hold each other's hands and kiss each other upon your lips. The Path of Patience is a continuation of that. However, it must be done slowly and with purpose, but most of all, it cannot be cheated."

"What do you mean?" I asked.

"You must both start small and build up your intentions with each other. This can, and will, take months, even years, before you are able to join physically. Be as one as other folks can be, as you put it. Any misstep, and your Talent will leave you. Done properly, and your Talent can be trained to accept your intentions as each other's true heart and soul."

I believed I understood him. "What you're saying is, that given time, we can have full physical love with each other as well as keep our Talent?"

"That is correct."

Tom asked, "Then why don't Talented folks know this? So many of 'em could have kept their gift before they had children or got a partner." He had glanced at his father.

"If you are true soulmates, your Talent will let you know when each step can be made—as I'm sure you have already felt," Master Xun Xiuying said.

I had felt something the last time I was with Tom alone. When I wanted to touch him with my hands after we came to our climax. The urge was so great and felt so right, but I didn't understand what it meant at the time. It was like something was deep inside me, lying entangled with the beast of my Talent but waking up, spurring me on. I didn't know what it meant at the time as I had been told not to touch Tom in any way other than what we already knew was safe.

The Dragon Master continued, "I must say, most understand this, but to understand something is not the same as accomplishing it. As I said, it is a very long path. Perhaps you may only be able to take the first step with the slightest breath upon your lover's intimate places. There will be no more than the ability to do so for weeks before you can move to the next step. Even then, the next step may only be a kiss. Most mortals do not have the patience for this. With biological needs swirling within them, the instinct to perpetuate the species far outweighs any other desires. Not so for you, Oliver and Tom. You are different. This is why I have waited for you for so long. Two men, both possessing the Talent, together as lovers and soulmates. That is worth a millennium in the waiting."

Tom and I glanced at each other. I took his hand, warm and clammy in mine. He was nervous, as I was.

The Path of Patience was going to be a long undertaking, but the reward at the end was something we could both wait for. I knew it in the depths of my being.

"Do you want to walk the Path of Patience with me, Tom?"

"Yes," was all he breathed.

We didn't need to say anymore.

Chapter Fifty-Three
The First Step

Back home, Tom and I paid a visit to my father within her chambers. I quickly discovered she'd suffered no more than the bruising of her ego and a few aches and pains from the ordeal at St. Giles. "I'm pleased you are both going to learn the Path of Patience," she said sombrely.

After being thanked for our efforts and excusing ourselves, Tom and I went to our chamber. Mimsee had informed me that Arthur had returned, deciding to stay in the house on a more permanent basis. He was given a room on the third floor.

She also told me of how he was to sell his house; it held too much bitterness for him. Another interesting titbit of information was dropped on me, one that raised Tom's eyebrows as well as my own: Peeler Stirling was attending Arthur in his chamber.

Mimsee had drawn us a bath. Tom and I took turns to bathe. We didn't want to risk washing each other. I knew the Path of Patience wouldn't allow that sort of contact, not for a long time. I didn't feel it, either. Don't ask me how, but I also had a feeling Master Xun Xiuying was right—our Talent would be required soon to aid others.

Perhaps it has something to do with the Dragon Master returning to his ancient form, but I couldn't really be sure. Although, I had to admit, for the moment I was just grateful to get out of my soiled clothing.

When we were in our bed, warmed by each other, Tom held

my hand. We didn't speak; there was no need. Our words would have spoiled the moment that was building, the anticipation of the first step we were going to take without using our Talent was more than enough.

I stirred already.

He came over me. We held hands but moved so our fingers were laced above my head. I gasped in expectation of what was to follow. I trembled, and my stomach quivered.

We kissed, deep and loving, touching tongues and enjoying the only foreplay we were able to perform upon one another. My mind spun, my thoughts only of Tom.

I relented myself to his control. He kissed me even more passionately. Many times, after we broke contact, my lips tingling, I gasped.

"More," I said with a groan.

We must have kissed for another age before I realised that the boiling Talent within me had subsided enough to let me know it was right to take the first step on our new journey. The beast slept while my urges rose, uncoiling itself to consume me.

Nerves found me.

I let Tom know by increasing the outward signs of my fervour, writhing and whimpering. He must have understood, because he moved so he could bring his lips to my chest. He exhaled, breathing his hot, sensual breath over my nipples. Lightning shot through me.

Instantly, they hardened along with my gentlemanly asset. I arched my back. He kept going, coming so close to me that I could feel the heat of his lips warm against the sensitive skin of my areola. Gooseflesh ignited across my whole body, including where he breathed across my nipples and chest. I inhaled deeply as he did so.

Moments later, I shuddered.

I came to conclusion, groaning in delight without having to

use my Talent or touch myself. It was a deep and long release. One as strong as I'd ever experienced, and very satisfying. The most satisfying I'd ever had.

"I still have my Talent," he whispered.

He must have been correct, because I still had mine.

If that was the first step on the Path of Patience and the result of it, I welcomed it with all my yearning. What would happen on the next step? The thought was almost too much to comprehend after the carnal pleasure I had just experienced from a mere breath upon my skin.

When I'd done the same to Tom, his climax as strong and revealing, he turned to go to sleep after kissing me goodnight. His breathing instantly slowed to become deep and regular.

I was too overwhelmed.

Then I had something else on my mind. I climbed out of bed, gathering up my nightshirt and slipping it over me. I had to tell Mimsee.

I didn't trouble with knocking on her chamber door; she never bothered to do so on mine. We had an understanding. No secrets between us. Besides, she was probably getting ready for bed. My visit would be welcome.

What I saw as I opened her chamber door, however, was something rather interesting indeed.

Chapter Fifty-Four
Peeler Stirling's Secret

There was Mimsee, lying on the bed without a stitch on, propped up by pillows. Her magnificent dark skin, lustrous and smooth, was beautiful. On the bed in front of her, Peeler Stirling was on all fours, also similarly unattired.

His face was deep between her legs.

There was a man behind Peeler Stirling. Arthur.

He was enjoying Peeler Stirling's fleshly wonders, moving so it was plain to witness what was going on. The young peeler was moaning, both in agony and ecstasy by the act of being ridden and pleasuring Mimsee at the same time.

I felt a pang of jealousy.

Not because of them, but because they could do to each other so easily what Tom and I would have to learn by walking the Path of Patience.

Before I could exit the chamber, leave them to their pleasure, Arthur and Peeler Stirling changed position. Peeler Stirling really did have enough for Arthur to worship and Mimsee to enjoy the sight of, even though he was all skin and bones.

I smiled, pleased for them both. As I backed out of the door, there were groans. I believed Peeler Stirling had come to give Arthur his appreciation. Mimsee remained ever delighted by what she witnessed and felt.

I left, closing the door quietly.

Returning to bed, I thought about how momentous everything that had transpired had been. My dreams were filled with my love for Tom, the pain of losing my mother, the defeat of the Skilamalink Man, thugs, filthy streets, good friends and new family, dragons, the Path of Patience, breath upon skin, and how I could keep my Talent in spite of it all.

The next morning at breakfast, a very filling and delicious repast of eggs, bacon, sausages, knobs of fresh bread, cheeses, and colds meats, Mimsee finally made herself known. She hadn't come into my chamber to draw the drapes, open the window, or attend either Tom or myself.

Not that it mattered if she hadn't. That was her decision to do so.

As she entered the morning room, I couldn't help but notice she didn't look as happy as I imagined she would, considering what I witnessed last night in her chamber.

"Good of you to finally grace us with your presence, Mimsee," my father said. If I wasn't mistaken, her words seemed more like a tease. Did she know about Mimsee's late night antics with Arthur and Peeler Stirling?

"Sorry, Mother. I overslept." She curtsied before seating herself and grabbing a plate to fill it with food. A large plate.

I had told Tom of my discovery, and how Peeler Stirling had been a rather busy young man. Tom snickered by the excuse of her apology, and I grinned at Mimsee cheekily. She poked her tongue out at me.

"How was it?" Tom questioned. I knew he couldn't hold his tongue. "Was Peeler Stirling good with his truncheon to you and Arthur?"

I glared at him; he shrugged.

We both tried in vain to suppress laughter. Mimsee rolled her eyes to the heavens. My father tutted but didn't say anything.

To be honest, she still hadn't composed herself from yesterday's ordeal, her hair not as tightly bound as usual. She didn't wear as much makeup, either. I imagined it would take a few days for her to return to her old self.

It was at that moment, I realised neither Peeler Stirling had left the house nor had Arthur announced himself.

Mimsee finally replied, "It was quite satisfactory, if you must know." She stuffed a lump of cheese into her mouth from off her dainty fork. After chewing it and swallowing, she added, "But once again, I 'ave come out second best. Stirling 'as made it clear what 'e prefers to do in the boudoir. And all I have to say on the matter is that Arthur's a lucky man, and we'll leave it at that, won't we?"

I felt saddened for my sister at those words. "Are you all right with that, Mimsee?" I asked seriously.

"I'm fine." A lady who spoke of being fine was usually far from it, but she continued to eat.

Before I could either console her or elaborate my thoughts, Oscar burst into the morning room, door clattering against the wall. "Got a guest!"

"Young man," my father snapped, almost scandalised. Once again, the sheer number of breeches in protocol from Oscar was almost mindboggling. My father wouldn't tolerate it for too much longer, but I found it amusing. "You are supposed to announce who the guest is!"

"Yes, my Lady," Oscar said forlornly. He was dressed in ankle boots, long white socks up to his knees, knickerbockers, a blue pinstriped shirt with

large, rounded collar, and a loose bow tie. He had certainly been looked after while he'd been staying in the house. He had also been well fed, with his skin clean and his hair shiny, too. He turned toward the foyer. "Oi! What's your name, Mister?"

"My name, *boy*, is Mister Fallow," a man announced in a voice I recognised.

Oscar was about to publicise what we already knew, when my father interjected, "Please tell Mister Fallow to come in, Oscar. Later, we will have to discuss how you perform your duties. For the moment I require you to stay. I have an errand I need attending to, but I will see to our guest first."

"Yes, Lady."

Mister Fallow waltzed into the morning room. He was the weedy man, all wet lips and sticky expression. After he bowed to my father, he roved his gaze over Tom and I. "Oliver! Tom! I almost didn't recognise you there."

Tom whispered to me under his breath, "That's because we've got our clothes on and our tackle ain't distracting him." Out loud, he was politer. "Good morning to you, Mister Fallow."

I gave the same formal greeting.

"What brings you here this fine morning, Mister Fallow?" my father asked impatiently. Having one's breakfast with family interrupted was also another transgression of etiquette I knew would rankle her like a loose thread on an otherwise finely stitched hem.

"I was just passing by and…" It was then Mister Fallow must have noticed Oscar proper, really drinking him in. I could almost see the moment clearly on his face when whatever he was going to say had left him. "Tell me, Lady Penelope, how long have you had that pretty little boy working here?"

I bristled at his words, hoping the situation wasn't going where I suspected. My father remained calm and composed. Also, she was never one to be slow on the uptake. "That *boy* has a name, and it is Oscar. He works here as an errand boy only. He is under my care and protection and has that privilege bestowed upon him because I owe him a great deal for helping my eldest son during his darkest hour."

"That's lovely, I'm sure. How old is he?" Mister Fallow licked his lips, almost salivating as he began undressing Oscar with his eyes.

This *was* going where I feared.

My stomach knotted. When Master Xun Xiuying said I'd need my Talent to help others, I didn't in my wildest imagination believe it would be so soon or for someone in my own home.

Oscar didn't seem deterred or was oblivious. "I'm nine."

"You see, Mister Fallow," my father snapped, "far too young for what you no doubt have in mind. As you well know, the age of consent is fourteen. As such, I will not have this house become mired in any illegal activities. I have a reputation to uphold and the safety of those who work for me to consider. If you want underage rent boys to do your depraved bidding, then Whitechapel is where you'll need to be. Not here."

I breathed a sigh of relief, realising I was holding my breath while I watched the predator try and gain his prey.

What Oscar said and did next, however, told me in no uncertain terms he knew exactly what was going on. That he was as clever as a fox, and he would fit into this house perfectly.

It all began with a wink. "Mimsee told me you gave five sovereigns to look at Oliver's willy. I'll show you mine for that, Mister, I will."

Mister Fallow cocked an eyebrow, intrigued. He moistened his lips once more, smiling hungrily as he kept his attention on the knickerbocker-wearing boy in front of him. "That would be most delightful…Oscar."

My father must have caught on to what I had, for there were no more words from her spoken on the matter. I had been mistaken: the hunter wasn't Mister Fallow, it was Oscar.

The man, as sick and twisted and creepy as he was, mustn't have caught on to the fact he was being lured in. He missed the wink at the beginning of Oscar's offer, obviously too involved in his own depraved thoughts to notice such small details.

I noticed.

Tom and Mimsee must have as well, for they tried to suppress a snicker behind their hands. I had a wonderful feeling that Mister Fallow was about to be duped, as they say.

Chapter Fifty-Five
Magic Peelers

"It's agreed then," Mimsee offered. I could tell by her expression she was enjoying what was unfolding.

"Agreed," Mister Fallow purred with the content of a well warmed house cat sitting by the fireplace.

He was about to leave the room, clearly thinking he'd be back later to enjoy the performance from Oscar he was paying for, when Oscar blocked the doorway.

Oscar stood stock still, hands on his hips. "Five sovereigns please, sir. Or I tell Peeler Stirling who's upstairs right now that you like to fiddle with little boys."

Mister Fallow was bright red, right to his ears. His fists were knotted to tight balls. The man stammered, "You…he didn't… I…he was supposed to…I didn't mean…that wasn't even…I…"

My father said, "I do believe you owe Oscar his dues or face the consequences, Mister Fallow."

"But…but…" The man, fooled and defeated, reached into this pocket, threw down the money and stormed out.

Oscar, I had to say, was brilliant.

After he casually picked up the coins and pocketed them, he said, "Used to get men like him all the time out on the street. I can handle 'em."

At that, and with a raised brow, my father added, "Oscar, I would like it if you were to move into one of the spare bedchambers on the third floor from your guest quarters. I will arrange for it to be legal that I look after you for as long as you desire. To put it plainly, you will be adopted into this house just as Oliver and Mimsee have been. After seeing how well you handled yourself, I really do think your cunning and street knowledge will be most useful when it comes to aiding my Oliver and his Tom in the future. You will join Mimsee in seeing that is accomplished. Would you like that?"

Oscar bowed. "Yes, my lady." The boy was glowing, beaming a smile. Mimsee stood, going to him. She took him by the hand, about to attend to his sudden change in fortune by escorting him to his new accommodation, when the boy added, "I think it would be good to help the magic peelers fight the monsters, it would."

Magic Peelers? I liked that. I never considered that was how Tom and I would be seen by others, especially by those without the Talent. But his term didn't quite have the correct connotation for what we did or what we could achieve. I thought for a moment. Then it struck me, and I clicked my fingers.

"I have it. We're not magic peelers, Oscar, but Supernatural Detectives. Aren't we, Tom?"

Tom, busy eating, nodded and grunted. His enthusiasm was as underwhelming as yesterday's cold porridge by my rather clever suggestion. He mumbled through a full mouth, "I like Magic Peelers better."

Father said, "That settles it. You will both be our Magic Peelers from now on if anyone enquires for your services."

Mimsee kissed the boy on his cheek. "Looks like it's you an' me, Oscar. Oliver an' Tom need us, so we best be on our guard from now on."

With that, the two of them left.

Mimsee had a new purpose, one that would hopefully take her mind off the events that led her to discover that Peeler Stirling liked playing backgammon with Arthur. She would find someone special one day; I knew in my bones it would be so.

No sooner had Oscar and Mimsee left the morning room, Hao and Tan came in, looking flustered.

My father dropped her fork. "Good gracious, what is it now? Surely no more visitors can come to our door this morning!"

Hao and Tan bowed, giving the fist in hand greeting as they did so. Hao, the usual spokesman of the two twins said, "My dear Lady Penelope, honourable Oliver, and honourable Tom, there has been a sighting of a spirit at the Regent Theatre in the Limehouse district. Mister Remington, the owner, informed the Dragon Master and our father that the man he employed as his nightwatchman was found dead on the stage, not a drop of blood left in him. You must come quickly. The Dragon Master informs us that the time has come once more for you to both be called upon, your Talent required."

I looked at Tom. He had stopped forking food into his mouth. He must have read my mind by my glare, because without further hesitation, he said, "Looks like we've got our first job as Magic Peelers. Spirit, you say. That's a ghost, right? Not what comes out of a bottle?"

Hao bowed again. "Yes, honourable Tom, it is."

"I take it there is a carriage waiting outside for us?" I questioned.

Tan said, "Of course. Ready when you are."

I turned to my father, about to request to be excused from the table, when she said, "You'd better go, the both of you. I will have Peeler Stirling and William join you at the theatre presently. I'll also inform Mimsee and Oscar of your whereabouts."

"Thank you, Father."

Tom said, "No more dancing for coin then for us, is there?"

"Which will be a relief for you, Tom my dearest," I teased. "You were terrible at it anyway."

What Tom said was the truth, though. I thought about how the Path of Patience I was undertaking with him. To be honest,

I didn't want to strip down to my skin for others anymore, either. He was all I wanted to see and be with from now on.

Tom was my world now.

"I was not…was I?"

"Let's just say I'm glad a new opportunity presented itself so soon."

Master Xun Xiuying was right. Tom and I would be required, and a lot sooner than I had hoped. Thankfully, when I got up early this morning, I'd inked a new Dragon Symbol of protection onto a piece of paper and placed it into my shoe. Again, whether through intuition or some other strange method of knowing, I had a feeling I would need it.

I joined Hao and Tan, bowing to my father to give her my leave. Tom did the same. He then grabbed my hand, holding me tightly, and letting me know without a shadow of any doubt that he was with me no matter what.

Tom said, "Together we walk patiently into the unknown then, Oliver."

"Together indeed."

The End

Glossary

Abbess: Brothel madam/owner.

Agony of Bliss: Orgasm.

Arbour Vitae: Penis.

Bagpiping: Act of giving a blowjob.

Beast with Two backs: Two people engaged in sexual intercourse.

Blowsy: Name for someone who gives blowjobs for money.

Bollocks: Testicles.

Bunter: A low class prostitute. Also referred to as a six-penny Bunter.

Cloven Inlet: Vagina.

Cock Lane: Vagina.

Fairest Flower: Vagina.

Kettle Drums: A woman's breasts.

Lickspittler: a sycophant/arse kisser.

Lobcock: A man with a flaccid penis (especially during amorous moments).

Mandrake/Mary: A gay man.

Molly Room/House: A place where gay people could socialise.

Monosyllable: Vagina.

Muckspout: One who swears a lot.

Peeler: Slang for policeman (derived from "Sir Robert Peel" who established the Metropolitan Police force in 1829).

Quim (quim-faced): Vagina. (used as an insult).

Rantallion: When balls hang lower than the penis (has a small penis).

Shivering Jemmie: Beggar.

Toff: A rich person.

Toffer: Upper class prostitute.

Truncheon: Penis.

Tupping Boy: A young male who receives anal sex from an older male.

White Staff: Penis.

About the Author

By day I'm a humble physical therapist…and by day I'm also a writer of sweet & saucy boyslove stories (18+). I sleep at night as an old fart like me should. I'm both self-published and traditionally published. Other than that, I live with my partner and two cats and live my best life.

Website: http://konblackeboyslovewriter.com
Twitter: http://www.twitter.com/blackekon

Also by Kon Blacke

Boyslove in the Gangland District
#1 Offering Gold Coins to a Cat
#2 Soft Boys Play Hard
#3 Catching Two Frogs with One Hand
#4 The Chirping Cricket Desires the Ripened Crop

The Saurian Love Trilogy
#1 My Tyrannosaurus Lover
#2 My Saurian Friends

The Legend of Hereward
(Published by Dreamsphere Books)
#1 Immortal Whispers
#2 Mortal Screaming

Also by Kon Blacke
Published by Dreamsphere Books

Immortal Whispers
Kon Blacke

The Whispering Monks have foretold change to the world, and it's fast approaching. They also speak of the mortals who'll be involved.

Hereward, a lord knight who only worships the steel at his side, as the mad magician Ealdræd has taken away everyone he had ever loved. Wymond, an oblate determined to find his true self, even if it means turning away from everything he has ever known. Beornræd, a powerful magician who fears to love again after the cruelties of his past. Kieron, a stable hand with dragon blood flowing through his veins and is the rightful heir to a realm of unimaginable beauty.

All four will travel their own paths, to destroy their pasts and rebuild their future, as they thwart the evil plans of Ealdræd and his conduit, the immortal Abbot Hosho.

The whisperings continue through epic battles, both on the ground and in the sky.

The whisperings shall continue beyond the aftermath.

As it has been foretold.

Also by Kon Blacke

Offering Gold Coins to a Cat
Kon Blacke

Tachibana Kushano goes to Michael Brock's gentleman's club, Badda-Bings, to give himself to many other men at once. All because his boyfriend, Riyu, orders him to.

Tachibana never questions Riyu.

He's his submissive, after all.

But when he's finished, Riyu still isn't happy, and Tachibana doesn't understand why. And as he quickly discovers, he's never been appreciated by Riyu either, even when he's done whatever he's been told without question. As a result of Riyu's anger, Tachibana is then punished, hurt beyond anything imaginable.

For Tachibana, it's the last straw.

The trouble is…how can he recover after being dominated by Riyu for so long? How can he learn to trust someone else again?

But above all, how can Tachibana love someone else, even someone who wants to care for him? Someone like Michael Brock, for instance?

Also by Kon Blacke

My Tyrannosaurus Lover
Kon Blacke

Karl Meddings is what you would call an ordinary guy in every way. He loves his best friend—with benefits—Sagan, with all his heart, and leads a good life. The only unusual thing about his world is the fact he shares it with saurians—the modern-day ancestors of dinosaurs.

But now, Karl's boss, a rather attractive tyrannosaurus by the name of Benedict Tumbold, has an interesting proposal for both Karl and Sagan—a proposal that could turn Karl from an ordinary guy with no real prospects to someone special.

A hero…

Will Karl accept his boss's offer? Will Sagan? Or will an ordinary life be all that Karl's destined for?

www.ingramcontent.com/pod-product-compliance
Lightning Source LLC
Chambersburg PA
CBHW021952010726
47494CB00003B/704